Trouble at
the Red Pueblo

To Mark!
Merry Christmas, 2014
We always remembered
how kind you were to my
children when we visited
your folks so many years
ago. You've probably
forgotten, but I never
will.

All best
Ivy (Teddy) Adair

OTHER BOOKS BY LIZ ADAIR

The Lodger, a Spider Latham Mystery

After Goliath, a Spider Latham Mystery

Snakewater Affair, a Spider Latham Mystery

The Mist of Quarry Harbor

Lucy Shook's Letters from Afghanistan

Cold River

Hidden Spring, a novella in the
Timeless Romance, Old West Collection

Trouble at
the Red Pueblo

Liz Adair

Published by Century Press, 496 West Kane Drive, Kanab, UT 84741

ISBN: 978-0-9905027-1-5

Cover design by Ron Shook
Cover design © 2014 by Liz Adair
Formatting by KristiRae Alldredge of Computers & More Design Services

Dedication

This book is dedicated to my two Kanab/Fredonia high school chums, George Ann Brinkerhoff Brooksby and Nayna Judd Christensen. Georgie, your spunk as you take what life throws at you is truly inspiring; and Nayna, who would have thought that we'd end up as two little old (ex-cheerleader) ladies walking in the morning? It has been a joy to pick up the threads again. The friendship threads, not the cheerleading ones.

Acknowledgements and Apologies

◆

I'll take care of the apologies first:

I somehow cannot get through a book without rearranging geography. For all of those who travel between Kanab, Utah and Fredonia, Arizona, you will know that the vacant Travelers Inn sits in Arizona. For the purpose of this narrative, I have moved it just across the state line into Utah. I apologize to all of the local citizenry who are bothered by this, but you'll see why it was necessary as you read the book.

For Spider Latham fans who have read the previous books, I'm warning you now. I've skipped fifteen or twenty years, updating to the present without Spider aging a whit. Don't let it throw you.

Now for the acknowledgements:

Thanks to my writing community for encouragement and cheerleading. Part of that community is my critique group: Terry Deighton, Ann Acton, Tanya Parker Mills, Christine Thackeray and Bonnie Harris. Thanks, ladies. Your tough love makes me a better writer.

Thanks to Steve and Darlene Judd for advice about horses and hooves, and to Kent Douglass. He not only was a beta reader, but he also gave me some tips about police procedure. If what I wrote takes literary license, it's not because I got bad information from Kent.

To Dixon and Launa Spendlove for support from the Red Pueblo Museum in Fredonia, and to Kendall and George Ann Brooksby, who introduced me to the museum—thank you.

Thanks to my brother Ron and his wife, Mary. Ron designed the cover, and Mary read the manuscript.

To all the people who read and gave me a list of mistakes found, I am so in your debt! In addition to my critique group and the already-named readers, these generous people include Nayna Christensen, Joyce Packard, Linda Chatterley, Joan Kirby, and Ross and Karalee Oblad.

Thanks to my friend Hani Almadhoun for giving me the inspiration and name for the wonderful character, Karam Mansour. Thanks to Heather Justesen for her unflagging support as she acted as midwife to my first foray into indie publishing.

And, as always, thanks to Derrill, my husband of fifty years. He is unfailing in his support of my writing.

Chapter 1

◆

ALL SPIDER LATHAM wanted to do was get home. He wanted free of the choking black necktie, free of the memory of his mother in a cheap casket. If he were a drinking man, he'd head right to the whiskey. Instead, he thought he'd fix the fence that ran along the south property line. It'd been on his to-do list for a while, and the work would be hot, hard and demanding.

Laurie, sitting beside him in the pickup, pointed at a small, square sedan parked in front of their house. "Isn't that the car you drove home from Las Vegas last year?"

"Yep. That's the one." Spider turned off the gravel road, rolled over the cattle guard and pulled up beside the orange Yugo with flames decorating its front end. "I don't know that I'm ready for company."

Laurie patted his knee. "Maybe company is what you need. You like that fellow don't you? What's his name?"

"Jade Tremain. Yeah, I like him. But today's not..."

"Life goes on." The moment he turned off the key, Laurie opened the door and slid down to the ground. Smiling, she walked toward the young man emerging from the compact car. "Hello, Jade. Welcome."

Jade took the hand she held out to him. "Did I come at a bad time?" His eyes went from Laurie, dressed in a black dress and high heels, to Spider, climbing out of the pickup wearing a black suit on a hot August Tuesday.

Spider ambled over, pulling down his Stetson to shade his eyes from the afternoon sun. He shook Jade's hand and nodded toward the Yugo. "Your dad still keeping you humble?"

Jade laughed and looked at his watch. "It was the only company car left in the garage."

Laurie patted the orange fender. "I never will forget having to rescue Spider when he drove it home that time he was doing some work for your dad."

Spider eyed the car. "I wonder why he hangs on to it. It must be more than twenty years old."

"Twenty-three, but it doesn't have that many miles on it. No one wants to drive it." Jade looked at his watch. "I've come to talk to you about doing some more work for Dad."

"Spider, take Jade out back," Laurie said. "You can sit in the shade while he tells you what he's come for. I'll bring out some ice water." She headed up the walk to the front door.

Spider jerked his head in invitation and led his guest across the lawn. At the back yard fence he held the gate open.

Jade passed through. "I tried to call, but it said the phone was disconnected."

"Things have been pretty tight lately. We figured that was something we could do without." Spider fished a cell phone from his shirt pocket. "The county gave me this to use for work, but I don't take any personal calls on it."

"So you're still deputy sheriff?"

Spider pocketed the phone as he headed toward a grape arbor. "Yeah, but the county's running out of money. Ever since this last recession hit, all employees have to take three unpaid furlough days each month. And then I had a funeral to pay for."

Jade stopped just short of the shade. "Oh, gee, Spider. Is that where you've just been?" He hit his forehead with the heel of his hand. "I bet you wish I hadn't come."

Spider sat in one of the chairs and pointed at the other. "Take a load off."

Jade hesitated, his hands in his pockets.

"Sit," Spider said.

Jade sat. "I'm sorry about coming today. Would you...could I...whose funeral was it?"

Spider crossed his legs, resting the ankle of his black cowboy boot on his knee. He took off his Stetson, held it in his lap, and turned his face away. "My mother's." As he looked off to the south, his eyes welled up, and a tear slid down his cheek.

Jade shifted in his chair. "I'd better go."

Still looking away, Spider made a negative motion with his hand. He drew a handkerchief from the inside pocket of his coat and wiped his eyes. "Don't go." He blew his nose and turned to face the younger man. "I don't know where that came from. I haven't cried a tear since Mama died."

Jade sat with his hands on his knees. He opened his mouth as if to say something but closed it again and folded his arms tightly across his chest.

Spider cleared his throat. "Actually, the old woman

who lived with us this last year wasn't my mama." He smiled at the confused look on Jade's face. "My mother had Alzheimer's. We've been saying we'd rejoice when she was finally released from that prison, but here I am crying. In front of company, no less."

Jade pursed his lips and looked down at his feet.

Spider uncrossed his legs and leaned forward. "So, what's on Brick Tremain's mind? Why'd your daddy make you drive the three hours from Las Vegas to Lincoln County to see me, aside from the fact that he couldn't talk to me on the phone?"

"He needs you to do some investigating for him, but he says it'll take longer than a weekend. He wants to know if the sheriff's office can spare you for a week or so."

"Shoot, the sheriff would probably kiss your daddy on both cheeks if he employed me for a week or more. That would mean he wouldn't have to take any furlough days himself. It's really chafing him that he's being treated the same as his deputy." Spider put his handkerchief back in the inner pocket. "What exactly does the boss want me to do?"

The screen door banged, and Jade waited to answer while Laurie approached with a tray holding three tumblers of ice water. He murmured thanks and set the glass on a table beside his chair. After she served her husband and sat with her own cool drink, he spoke. "Dad's on the board of directors of a small museum in Arizona. Anasazi artifacts and stuff like that."

Spider took a sip. "The Anasazi were early Pueblo Indians, right? That's about all I know about them."

Jade smiled. "Well, that's more than I know."

"Where is this museum?" Laurie asked.

"It's in a little town called Fredonia, right on the Utah-Arizona border."

Laurie's smile was huge. "You're kidding! I have cousins in Fredonia."

"Dad says the museum director lives in Kanab, Utah. I guess it's near Fredonia."

Laurie nodded. "Seven miles north. I have cousins in Kanab, too."

Spider leaned back and smiled at his wife. "Never mind about your relatives. Let's hear what Jade has to say about the problem this museum has and what his daddy wants me to do."

"I don't know the particulars." Jade stretched out his legs and jingled the keys in his pocket. "I just know they're in trouble. Someone is threatening to close down the museum and ruin the director financially. They need help right away, like by the end of next week. Dad wants you to go over and lend a hand." Jade looked at his watch again.

"That's mighty slim—" Spider was about to go on when Laurie put her hand on his knee.

"Do you need to leave?" she asked Jade.

The young man ran his hand through his hair. "I'm sorry. I didn't mean to look impatient. The truth is, my wife is supposed to call me. She went to the doctor this morning."

"Is anything wrong?" Laurie's concerned look deepened.

Jade's cheeks grew rosy and he shook his head. "We're expecting a baby. It's our first."

"Congratulations!" Spider stood and held out his hand. "If you don't have any more information for me, I'll let you get on your way back to Vegas. Just tell me who I talk to at the museum."

Jade stood, patting his shirt pocket before extracting a business card. "Here's the director's contact information. He can tell you the whole story."

Spider walked with Jade toward the gate, reading the name on the card as he went. "Martin Taylor. Should I call him or just show up?"

"We'll just show up," Laurie said. "Since we don't have a phone."

Spider stopped and looked down at his wife. "*We'll* show up? Are you coming with?"

"There's no need for me to stay home now," Laurie said. Her voice quavered at the end of the sentence, and her eyes filled with tears. She accepted the handkerchief Spider proffered and turned away for a moment to wipe her eyes. "Excuse me," she said to Jade. "I didn't expect to get weepy."

Jade stopped at the gate to let her go through first. "Please don't apologize. I should have come on another day."

She shook her head. "No, I think it's wonderful you came today. This will give us both something to think about instead of the empty chair in the living room."

Spider put his arm around his wife as they walked Jade to his car.

The young man stopped with his hand on the door handle and looked at the roof of the Latham vehicle. It still showed the dents Spider hadn't been able to completely hammer out after the rollover accident he'd had on one of his first cases. "I see you're still driving the same pickup."

"It runs good," Spider said. "And it's easy to spot in a crowded parking lot."

"My dad would approve," Jade said with a smile, opening the door of his own car. He paused and leaned against the top. "If things are so tight here, why don't you come to Vegas and work for Tremain Enterprises? Dad'd hire you in an instant."

"I know that," Spider said. "He told me the same thing last time I worked for him, but Lathams have been living in Meadow Valley for four generations. Five if you count my boys. We've got good pasture and plenty of water. It's worth hanging onto, even when times are lean."

Jade slid into the driver's seat and closed the door, speaking through the open window. "Dad says there's a room for you at the Best Western in Kanab. It's there on the main drag. He wants you to call him once you're settled in and understand the lay of the land."

"Will do." Spider drew Laurie back a pace as Jade started the engine. They watched as the car turned around in the drive, and they waved as it rattled over the cattle guard.

"I'll run over to Bud's and ask him to check on the cattle for me every few days," Laurie said. "Then I'll stick all those funeral casseroles in the freezer and pack something for us to eat for supper on the way."

"We're leaving this afternoon?"

"You heard what Jade said. They're in trouble, and there's a deadline."

Spider took the phone from his pocket. "All right. I'll call and make sure it's okay for me to take the time off."

Laurie headed toward the barn. "I'm getting my saddle right now and putting it in the pickup, so I don't forget it."

Spider paused with his thumb on the key pad. "Hold on a minute. You're taking your saddle?"

Laurie stopped and turned around. "Yeah. I thought I'd spend some time with Jack."

"Jack?"

"Jack Houghton, my cousin. We used to ride all around that red rock country when I was sixteen. It would be fun to do it again."

"Isn't he a dentist? How do you know he has horses?"

"He's an orthodontist. His cousin Sally was at the funeral today. She told me he's bought the old family ranch and built a new house and stables on it."

"Huh," Spider grunted. As Laurie turned again toward the barn, he went back to scrolling through the menu on his phone to find the sheriff's number.

Chapter 2

◆

SPIDER SHUT THE hotel room door behind him with his foot as he balanced Laurie's saddle on his shoulder with one hand and carried her guitar case in the other. He dumped them both on one of the two queen size beds. "I didn't know you packed your guitar."

She put down the phone receiver. "Jack and I used to sing together. I brought it just in case."

Spider pulled down the corners of his mouth.

Laurie smiled. "Don't give me that look. What have you got against Jack?"

"What look? Why would I have anything against Jack?"

"I don't know. You tell me." She walked over and put her arms around his neck. "You look like you've bitten into a persimmon every time I mention his name."

"Not a persimmon." Spider dropped a kiss on her lips. "Maybe a horse biscuit."

Laurie laughed and turned away. "You're terrible. What has poor Jack done to make you dislike him?"

"I don't like the way he looks at you, and he never misses a chance to put his arm around you."

"He's my cousin. We spent a lot of time together when I was a teenager."

"He's a third cousin." Spider pulled a card from his shirt pocket. "And I particularly don't like the way he's always quoting poetry."

Laurie hefted a suitcase up onto the bed. "He's a fourth cousin, and it's cowboy poetry. He writes it. He's pretty good, too."

"I wouldn't mind it so much if he didn't do those gestures." Spider struck a pose with one foot forward, one hand in the air, fingers spread apart. Then he shook his head and picked up the phone.

Laurie grinned. "Well, we're having dinner with him tonight."

Spider rested the receiver on his shoulder and looked at her, eyes narrowed. "Not really."

She nodded. "I couldn't tell him no. Besides, you said you were hungry."

He looked at his watch. "When?"

"In about ten minutes." She began transferring clothing from a suitcase to a drawer.

Looking at the card and punching buttons on the phone, Spider muttered, "I think I just lost my appetite."

Laurie glanced up. "What did you say?"

"Nothing." Spider turned away as his party answered. "Mr. Taylor? This is Spider Latham. Yes. Brick Tremain asked me to come over, see if I could help." He listened a moment and then asked, "Can I come by and talk to you this evening? That would be fine. Seven-thirty it is."

Laurie poked Spider in the back with a clothes hanger. "Seven-thirty? That doesn't give us much time for dinner with Jack."

Spider hung up the phone. "What can I say? Today's my lucky day."

♦ ♦ ♦

Spider and Laurie walked the two blocks to Parry Lodge where a fresh-faced young woman with spiky black hair and dangly earrings met them in the foyer of the restaurant. Carrying a sheaf of menus on her arm, she welcomed them with a smile. "Would you prefer the dining room or the coffee shop?"

Laurie tucked her hand inside Spider's arm. "We're meeting someone here. Jack Houghton?"

"Oh, yes. Dr. Houghton is in the dining room. I'll take you right in." She led them through a wide archway to a pleasant room done in blue and green. Widely-spaced tables with heavy white linen tablecloths, napkins, and fresh flowers gave the room an air of elegance.

"Laurie!" At a corner table, a tall man, handsome in an angular way and graying at the temples, stood and beckoned.

"Geez." Laurie grabbed Spider's hand and whispered, "Look how thin he is."

Spider nodded his thanks to the spiky-haired hostess and allowed himself to be pulled over to Jack Houghton's table.

Jack planted one foot forward and held up his right hand, fingers lightly flexed, as he began quoting.

> *I saw her comin' from afar,*
> *That gal with auburn hair,*

And my heart, which had been workin' fine,
Just stopped and stuck right there.

She was such a pretty thing,
It scattered all my wits,
And I'd a-give my heart to her,
If it wasn't on the fritz.

"Hello, Jack." Laurie kissed his cheek. "You are sweet and funny. Do you remember my husband, Spider?"

"I remember the face," Jack said, shaking Spider's hand, "but I thought his name was Spencer."

"Spider's a nickname." Laurie took the chair that Jack held for her. "I don't think many people know what his real name is."

Jack sat opposite Laurie and leaned on his elbow, regarding her. "So tell me."

Laurie's answer was interrupted by a young waiter in a white shirt and tie. He introduced himself and asked if they would care to order drinks.

"We're in a bit of a time crunch," Spider said. "We'd like to order now, if that's all right. What can you recommend that will be fast?"

Jack held up his hand. "Wait, wait, wait. You can't eat at Parry Lodge and have a time constraint. Why, look around. Look at the pictures on the walls. Famous people from all over have eaten here. The place is famous for its food and famous for its ambiance."

Spider didn't reply to Jack. He kept his eyes on the server, waiting for an answer to his question. The young man stepped around in back, so he could point out items on Spider's menu that took less time, and soon he was on his way to the kitchen, having promised expedited service.

"Famous people," Spider mused. He looked around at the black and white photos. "John Wayne I recognize, but—" He peered at the names under the pictures on the wall next to his chair. "—Lex Barker? John Agar? If the food is equally famous, I hope I'll recognize the lasagna."

Spider felt Laurie kick him in the ankle and obligingly turned the conversation. "I hear you built a new house, Jack."

Laurie's cousin needed no more encouragement and entered into a detailed description of the art of building a straw-bale home. His narrative lasted through the salad and entrée, and he broke into poetry only once when he described the building site. He was deep into the stucco finish when Laurie looked at her watch.

"We've got an appointment at seven-thirty," she said, putting her napkin by her plate.

Spider stood and helped with her chair. "Thanks for inviting us to dinner, Jack. Sorry we have to run."

Jack stood as well. He kissed Laurie on the cheek. "I've got some braces I've got to see to tomorrow, but the day after that I'm free. We can spend it together. Remember that ride we used to take out to Inchworm?"

Laurie smiled. "Yes. I'd love to go there again."

Jack turned to face Spider. "Uh, you too, Spencer. Glad to have you come. Do you ride?"

Spider offered his hand. "Yes, but this is a working trip for me. I'd better not make any plans."

The two men shook, and then Spider walked behind

Laurie, his hand on the small of her back, as they wove through the tables and across the foyer to the exit.

Night had fallen while they were having dinner, and the evening was pleasantly warm as they walked back to the hotel. Laurie linked her arm through Spider's. "Nicely done, Spencer."

"Yeah, well don't try to talk me into going riding with you two."

A couple walked by, having an animated conversation in what appeared to be Japanese. Spider waited until they had passed and then remarked, "I've heard about three different languages tonight. I didn't realize Kanab was such a crossroads."

"I think that's why that summer I spent here was so exciting. People come from all over the world to see the nearby national parks, and I got asked out in five languages."

"But you didn't go because your true love was Cousin Jack."

"I didn't go because I was a shy, small-town waitress, afraid to move out of her protected circle."

They reached the pickup, and Spider opened the passenger door for Laurie. As he walked around to his side, an ambulance went by, siren wailing. He got in and waited until the sound faded before asking, "Are you sorry you never ventured beyond the small-town life?"

She shook her head. "No. Our sons moving so far away and doing great things showed me that distant places and different people aren't scary. I guess a small town just suited me." She looked both ways as the pickup stopped at the edge of the parking lot. "Do you know where you're going?"

"Yeah, I think. The highway is Center Street, and the stop light is Main. We need to go north a couple blocks and then east."

They drove away from the city center to where street lights were fewer, and Laurie rolled down her window. "I always loved the summer nights in Kanab. They seemed more exciting than the nights at home." As they turned a corner, she pointed at flashing lights a couple blocks away. "Some family's got a tragedy going on."

"Yeah, and by my reckoning, that's just about where we're headed. Can you see anything?"

"Even numbers are on this side."

Spider pulled up behind the ambulance and peered through the windshield, trying to locate the address on the house that stood with its front door open. "That's it," he said, reaching for the door handle. "I don't like bothering people when they've got something like this going on, but I've got a bad feeling about this."

"At least the police aren't here," Laurie said.

"Not yet, anyway. Stay here." He got out and crossed the lawn, reaching the edge of the yellow circle thrown by the porch light as a uniformed man backed through the doorway on one end of a wheeled stretcher. His partner followed on the other end, and they passed by Spider on the way to the ambulance. In the shadows, Spider was aware that the man on the stretcher had gray hair and an oxygen mask. Two people trailed behind—a young man with his arm around an older woman. She walked with hunched shoulders and folded arms. They stopped near Spider as the EMTs slid the stretcher inside, and the sound of the legs folding rang loudly in the quiet of the night.

The ambulance doors slammed shut, and the young man said, "Come on, Mom. We'll meet him at the hospital." He tugged on her arm. "You go get in the car. I'll close the front door."

Feeling uncomfortable and intrusive, Spider followed him across the lawn. "Excuse me. Are you...is this where the Taylors live?"

The young man whirled, obviously startled. "Yes?"

"I know this is a bad time."

"This is a very bad time." He jerked the front door closed and strode to the car with Spider in his wake.

"Who is it, Mattie?" The woman's voice was querulous. As she stood in the driveway, she looked like she was ready to fold in on herself, and Spider veered to her side of the car.

Her son reached the driver's door and opened it. "Get in the car, Mom."

Spider took her arm and opened the passenger door, supporting her as she slid into the front seat. "My name is Spider Latham. I was supposed to be talking with Mr. Taylor right about now. Brick Tremain asked me to come over, see if I could lend a hand with the trouble."

The driver leaned over and frowned up at Spider as he stood by the open door. "Come to the museum at nine tomorrow morning. We can talk then about 'the trouble' as you call it. I'll tell you one thing, Mr. Latham. When I find out who did this to my father, I'm going to kill him." He started the car and shifted into reverse. "Now shut the door. We're going to the hospital to see if my dad is going to survive the night."

Chapter 3

———◆———

THE NEXT MORNING, Laurie stood on the balcony of their hotel room and called through to Spider, brushing his teeth in the bathroom, "Have you ever seen sky so blue?"

"Not from where I am right now." He rinsed, put the cap on the toothpaste, and strolled out to join her. "What makes this sky bluer than the one in Lincoln County?"

"I think it's the red cliffs. They just bring out the blue."

"Well, I'll give you the red cliffs, but I'm not sure about the sky." Spider tapped his watch. "We're due at the museum in fifteen minutes."

Laurie leaned on the railing, looking at the towering sandstone mesas that ringed the town. "I'd forgotten how beautiful it is."

"You said that as we drove in last night. C'mon. We've got to go." Shooing her through the sliding glass door, he closed it behind her and followed through the room and out the door, making sure it was locked.

When they were in the pickup headed south on Highway 89A, as the country faded from red sandstone to brown, Laurie asked, "What is the son's name?"

"His mom called him Mattie. He looks more like a Matthew. Or a Matt."

"Does he work at the museum?"

"Don't know."

They rode in silence, dropping down in elevation as they crossed the state line. A few houses perched among the rocky cliffs to the left, and a tumbledown package liquor store stood next to the highway, ready to serve thirsty Utahans willing to travel the few miles into Arizona.

Topping the next rise, they could see Fredonia below.

"I wonder how Mr. Taylor is," Laurie said.

"We'll know soon as we find the museum."

"It's on this end of town. Just beyond all the refinery tanks."

"How do you know?"

"I saw the sign when we came through yesterday afternoon. It's called the Red Pueblo."

"Huh." Spider scanned the small town's outskirts, noting the missing metal on the huge steel tanks of the idle refinery and the vacant appearance of the surrounding buildings. "It doesn't look like a prosperous place."

"But the museum looks good. See the sign ahead?" Laurie pointed.

Spider followed the line of sight from her finger and saw three adjoining small square buildings painted red ochre. He looked at his watch. "We're five minutes late, but it doesn't look like it's open yet." He slowed and turned left into a drive that led to a padlocked gate painted the same hue as the buildings. He pulled up beside an older SUV with a dimpled roof that looked like a near kin to the one on his own pickup.

An older couple sat inside. The lady in the passenger seat had her silver hair trimmed short with bangs that fell over her brow. She turned and smiled so broadly at Spider that her eyes crinkled shut. She motioned him to roll down his window and lowered her own. Spider noticed for the first time that she had oxygen tubing over her ears and going to her nose.

She pointed to an area above him. "What happened to you?"

It took Spider a moment to realize she was asking about the roof of his truck. He had rolled it on Barkley Mountain, trying to outrun someone who was shooting at him, and he hadn't been able to pound out all the dents. "I missed a turn on a switchback," he said.

Her eyes crinkled. "We got ours on the hogback up on the Pinnacle Trail." Waving her hand to indicate the driver, obviously her husband, she said, "Dad got too close to the edge, and over we went. But we landed on the wheels."

Wondering at the wisdom of senior citizens on hogbacks, Spider said, "That was lucky."

"Dad says it was good management. He just hitched up the winch and hauled us back up. We were out getting rocks for Mattie's ax heads."

"Now, Mother." The SUV driver's voice was admonishing. "We're not to call him Mattie anymore. He's got a master's degree."

She spoke over the whoosh of her oxygen canister. "Mattie was good enough when I used to babysit for his mom. It's good enough now."

Spider glanced at his watch. "We were supposed to meet him here ten minutes ago."

"Mattie? He's not here until this afternoon. His father's scheduled to open today." She turned her head to look up the road toward Kanab. "He's always here early. I hope nothing's happened."

Spider cleared his throat. "Well, as a matter of fact—"

Her husband interrupted. "Here comes Mattie."

A mid-sized red pickup with a rack of lights on the cab pulled up behind the SUV, skidding on gravel that had migrated from the shoulder to the blacktop driveway. Matt Taylor got out of the cab, strode to the gate, and unlocked it. Pushing it open, he stood grim-faced while the two waiting vehicles passed through.

Laurie let out a breath. "Things don't look good."

"Well, let's wait and see what he says." Spider parked in front of the entrance to the well-kept museum building. To the right, a fence encircled a log cabin, a small replica of a dugout dwelling, and several different kinds of wagons.

The SUV pulled up beside them, and the red pickup followed. As Matt got out and stalked across to the double glass doors, his angular form reminded Spider of a coiled spring.

The senior couple met Matt at the entrance. Her oxygen bottle was slung over her shoulder in a canvas grocery bag as she waited for him to unlock the door. The husband, tall and heavy set with iron gray hair and a cookie-duster mustache, frowned as he listened to what Matt was saying.

"I hope we haven't come too late," Laurie said. "Are you going to talk to him?"

"Yeah." Spider watched Matt let the gray haired couple in and then turn to acknowledge the Lathams' presence, raising his hand and giving a *come on in* gesture.

"I'll look around the museum while you two talk," Laurie said.

Spider opened his door. "No. You've got good instincts. I'd just as soon you hung close by." He got out and waited for her to join him on the sidewalk and then held the door for her as they entered.

The museum lobby, though small, was well laid out. A receptionist's area sat behind a U-shaped glass showcase filled with pottery, baskets, stone axes and other Native American wares to sell. Books, pamphlets and maps lined one wall, and on the opposite wall, a wide arched doorway led into the museum proper.

Matt and the senior couple were behind the glass counter. All three looked up with solemn expressions as Spider and Laurie stepped through the doorway.

For a moment, nobody spoke. Spider, expecting the worst and wishing he had stayed home in Panaca, took off his Stetson and introduced himself and Laurie, explaining that he had come at Brick Tremain's behest. Turning to Matt he asked, "How's your father?"

"He's alive." Matt ran his hand over the dark stubble on his chin. "I sat with him all night. You'll have to excuse how I look."

"I'm LaJean Baker." The gray haired lady reached across the counter to shake hands with Spider and

Laurie. "This is Isaac. We volunteer here at the museum, and Isaac's on the board with Brick Tremain."

"We knew he was sending someone, but we didn't know it was you," Isaac said.

LaJean smiled. "I guess we didn't expect you'd be driving a pickup that had turned its oil pan to the sun."

Spider smiled back at her. "I like to keep a low profile. Glad to meet you both." Turning his attention to Matt, he asked, "What happened that sent your father to the hospital in an ambulance?"

"We thought it was his heart, but the doctors said that it was stress mimicking a heart attack."

"Then it wasn't an injury?" Laurie asked. "He wasn't attacked?"

Matt's brown eyes flashed. "Nobody came at him with a gun or a club, but I assure you, he is under attack."

At the sound of a car pulling into the driveway, Spider glanced out. A bespectacled child sat in the backseat, nose to the window. "Looks like you've got customers," Spider said. "Is there a place we could talk privately?"

"In here." Matt opened a door behind the counter leading to an office. The wall between the office and lobby was mostly glass, but it would offer a place where conversation couldn't be heard by strangers.

Spider stepped aside, so Laurie could precede him and then followed her in. The office was a study in organization, with labeled cupboards, cubbies and mail slots lining the walls. Matt sat at a desk located in the middle of the room, and Laurie and Spider took the chairs in front of it.

Setting his hat on the corner of the desk, Spider

pulled a small spiral notebook and pen out of his shirt pocket. He looked Matt in the eye and said, "I know you're angry enough to go bear hunting with a switch, but I need you to take a couple of deep breaths and tell me what's going on. All Brick said was that there was some kind of trouble."

Matt had his elbows on his chair, hands clasped in front of him, and his dark hair fell over his brow as he looked down and muttered through clenched teeth, "Some kind of trouble."

Spider waited, and the moments stretched out as Matt continued to examine his hands.

Laurie was the first to speak, and her voice was gentle. "Tell us when the trouble began. What was the beginning of your father's stress?"

Matt exhaled, a great whooshing sound like a deflating balloon. He unclasped his hands and rubbed his forehead, though he still kept his eyes lowered. "I guess the beginning of it was last year with the bathroom incident."

Spider opened his notebook. "Can you tell us what that was?"

The younger man made a motion with his hand as if trying to dismiss the memory. "The museum was built on what used to be a rest stop. The foundation got it from the state when they were going to close it down but with the proviso that we keep the restrooms open for travelers."

An electronic bell sounded a two-tone alert, and Spider glanced through the window into the lobby as a ten-ish boy shouldered his way through the door. His mother hung onto his shirttail, giving what seemed to be instructions as they entered. The boy pushed his glasses up on his nose and nodded as he towed her to the counter and began asking Isaac questions.

Spider saw that Matt was watching as well, and the sight of the boy's eager interest seemed to make his countenance lighter.

"The bathroom incident," Spider prompted.

"Yes." Matt sat up straighter. "A woman said she slipped on water from a leaky pipe. She sued for injuries and pain and suffering, said she lay there for two hours calling for help."

Laurie leaned forward. "How much was she asking for?"

"Two million dollars," Matt said.

Spider whistled. "Two million! She must have really busted herself up in the fall."

Matt snorted. "She didn't have a scratch on her. She said she hurt her back." Apparently sensing Spider's next question, he added, "There was no leaky pipe, either. There was water on the floor, but we were never able to find out where it came from."

"But that's ridiculous!" Laurie's eyes flashed. "I can't believe the courts would even consider the case."

"Oh, it was well presented. She had a good lawyer and a couple of doctors who gave convincing testimony."

"So what happened?" Laurie asked. "I suppose your insurance covered it?"

Matt shook his head. "Our limit was half that. We had to fight it, and in the end we settled out of court. The whole thing cost my father a quarter million."

Spider looked up from writing in his notebook. "Cost your father or cost the museum?"

"The museum doesn't have that kind of resources. We skate along on the edge of insolvency as it is. Some months, after everything else is paid, there's nothing left over for my salary." Matt raked his hair back with his fingers. "Dad raided his retirement fund and mortgaged the house, and he still came up short."

"What happened?" Laurie asked.

Matt indicated the gray-haired couple with his thumb. They were still at the counter, talking with the boy and his mother. "LaJean and Isaac got together and threw a fund raiser. Navajo tacos, a silent auction, concert and a dance. Folks turned out in droves and saved the museum."

"But it left your father a poor man," she said quietly.

"It depends on your definition of poor." Matt's gaze turned to the interior of the museum, seen through the arched door in the lobby. "He feels very rich to be able to share fifty years of exploring this area with the world. People come here from all over the globe, and he's able to tell them about finding an Anasazi medicine bundle or a bowl that's 700 years old in a cave up a box canyon."

Spider leaned back and crossed his legs. "So, your father's philosophical about what happened. The suit's settled; the museum's safe. What's the trouble that Brick Tremain was talking about?"

The front door signal sounded again, and Matt glanced up through the window into the lobby. He immediately turned away and picked up a pencil, twisting it in his hands. "I'm sorry. What was the question again?"

Spider examined the young woman entering the lobby, wondering why Matt was so determined not to look at her. Tall and angular, she had bronze skin and honey-colored hair pulled back in a ponytail. Her face had an open, honest look about it and, when she smiled at LaJean, a certain kind of beauty.

Laurie supplied a rephrasing of the question. "Why did Brick Tremain send us here?"

Matt opened the desk drawer and carefully set the pencil inside. His eyes slid sideways for a quick glance into the lobby.

Spider looked through the window, too, and saw the young woman, still smiling, take a key from a hook. She glanced beyond LaJean to the office where he, Laurie and Matt sat. The smile faded, and she turned and left the museum through a side door opening onto what a sign said was the Heritage Yard. Isaac and LaJean shepherded the mother and son into the yard right behind her.

A chime signaled the mass exit, and at the sound, Matt stood. "To explain about the current problem, I need to show you one of the exhibits. If you'll follow me, please?"

Passing through the archway and into the single exhibit room of the museum, Spider's first impression was of antiquity and neatness. Floor to ceiling display cases presented pottery, baskets, and other Anasazi artifacts in well-lighted, meticulously labeled order. "Are these all from around here?" he asked.

"Yes. Most of them were found by my father."

Laurie examined a pair of sandals made out of twisted grass. "He must have spent a lot of time exploring."

"He was a teacher. From the time I was a little boy, we spent every summer roaming the hills. But what I want to show you isn't Anasazi. It's right here." Matt stood just inside the archway.

Spider and Laurie joined him at a lighted case in the corner that held several artifacts that didn't seem to be Native American.

"Oh, look at that saddle!" Laurie bent over to examine it. "I don't think I've ever seen one like it."

"It's Spanish," Matt said. "It dates to the seventeenth century, but originally it wouldn't have been covered in tooled leather as this one is. It has apparently been refurbished at some time."

"Some time quite a while ago," Spider said. "There's not much leather left on it. And look, one of those rifle barrels is an old muzzle loader."

Laurie tapped on the case above where the information card was posted. "So, all these things were found together?"

"Yes," Matt said. "Somebody cached them in a cave. Probably in the late 1880s. Notice the woman's handkerchief?"

Laurie's eyes got wide. "You're not saying it was a woman who left them?"

Spider chuckled. "Where's your sense of romance? It was some lonely fellow, carrying his sweetheart's hankie next to his heart when he came out west. I wonder why he left it in the cave."

"Hard to say," Matt said. "He left some other things, too, like this brass match box and ammunition for the rifle. And—"

The door chime sounded. Matt stopped in mid-sentence and looked toward the entrance. Seeing his fixed gaze, Spider followed it.

A striking blonde had just entered. Dressed in Levi's, high heel sandals, and a champagne-colored knit top that accented the highlights in her hair, she took off her sunglasses and looked around.

"Excuse me," Matt said. Without waiting for a reply, he walked to the lobby.

Spider listened to the younger man's murmured greeting and watched as he stood, head bent, talking to the lady in low tones. Without a glance at Spider and Laurie, he took her arm and led her outside. They walked to the curb and stood in front of what was obviously her car, a red BMW convertible.

"I wonder if that's the trouble Brick Tremain was talking about," Spider mused.

"Well, she's trouble to somebody." Laurie pointed to the glass door that led to the Heritage Yard. Through it they could see the young woman who had been talking to LaJean. She stood near the dugout house, wearing a canvas apron and a bandana tied around her head. Her shoulders sagged, and her hands hung loosely at her sides as she stared at Matt and the elegant blonde.

Feeling uncomfortable at watching the naked despair on her face, Spider looked back at Matt, who was talking on his cell phone. He covered the receiver, said something to his companion, and walked back to the museum, finishing his phone conversation as he entered.

"Good news," he said as he dropped the instrument

in his pocket. "Dad is home. He'd like to have you come up to the house and talk to him."

Laurie clasped her hands. "That's great news."

Spider gestured toward the case that held the saddle and other items found in the cache. "Do you want to finish telling us about this?"

"Uh, no." Matt put his hands in his pockets and actually shuffled his feet. "I've, uh, got to talk to Tiffany Wendt." He nodded toward the blonde, now sitting in her convertible. "She's a museum patron. Gotta keep her happy."

He turned and quickly walked across the lobby and out the door. Through the window, Spider saw him break into a trot halfway to the car. Hopping in, he smiled at something she said as she backed away from the curb.

The bell sounded as the side door opened, and the girl in the apron and bandana came in. She kept her eyes on the floor as she went around the U-shaped counter and opened the door to the office beyond.

"She's gone in there to cry," Laurie said.

"Aw, shoot," Spider muttered.

"I know. Men are hard on women's hearts."

"No, that wasn't what I meant. I left my hat in there."

"Want me to get it for you?" Laurie raised a questioning eyebrow.

"Thanks, Darlin'. And see if you can find out what's going on."

Spider moved into position, so he could see through the window as Laurie opened the office door. He watched as she picked up his Stetson and said something to the girl. The girl didn't look at her but shook her head. Laurie sat by her, put her hand on the girl's back, and continued speaking.

After a while the girl sat up straight. Laurie pulled a tissue from a box on the desk and offered it, and they began to converse. Spider hung around where he could observe, but LaJean came into the lobby, so he moved over to the bookcase, pretending to read titles.

He watched LaJean hang a key on a hook behind the counter and peek in the office. She turned, met Spider's glance, and looked like she might say something, but at that moment Laurie came out.

Laurie smiled at LaJean and held out her hand. "It was nice to meet you and Isaac," she said. "I don't know if you heard, but Mr. Taylor is home from the hospital. He wants to see Spider, so we're heading up to Kanab right now."

"Well, that's the best news I've heard in a long time," the older lady said. "Lord knows, we haven't had much good news lately." She motioned toward the office.

Spider couldn't think of a reply, so he stepped toward the door. "I imagine we'll be meeting again," he said, nodding a good-bye. He held the door for Laurie, taking his Stetson from her as she passed through. Following her out, he waved to Isaac, who stood at the cabin door with the boy and his mother.

When he was in the driver's seat of the pickup with Laurie beside him, he asked her what she had learned when she went in to get his hat.

"Well, that girl's name is Linda Russell. She's been working at the museum since the first of the year." Laurie paused to secure her seat belt. "And up until five days ago, she was engaged to marry Matt Taylor."

Chapter 4

◆

Spider waited for a minivan to make a left turn into The Red Pueblo driveway before pulling onto 89A, heading north to Kanab.

Laurie rolled down her window to let the heat build-up escape. "Did Matt Taylor strike you as a little flakey?"

"What do you mean by flakey?"

"Well, there was something odd about the way he was acting. First he was almost hostile, and next he got all misty-eyed about his father's museum collection. Then he was going to explain what was going on but never got around to it. Finally, he left us high and dry when that blonde, manicured, city-type woman came."

"Driving a BMW," Spider added.

Laurie laughed. "Yeah. That blonde, manicured, BMW-driving, city-type woman. He couldn't get over to her fast enough when she walked in."

"Kind of like how ol' Jack is with you."

"I'll let that pass." She rolled up her window and turned the AC vent to blow directly on her. "The thing is, Matt didn't tell us diddly-squat. We don't know any more about Brick Tremain's trouble now than we did last night."

They crossed the state line, halfway to Kanab, and Spider set the cruise control on fifty-five. "I think we found out several things from ol' Matt. Some he told us, some he showed us."

"So, what did he tell us? Let me see your little notebook."

Spider handed the spiral pad to Laurie.

She opened the cover and looked at the list he had written. "What is this first thing? *Bakery implement*? *Halters imminent*? I can't tell if that's a B or an H."

"Let me see." Spider reached for the notebook and held it up so he could glance from the road to the list and back. "It says *bathroom incident*."

"Oh, I remember. He said that was the beginning of the trouble. But that all got settled."

"After Martin Taylor shelled out a quarter million dollars."

Laurie took back the notepad. "You've got number two as—" She squinted. "—*fall boat*? That can't be." She held the paper up so he could look at it.

"That's *flat broke*. Remember, he said his father cashed out his retirement and mortgaged the house?"

"That's scary to lose your retirement. I wonder how old his dad is."

"Don't know. Let me see what's next on the list." He glanced over as she held it up. "The next one says *fifty years of collecting*, and the one after that is *ponytail*."

"Ponytail? What's that for?"

"When that gal first came in—the one that ended up crying in the office—"

"Linda Russell."

Spider pulled up at the stop light at Main Street in Kanab. "Yeah. When she first came in, it was obvious there was tension between her and Matt. It was something I wanted to follow up on."

"Well, maybe Mr. Taylor can fill us in. Linda didn't want to talk about what happened, and from the way Matt was acting, I don't think he even knows she exists anymore."

Spider turned left, retracing the route of the night before to the Taylor residence. "Oh, he knows she exists, all right. But there's more that's come between them than someone in a red convertible."

"How do you know that?"

"Just a hunch. Something about the way he couldn't look at her."

"But that's because he's got that city gal panting after him."

Spider pulled to the side of the street, parking where the ambulance had been the night before. "Maybe, but when she first came in, he turned away and hunched one shoulder. Looked to me like a man in pain."

"He wasn't in much pain when he drove away with that woman."

"I noticed that he looked back at Linda, though, as they were going out the gate, and he looked like someone who'd been waiting for his ship to come in, and the pier collapsed." He opened his door. "Shall we go in and see what Mr. Taylor can tell us?"

The house, a fifties-vintage, red-brick rambler, had a patchy front lawn and tired side fence that seemed incongruous after the spit, polish, and order of the museum. It was obvious where Martin Taylor spent his time.

The aging concrete sidewalk had lost its smooth finish, exposing the aggregate beneath. Laurie and Spider followed it and mounted the two steps to the small front porch. Spider pushed the doorbell button, but not hearing a chime from the interior, he knocked on the door. It was immediately opened by Mrs. Taylor. She seemed to be the full color version of the pale woman he'd met the night before. A blue headband kept her shoulder-length hair away from her face and accented the color of her eyes.

"Mr. Latham? I met you last night. How do you do?" She opened the door wide. "I'm Geneva, but everyone calls me Neva."

"Nice to see you again in better circumstances." Spider took off his hat, and he and Laurie entered. "And you, too, sir," he said when Martin Taylor stepped forward. "This is my wife, Laurie."

Martin shook first Spider's hand and then Laurie's. "I can't tell you what it means to have you come." He pulled a handkerchief from the back pocket of his Levi's and wiped his eyes.

Spider regarded him, trying to get his measure. Of medium height and wiry build, Martin had graying hair, rimless glasses, and the look of a scholar.

"We haven't done anything yet." Spider looked around the living room, noting the serviceable-but-worn furniture. "We don't even understand what the problem is. Can we sit down and have you fill us in?"

"Didn't Mattie tell you?" Neva pulled a side chair closer to her husband's recliner and sat in it. With a sweep of her hand, she invited the Lathams to sit on the couch.

"He got called away on business," Laurie said.

"Oh?" The question was voiced by Neva, but both she and her husband looked expectantly at Laurie.

When Spider saw Laurie hesitate, he supplied the information. "Tiffany Wendt showed up just after word came you wanted to see us. He said you'd brief us and went somewhere with her."

There was a long pause during which neither of the Taylors met the eyes of anyone in the room. Finally, Martin spoke. "I see."

Spider set his hat on the couch. "Can I ask some questions?"

Martin grasped the arms of his recliner as if steeling himself. "Certainly."

"Brick mentioned trouble. He said it was serious, said I needed to get over here right away and needed to figure on investing a couple of weeks. As I said, no one as yet has told me exactly what that trouble is."

Martin ran his hand over a seam in the upholstery. There was a slight tremble in his fingers. "The trouble is, we're about to lose the museum. Or the Goblin Valley Ranch. Or both."

Spider took out his notebook and pen. "How?"

"A lawsuit."

Laurie sat forward on the couch. "Matt told us about that. He said it got settled."

"That was the first lawsuit," Neva said. "This is a new one."

Spider's brows went up. "Really? Another accident?"

Martin shook his head. "A family is suing us to recover the contents of the cache."

"The saddle and guns?" Spider handed the notebook and pen to Laurie. "Darlin', can you take notes? This will go a lot faster if I can just talk."

Martin spread his hands. "The cache contained quite a few items besides the saddle and guns. Most of them are in the display case. The value is, for the most part, only historical."

"I didn't get a chance to ask Matt where they were found," Spider said.

Martin pointed to his chest. "On land that belonged to my family."

Spider thought a moment. "And what is the law about finding things like that? Are you within your rights to keep it?"

"Yes," Neva said. "Things like the cache are considered the same as abandoned property. Because they're so old, and because they were found on our land, Martin, as finder, has ownership rights."

"But that doesn't matter," Martin said bitterly. "We're on our butts financially. We can't afford to go prove in court that we're within the law."

Spider frowned. "Wait a minute. I don't understand. How can these people even think to have a claim if you don't know the name of the person who left the cache in the cave? It seems like you would be able to go defend yourself without hiring a lawyer. All you have to do is show they have nothing to base a claim on."

Laurie cleared her throat. "Can I interrupt? Martin, you said most of the items found in the cache are in the display case, and most have only historical value. Was there something in the cache—something that's not in the case—that is worth a lot of money?"

Martin stood. "I was coming to that. Just a minute, and I'll be able to address both of your questions." He left and returned presently with an envelope in one hand and a pair of white gloves in the other. "Let's go sit in the dining room. The light is better there."

Neva led the way through an archway into a room where a mahogany table stood in the center, ringed with cardboard boxes stacked three high against the walls. "Please excuse the way it looks in here," she said. "We do lots of cataloguing at the table."

"Let's sit at this end." Martin placed the envelope on the table and put on the gloves. He seated himself at the head and waited for the others to sit. From the envelope, he solemnly pulled a piece of paper about the size of a three-by-five card that bore creases from having been folded several times. He showed them one side and then the reverse. "This was in the match box."

Spider leaned forward and examined the document lying in Martin's hand. "It looks to be part of a larger sheet of paper. On the underside, you've got pieces of sentences that have been cut away. What is it?"

Martin pointed to some writing. "Look at the signature."

"Great suffering zot," Spider murmured. "Does that say what I think it says?"

"His writing's better than yours," Laurie said to Spider. "A. Lincoln." She looked at Martin. "Is this authentic?"

"Yes, ma'am. Mattie has been working for six months to find out. We just got a definitive decision two weeks ago." Martin turned the paper over. "Apparently the two lines written by Lincoln were on the back of a letter from Archibald Dixon petitioning that Oscar Goodman, a confederate prisoner of war, be allowed to take the oath of allegiance to the union and be set free."

"Could I see the Lincoln writing again?" Spider peered at the scrap as Martin held it out to him, and he read aloud the two lines above the signature. "Sgt Oscar Goodman, as noted in Archibald letter, take Oath of Dec 8 and be discharged. Jan 16 1864."

"Who was Archibald Dixon?" Laurie asked. "And why was he writing to Lincoln? Wasn't Kentucky a confederate state?"

Martin shook his head. "The government was pro-union, the people pro-confederate, so officially Kentucky was neutral. Archibald Dixon was a union-leaning government leader."

Neva picked up the thread. "On December 8, 1863, Congress passed a bill allowing people from confederate states to take an oath of allegiance to the union and receive amnesty."

"So the oath was a get-out-of-jail-free pass for prisoners of war?" Laurie asked.

Martin raised a finger. "Not for soldiers from Kentucky who fought for the gray. Sergeant Goodman's family probably got Dixon to speak for them."

Laurie sat back in her chair and folded her arms. "But was Goodman the person who stashed everything in the cave?"

Martin shrugged. "Maybe so. Maybe not. The fact that Lincoln's note and signature were cut from the letter makes it look like someone was collecting a souvenir.

There's no way to know how the paper ended up in that cache."

Spider rubbed his chin as he digested the information Martin had just given him. "Okay. I understand about the signature, but you haven't said anything about who is bringing suit. Or on what grounds."

Martin slipped the paper back in its envelope. "Alyssa Goodman is the plaintiff. She says she's a direct descendent of Oscar Goodman."

Laurie looked from Neva to Martin. "But what does that matter? You said there's no way to prove he was the one who left the cache."

"What does your lawyer say?" Spider asked.

Martin's mouth opened, but no sound came out. His eyes widened, and he looked like a goldfish, his mouth forming an O and working uselessly as the skin around it took on a bluish tint.

Seeing Martin's hands begin to tremble, Spider stood. "Are you all right, sir?"

Neva stood as well. "No, he's not all right. I think he's going to faint again. There he goes; don't let him fall!" She turned around and hurried through a door behind her.

Martin's head fell forward, and he listed to the side. Spider stepped close to the chair and held the other man's body erect until consciousness returned.

Martin's eyes fluttered and then opened. "I'm going to—" His diaphragm began to constrict, and Spider looked around for something to use as a basin.

Neva reappeared and slid a mixing bowl onto the table just as Martin's breakfast reappeared in liquid form. She sponged his brow, cheeks and the back of his neck with a cool cloth, and she spoke in soothing tones. "Let's get you in to the couch, honey. You can rest and get over this dizzy spell." She looked up at Spider. "Can you support him? I think he can pretty much walk there."

Spider pulled Martin's arm around his neck and hoisted him out of the chair, but his legs were like wet noodles. Laurie stepped in on the other side, and between the two Lathams, they were able to get Martin from the dining room to the living room couch. Neva propped his head up with a pillow and bathed his face again.

When the color returned to Martin's cheeks, Neva moved away from the couch, pulling Spider with her. "I need to talk to you," she whispered. "Can you wait on the patio?" She pointed to the flagstones outside the sliding glass door.

Spider nodded. He picked up his hat, and he and Laurie stepped out into the shade of a huge cottonwood tree that stood in the back yard.

"Over here," Laurie said, walking toward a cluster of green resin chairs surrounding a table. He followed her, and they sat, waiting only a few minutes before Neva stepped through the door from the living room with a business card in her hand. She left the door open.

"He's better now," Neva said.

Spider stood. "You're sure you don't want to take him to the emergency room?"

"It would just be a repeat of yesterday. They'll tell me it's stress, and, frankly, we can't afford another trip to the hospital." Neva sat in a chair and patted the one next to her.

Spider sat but said nothing, simply watching as she fidgeted with the card in her hands.

"I don't know if this has anything to do with..." Neva flapped a hand in the direction of the living room where Martin lay on the couch.

Spider set his hat on the table. "Yes?"

"Well, a couple months before the accident in the bathroom—the first lawsuit—out of the blue, someone sent us a letter wanting to buy our Goblin Valley property."

She paused, and Spider waited for her to tell it in her own way and time.

"I thought it was odd," she went on, "because everyone in the county knows that Martin would die before he sold an acre of that land. It's got good water, plenty of it, and it's been in the family for five generations."

Spider caught Laurie's eye. "I feel the same way about our place," he said.

Neva went on. "The letter was from someone over in St. George who said they'd buy it sight unseen. They offered more than it's appraised for, and something about the whole thing just felt off. I mean, who does something like that?"

"So what did you do?"

"Martin wrote them a nice letter and told them he didn't intend to sell, no matter what the price. But then—"

"Yes?"

"After we settled the lawsuit for the accident and were flat broke—I mean sometimes I can't even afford to buy milk—we heard from them again, wanting to buy the property. This time for less money."

Spider patted his pocket, looking for his notebook. "Can you give me the name of the person in St. George who made the offer?" Looking around, he noticed that Laurie still had his pen and pad, and he signaled to her to write the information.

"I've got her card." Neva handed it to him.

"Leona Rippley," Spider read. "Earnest Endeavors? That's an odd name for a company. What did Martin do when the second offer came?"

"He wrote a very firm letter saying that there was nothing that could make him want to sell the ranch." She looked over her shoulder at the living room. "Three weeks later, we received the summons about the cache."

Spider put the card in his pocket. "And when did that second offer come?"

"Right after Fourth of July."

"Wait a minute." Laurie sat forward in her chair. "You think the offer and the lawsuit are connected?"

"They have to be. It looks to me like someone is determined to get us into a position where our only option is to sell the property. I'm scared we'll lose the museum. Scared we'll lose the ranch." Tears spilled over and ran down her cheeks. "Scared I'll lose Martin."

Spider fished in his pocket for the neatly folded handkerchief he'd put there this morning and handed it to Neva.

She held it to her eyes as if the layers of cotton could shut out the cares of the world. Leaning over, her elbows on her knees, she exhaled a great, drafty sigh. "And I'm afraid of what Mattie might do."

Laurie stood and scooted Spider off his chair next

to Neva, putting her arm around the woman's sagging shoulders. That compassionate act opened the flood-gates, and Neva began to sob, leaning against Laurie for support as the salty byproduct of her fear and helplessness freely flowed.

Spider walked to the trunk of the cottonwood and leaned against it, watching the way Neva sat in a semi-fetal position in the circle of Laurie's arms. Uncomfortable to be intruding on her misery, he walked around the tree and surveyed the back-yard neighbors' garden plot. While he examined the corn, green beans and ripening cantaloupe, he listened to Neva's lessening sobs and the encouraging tone of Laurie's murmured words. Finally he judged it was safe to walk back around.

Approaching Neva, he cleared his throat. "Could I ask what you meant when you said you were afraid of what Matt would do?"

Laurie's head whipped around and her eyes flashed. "Spider Latham, you leave this woman alone. She needs peace and quiet, not someone stirring the pot."

Neva held up her hand. "It's okay, Laurie." She wiped her nose with the still-folded handkerchief and turned red-rimmed eyes to Spider. "I don't know what I meant. Truly I don't. It just came out."

Laurie stood. "How about a little rest? Wouldn't that be good?" Her voice was soft and soothing as she helped Neva up.

The two women walked together to the house. Spider heard them talking to Martin as they stepped through the sliding glass door, and then Laurie reappeared.

"I think I'll stay here while Neva rests," she said.

"Why don't you go back to the hotel? It's just a few blocks. I'll walk back when I'm done here."

"All right." Spider waited a moment after Laurie disappeared inside, wondering if he should try to talk to Martin again. Deciding against that, he picked up his hat and walked around the house to where his pickup was parked.

He took an alternate route to the hotel and noticed a crew setting up a portable stage by the Kanab Museum steps. A banner over the road advertised that the Western Legends Roundup was this coming weekend. Spider inwardly groaned, seeing visions of what his father used to call 'drugstore cowboys' thronging the streets. And cowboy poetry. There would be lots of cowboy poetry.

It was with that depressing thought that he turned left into the hotel parking lot and braked at the sight of the car in the fourth parking space. "Turns up like a bad penny," he muttered. Cars on both sides obscured the front of the square little orange car, but he'd lay money that it was a Yugo and had black flames flowing back on the front and sides.

Chapter 5

◆

"Hey, deputy latham!"

Recognizing the voice, Spider rolled down the window. "Hello, Jade. I thought you might be around. Your car gave you away."

Jade crossed from the direction of the hotel lobby, fishing an envelope from his pocket as he walked. A young man trailed behind, carrying a yellow plastic shopping bag. "It's not my car," Jade said.

"The company car, then."

Jade grinned. "Not anymore. Now it's yours."

"Say again?" A minivan beeped the horn behind him, and Spider waved an apology. "Let me park," he told Jade. "Then we can talk."

He swung into a vacant space and got out of the truck. "What are you doing here in Kanab?" He shook his friend's hand and then took the proffered envelope.

"Special delivery. Oh, this is Raul. He's my brother-in law."

Spider greeted Raul and then opened the envelope. Pulling out several sheets of paper, he examined the first one and his eyebrows shot up. "Great suffering zot! Is this for real?"

Jade hadn't quit grinning since he had first greeted Spider. "Yeah. You're now the proud owner of a 1991 Yugo. Allow me to personally thank you, along with all the other people at Tremain Enterprises. Keys are in it."

"I don't understand."

"Nothing to understand. Dad has given you the Yugo."

"But why?"

Jade drew them both into the shade of a covered walkway where heat wasn't radiating off the black asphalt. "I told him you were driving that same pickup, and he felt you ought to have another car. He knows you can't use your county cruiser when you're doing work for him. He says driving the Yugo gives you an edge."

"Oh? How's that?"

"He says people will underestimate you. Let their guard down."

Spider folded the papers and put them back in the envelope. "You sound like you don't quite believe him."

Raul laughed and Jade nodded, a rueful look on his face. "Yeah. I think when he bought the Yugo he thought it would appreciate in value. Having it in the garage reminds him that he may know lots about mining but not much about cars."

Spider held up the envelope. "So, it's mine?"

"The car is yours. The tax write-off is his." Jade looked at his watch. "We've got a four hour drive ahead of us. We've got to get on the road, but here, take these." He motioned to his companion.

Mystified, Spider took the sack Raul handed him.

"Dad wants to be able to get hold of you," Jade said. "And, since the Yugo has the problem with the gas gauge—"

"I remember," Spider interrupted.

"—he wants you to be able to get hold of Laurie."

Spider looked in the bag and took out a smart phone in a blue case.

"That one is Laurie's," Jade said. "Yours is black. You've got a service contract for a year, courtesy of Tremain Enterprises. All the company numbers are already in it. Keep it charged and on."

"Charged and on," Spider said. "I may be able to manage that."

Jade walked back out onto the asphalt. "Dad kept the insurance on the car. It's good for six months. His assistant will let you know when you need to change it over."

Spider dropped the envelope in the plastic bag and followed Jade into the sunshine. "I don't know what to say."

Jade laughed. "Admit it. You don't know whether to thank dad or curse him."

"No, no. Tell your dad thank you. Shoot, I'll tell him myself. I've got his number and a phone to call him with."

"It's a smartphone," Raul said. "It'll do more than call. You can access the Internet from anywhere, send emails, do research."

"Sounds like it's smarter than I am," Spider said. "My son Robby tried to show me how to use one last time I visited him in Seattle. I don't know who was more frustrated, him or me."

"It has a GPS to help you find an address," Raul said. "You want me to show you how to use it?"

Jade clapped his brother-in-law on the shoulder. "No time, *hermano*. We have to get on the road." He waved a farewell to Spider as he backed away. "Remember, Dad wants a report."

"I don't know much yet. Got a lot of questions but dang few answers."

Jade and Raul got in a small sedan parked near the office, and Spider walked over to the Yugo. He stood, hands on hips, the corners of his mouth lifting in a wry smile.

Jade backed up and rolled down his window. "I left a couple bottles of water in the back."

"Thanks." Spider waved as Jade pulled away then opened the door of his new car and leaned in to get the key.

A voice spoke from behind. "I had a car just like that when I was seventeen."

The accent was slightly British, and Spider straightened up and looked around to see who had spoken. The only person nearby looked decidedly un-British. Of medium height and slender, he had black hair, dark eyes and skin the color of honey.

The fellow smiled. "Of course it was a different color and didn't have flames all over the bonnet."

"I'd like it better if this one was a little less conspicuous." Spider stepped into the shade under the awning. "So what did you think of it at seventeen?"

"I thought I would rather have an E-type Jag."

Spider rubbed his jaw as he did the math. "Didn't Jaguar quit making the E-types in the mid '70s?"

The stranger's dark eyes twinkled. "Yes. My father

wanted to keep me humble. I told him driving a twenty-year-old E-type would do the joke."

"Do the joke? Oh, you mean it would do the trick."

"Yes. Do the trick. I have to practice that one.

"I take it he didn't buy your argument?"

"He did not buy the argument or the Jag. He bought a brand new Yugo."

Spider chuckled and stuck out his hand. "By the way, my name's Spider Latham."

"Spider, you said?" The stranger clasped his hand. "I am Karam Mansour."

"Where you from, Karam?"

"By birth and," he touched his heart, "in here, I am Palestinian, from Gaza. But I live and work in Dubai."

"Is that so?" Spider leaned a shoulder against one of the pillars supporting the awning. "So what brings you to this neck of the woods?"

Karam's brows came together. "I do not understand this...neck in the...woods, was it?"

Spider stood. "Sorry. I was just wondering what you're doing in these parts. Around here. In Kanab."

Karam's white teeth flashed. He took out his phone and tapped the screen several times and then began keying in the phrase, saying each word softly as he spelled it. "I collect American idioms, since I teach American History." He put the phone back in his pocket. "To answer your question, I was on my way to San Diego, and my car broke down. The man at the garage sent me to a man who is confident he can fix it, but we are awaiting parts."

"Oh. How long's it going to take?"

"Two weeks."

"Two weeks? Great suffering zot! Where do the parts have to come from?"

"Unfortunately, from London."

"What kind of a car do you have? No, don't tell me. A 1974 E-Type Jag?"

Karam raised his hands in surrender. "It's a '73, and I perfectly understand why my father would not buy me one."

Spider laughed. "Speaking of being humble, there's nothing lower than being afoot in a one-horse town."

Noting the confused look on Karam's face, Spider changed the wording. "There's nothing worse than not having transportation in a very small town."

"It is very inconvenient. There is a museum in the next town that I wanted to see, but there is only one taxi in Kanab. He is already booked."

"The Red Pueblo? I was just getting set to go down there myself. Want to come with me?"

"That would be excellent."

"Tell you what. How about you drive the Yugo and follow me, so I can drop my rig off for my wife. Then we'll head on down to the museum."

Karam agreed, and the Yugo shadowed Spider's truck to the Taylor residence. When Laurie answered Spider's knock, she put her finger to her lips and said, "They're both sleeping."

"I just wanted to give you this." He held out the pickup keys in one hand and the plastic bag carrying her cell phone in the other.

As she took them, she spied the Yugo sitting at the

curb and looked questioningly at Spider. His whispered explanation about Jade, the Yugo and Karam only seemed to confuse the issue.

"We'll sort it out this afternoon," she said. "Thanks for bringing me the pickup."

"Call me," he said backing away. He pointed to the yellow bag.

Laurie's brows drew together, and when Spider motioned for her to open the sack, she looked inside. Letting the door close behind her, she stepped to the edge of the porch. "What's this?"

"Brick Tremain wants us to stay in touch. Call me when you're on your way home. My phone number's in it."

Spider walked back to the car and got in the passenger seat. "Just head on down to the end of the block and hang a right."

Karam put the car in gear. "Go straight then turn right?"

"That works, too." As they pulled away, Spider adjusted the air conditioning, sat back, and looked around. From the inside it wasn't a bad looking car. A little Spartan, perhaps, but the price was right.

Karam broke into his thoughts. "Your wife is beautiful."

"I've always thought so."

"I will be marrying this winter. She is my cousin. We have been promised for several years, but getting in and out of my country is hard. If she emigrates successfully, we will marry in Dubai."

"Your cousin? First or second?"

"This will be my first wife."

"No, I mean is she your first cousin? The daughter of your father's brother?"

Spider watched while Karam whispered the words to himself, working out the connection.

"Yes," he said.

"Does that happen much in your country, marrying your cousin?"

Karam nodded. "Young men know they owe it to their families to make sure the young women have husbands."

Spider grunted. "Huh."

"Young men have an obligation to see that their cousins have the chance to marry."

"You just said that."

"But you said 'huh.' Does not that mean you do not understand?"

Spider thought a moment. "I guess it does, depending on how you say it. Sometimes it means you got the message."

"So, depending on how you say it, it can either mean you do not understand or you do understand?"

"That's about the size of it."

"Size of what? What are you talking about?"

"That means what you said is right. Correct. True."

Karam pulled over to the side of the road at the Arizona state line. "Will you please drive? I need to record these notes."

Spider took the wheel, and as they dropped down into Fredonia, Karam whispered, "That's...about...the...size...of...it," as he keyed the phrase and meaning into his phone.

Spider made the left turn into the museum parking lot. The Bakers' SUV was still there, as was Matt's red pickup and Linda's beige Kia SUV. Spider pulled up beside two out-of-state cars. "I'll introduce you to Isaac, and he'll show you around. I need to talk to a couple other people."

As they walked to the entrance, Spider noticed Linda and Matt in the Heritage Yard with a cluster of people around them. Matt was bent over a workbench, pounding on a rock while Linda addressed the group.

LaJean and Isaac were behind the counter when Spider and Karam pushed open the glass doors. She hitched up the canvas bag holding her oxygen bottle and said, "Hey, Stranger. That's quite the rig you're driving."

"Just trying to impress the ladies." Spider took off his hat and gestured toward his companion. "Let me introduce you to Karam Mansour. He's interested in American History."

"Glad to meet you, Karam." Isaac offered his hand. "You've come to the right place."

Spider indicated the knot of people around Matt and Linda. "What's going on out in the yard?"

"Mattie's demonstrating how to make an Anasazi ax head," Isaac said. "It's quite a skill."

Karam took out his phone. "I would like to see it. May I take pictures?"

"Take as many pictures as you like." Isaac motioned for Karam to follow him to the door that led out to the Heritage Yard. "You can even give it a try."

When they were gone, LaJean cocked her head. "You don't want to learn how to make a stone ax?"

"No, I'd like to talk to you about what's been going on at the museum."

"Well, you might as well come around behind the counter, so we can sit down." She pulled the two folding chairs into a conversation position and sat. "What do you want to know?"

Spider took the chair opposite, his hat in his lap. "I want to know how word got out about the name on the Lincoln document."

LaJean stared at Spider for a moment. She took the canvas bag from over her shoulder and set it on the floor beside her. "Who told you about the Lincoln document?"

"Martin showed it to me. He had another spell before I could ask him what I'm asking you, and Neva's not doing well, either. I thought if I could get the information from you and Isaac, it might be better for all concerned."

LaJean leaned forward and glanced through the side door at the group in the Heritage Yard. "Here's what I know. There were six people who knew about the Lincoln letter." She held up six fingers, lowering one each time she named a name. "Isaac. Me. Martin. Neva. Mattie. Linda."

"So, who leaked the name?"

"I only know that Isaac didn't, and I didn't. We haven't mentioned it to a soul. I'm almost as sure about Martin and Neva. There are lots of secrets here—where things have been found and such. They'll probably take those secrets to their graves. Why would they spill the beans on this?"

"What about Matt?"

"Mattie's like his father. He can keep a secret."

"Which leaves Linda."

"Yes" LaJean sighed. "Which leaves Linda."

"Who would she have told? And why?"

"Who? I don't know. Why? That old green-eyed monster. It makes people do things they never would if they were in their right mind."

"Jealousy? Is that what you mean?" Spider looked at the two young people in the Heritage Yard. They were engaged in a common task yet they didn't speak to each other, didn't even look at one another. "Who is Linda? When did she come to the Red Pueblo?"

"Mattie brought her here last January. He knew her at the university, and when she graduated, he talked Martin into hiring her. She's had a lot of great ideas for the museum, like the demonstrations and classes in the Heritage Yard. She teaches flint knapping—"

Spider broke in. "—which is?"

"It's how you make arrowheads." LaJean pointed at a tray in the glass case. "She made all of these. See how the stone is flaked away at the edges?"

"Is that what they're doing out there now?"

"That's another process called pecking and grinding. Check out that ax right there." She tapped the glass case. "You just hammer away with another rock until you get it the shape you want, and then you grind it on a harder rock until it gets an edge to it."

Spider bent forward and studied the stone implement. "That's not much of an edge."

"It'll cut wood," she assured him. "It's been a big boost to the museum's stature to have the classes, and it helps the people appreciate the Anasazi's ingenuity. And, it's all Linda's doing."

"Okay." Spider sat back and stretched out his legs. "So she comes here. She's an asset. Hard worker. Then what?"

"It was obvious to me when she came that she was in love with Mattie. They make a great team, and I think he saw that in her—saw them taking over where his parents will leave off some day. It seemed to me he made the decision to marry her more with his head than his heart, but that's not a bad thing." She lifted the green oxygen bottle out of the canvas bag beside her chair and looked at the gauge. "If you'll open that cupboard beside you, there's another one of these in there. Thanks." She used a small wrench hanging on a chain around her neck to exchange bottles and gave him the empty one to put back on the shelf.

"Now," she said, "what was I saying? Did it make any sense? Sometimes I don't when I run out of oxygen."

"You were telling me that Linda gave Matt her heart, and he gave her the museum in return."

LaJean dropped the bottle in the bag and took out her knitting. "That's one way to put it, though I think he's fonder of her than he realized. It really hurt him when she took up with that fellow from St. George."

Spider sat up. "Wait! What fellow from St. George?"

She looked up, needles poised. "No one has mentioned Austin Lee?"

Spider shook his head. "This is the first I've heard of him."

LaJean leaned forward again to check on the status

of the people in the yard. "Smooth as honey butter, he is. Handsome, in a California surfer kind of way."

"How's that?"

"Oh, you know. He's got sun-streaked blond hair and broad shoulders. Of course he's tall, and he dresses real sharp. Drives an expensive car. I don't blame Linda for falling for him. If he'd come in and started paying attention to me, I might have fallen for him myself."

Spider rubbed his jaw. "I need to visualize a timeline on this. Can you tell me the order that things happened in, from Linda coming and getting engaged—did Matt actually give her a diamond?"

"It was a turquoise ring that belonged to Martin's mother."

"Okay. When did that happen?"

"Memorial Day weekend. They announced it at the museum picnic.

"When did they break up? I take it Austin Lee entered the picture before that. And don't leave out Tiffany Wendt, either. I'm assuming she's the cause of the green-eyed monster."

LaJean put down her knitting, hefted herself out of the chair and walked around the counter to get the guest sign-in book, trailing her oxygen hose behind her.

Spider peeked in the bag. "How long a tether you got on that thing?"

"About forty feet." She returned to her chair and opened the guest book. "I can tell you the exact day that Tiffany Wendt showed up. And you're right. I think if she hadn't appeared on the scene, Linda wouldn't have looked twice at Austin Lee."

"So who called it quits? Do you know?"

LaJean snorted. "I think everyone in the county knows. They had an argument at about ninety decibels out in the yard." She opened the visitor log. "But I'm getting ahead of myself. You wanted a time line."

Spider waited while she paged through the book.

She finally stopped. "Tiffany visited for the first time on July third."

"What's her story? Is she local? Move-in? Married?"

"She's a returnee. She went to high school in Kanab, and then her family moved away. She grew up and married the owner of a software company. He apparently had a roving eye, found something he liked better, and gave her a pile of money in a divorce settlement. She remembered being happy here and decided to move back."

"I see. Did she know Matt in high school? Were they sweethearts?"

LaJean shook her head. "She was a cheerleader, prom queen, that kind of thing. Mattie was always out roaming the hills when he wasn't in class. Roaming and thinking." She tapped her temple. "He's got a lot upstairs."

"And Tiffany?"

"I think she's smart, but in a different way."

Spider raised a questioning eyebrow. "How so?"

"Oh, socially. Always knows the right thing to say and the right person to say it to. Never puts a foot wrong. Linda, on the other hand, doesn't have a social grace to her name."

Spider looked through the door at Matt and Linda.

The group of people that had surrounded them, Karam included, had moved on to the dugout, and the couple stood, heads bent, working on shaping ax heads. "They're a good-looking pair, seeing them like that," he said, turning back to LaJean. "But let's get back to the timeline. Engaged Memorial Day weekend. Tiffany shows up around the Fourth of July. What was that like?"

La Jean picked up her knitting again. "It wasn't like anything. She came to see the museum. Visited with Martin and Mattie. Visited with Isaac and me. Visited with Linda. We all thought she was great."

"All? Even Linda?"

"I told you, Tiffany never puts a foot wrong. She made Linda think she was her biggest fan. And I think she was sincere."

"So what changed?"

"All I can tell you is what I think." LaJean paused to count stitches. "Tiffany fell for Mattie, and she was determined to have him. She saw that his life is the museum, and she played to that. She offered to donate a sizeable sum to the Red Pueblo Foundation."

"How sizeable?"

"A quarter million dollars."

Spider whistled. "So he drops Linda because a gal with money comes along?"

LaJean pointed a knitting needle at him. "I hear the disapproval in your voice. You're way off base. Mattie's not like that."

"So, tell me what he's like."

"He's loyal and true, and he'd walk through fire

to help his dad. Sure he's paying attention to Tiffany. A quarter million dollars would go a long ways toward getting the museum back on its feet."

"But she hasn't given the money yet? Is that why he's being so attentive and laughing at her jokes? Would that classify as walking through fire?"

"I think so, yes." LaJean finished the row and jabbed her needles into the ball of yarn. "Let me finish your wretched timeline." Her smile took the bite out of the comment.

Spider returned the smile. "Last thing on it was Tiffany's arrival the first part of July."

LaJean picked up the visitor log and scanned through the pages. "Here it is. Austin Lee showed up on July twentieth."

Spider leaned over and looked at the name printed in precise block letters. "Do you remember anything about that day?"

"You mean besides having three tour busses stop at the same time?" Her eyes twinkled. "I'm kidding. I know what you mean, and yes, I do remember several things."

LaJean's brow furrowed as if trying to marshal her thoughts. While he waited, Spider glanced around the Heritage Yard. Isaac was talking, making sweeping gestures in the air, and Karam was listening intently to what he was saying.

"First," LaJean said, calling Spider back to attention, "when Austin showed up that day, Tiffany was out in the yard with Mattie while he was demonstrating the making of ax heads for one of the tour busses. Linda was in here minding the counter with me."

"Why does that stick in your memory?"

"Well, Mattie and Linda have always been a team—like today. They have a routine worked out that they go through, and all the tourists enjoy it." She tapped the page in the book. "This was the first time that Mattie did the routine with someone else."

"You say it was the first time. Does that mean he and Tiffany have partnered up other times?"

"Yes. Quite often."

"Whose idea was it the first time? Did she volunteer or did Matt suggest it?"

LaJean's eyes crinkled at the corners. "I told you she was good. She made it seem like Linda invited her to work with Mattie that day."

Spider nodded. "What else did you notice? You said 'several things.'"

"I noticed that Linda couldn't keep her eyes off Mattie and Tiffany and that every now and then, her chin would quiver." She pointed to the oxygen bottle. "If my heart wasn't already in such tough shape, I'm sure it would have broken to see her like that."

"Okay. Anything else?"

"Yeah. There's one more thing I've been wondering about. Say you're a good-looking fellow, drive a fancy car, dress sharp. Say you're the kind of guy that sets the ladies to swooning."

"That stretches the imagination, but, okay. Say I'm that kind of guy."

"You come into the museum, and you've got two ladies working here. One's mousy and shy—not to mention red-eyed from crying. The other is good looking, dressed to the nines, and outgoing as all get out. Who are you going to try to spend time with?"

"You mean would I hang around Tiffany or Linda? Well, if I'm a fancy dresser, driving a car less than twenty years old and without flames all over the front of it, probably Tiffany."

"That's what I thought, too, but he didn't even go out into the yard. He came in, looked at the displays, and then spent about half an hour here at the counter talking to Linda."

"What about?"

"Anasazi stuff. She was telling him about the axes. She tried to get him to go out and see the demonstration, but he stayed in here. He ended up buying one but wanted to be sure it was one she had made."

"Huh." Spider took a moment to consider. "That was just over three weeks ago. What happened after that?"

"They started spending time together."

"Linda and Austin? What kind of time together? Wasn't she still engaged?"

"Officially, yes. But Mattie would take off with Tiffany, and Linda would be here feeling left out. Naturally she's going to appreciate someone paying attention to her." She marked her place with her index finger and closed the guest book, holding it in her lap. "I tried to tell Mattie that he was shooting himself in the foot. I told him that Austin was going to cut his grass, but he said that Linda understood what he was doing. He said she was 'above jealousy.'" LaJean snorted. "Roaming the hills instead of going to dances doesn't teach a young man anything about women."

"So, for three weeks Matt has been courting a quarter million dollars."

"That's one way of putting it."

"And for those same three weeks, Austin has been courting Linda."

LaJean shook her head. "Austin dropped out of sight."

Spider's brows arched. "He did? When?"

She opened the book and leafed through it. "The last day he was here was when we had the Lithuanian tour bus stop in. Yes. It was on August third, about a week and a half ago."

"Was there some kind of squabble? He didn't just quit coming without saying anything?"

"Afraid so."

"Well, no wonder she's trailing wet tissues everywhere." Spider thought a moment. "There's one more thing. You said everyone heard Matt and Linda break up. What was the problem?"

"I can only guess. Most of the conversation took place inside the dugout in what you might call civilized tones. But Mattie must have said something that set her off. She came busting out of the door, screaming at him."

"What was she saying?"

"She was asking a question. 'I betrayed you?' Emphasis on the 'you.' Said it twice. Then she ripped off her apron and bandana and threw them on the ground and said she quit. He could consider that the beginning of her two weeks' notice. And she said the ring was in the apron pocket."

"And when was this, exactly?"

"Last Friday." She closed the book and set it on the counter. "Does that complete your timeline?"

"Looks like it." Spider picked up his hat and stood. "Thanks for spending the time with me. I think I'll have a word with Linda now."

"Linda just left. She drove off not two minutes ago."

Spider looked out at the empty parking spot where the Kia had been sitting. "Shoot. Well, in that case, I'll talk to Matt."

LaJean stood, pushing herself up with her arms and slowly straightening. She picked up the guest book. "I hope you can get this all sorted out," she said as she carried it back to its resting place.

"I hope so, too." Spider held his hat up in salute and headed toward the door to the Heritage Yard.

Out in the yard, Spider found Matt putting his ax-making tools into a basket which he then stowed on a shelf under the rough-hewn workbench. The bench was on wheels and had handles like a wheelbarrow, and he began wheeling it toward the fence.

Spider put on his hat and angled over to open the gate.

"Thanks," Matt said, passing through without looking up.

Closing the gate, Spider followed to the storage room and paused at the doorway. "You got a minute?" he asked.

Matt, inside, parked the workbench and put the basket of tools up on a shelf before he answered. "What for?"

"I'd like to ask you some questions." Spider ignored

Matt's impatient gesture and stepped inside. "Just a couple. I've got the lay of the land from your dad and LaJean, but there are some things only you can tell me."

Matt looked at the floor and rubbed his hands on his pants. "Like?"

"Like, what did you say to Linda last Friday about betrayal?"

Matt reached up to straighten the basket and then held onto the shelf, leaning his head against his arms.

Spider waited a moment and then said, "You haven't been much help thus far, you know."

Matt spoke, head still down, voice muffled. "I know. I've got myself into such a jam that it's hard to talk about it. It's like, if I don't say it aloud, maybe it isn't so. I knew I'd have to say it aloud to you."

"I'm not here to judge, son. What kind of jam are you talking about?"

Matt cleared his throat, stood, and met Spider's eyes. "For starters, I accused Linda of leaking the news about the Lincoln letter."

"How did you frame the accusation? What did you say?"

"I said she had betrayed the museum."

Spider grimaced. "That covers a whole range of things. Did she deny it?"

Matt blinked. His eyes shifted back and forth, as if he were working something out. "No. She didn't deny it."

"But she was angry?"

"She was angry about the time I spend with Tiffany, about the attention I pay her."

"Without cause?"

Matt put his hands in his pockets and kicked at the caster on the workbench to straighten it. "No. She had cause, all right, but I couldn't see it then. All I could see was that I had to spend time with Tiffany, be nice to her. I thought she was going to save us."

Spider folded his arms and leaned against the wall. "Do you still think she's going to save the museum?"

Matt looked past Spider at something in the distance. "I've begun to wonder what she would want from me in return."

Spider followed his gaze to the landscape framed by the storeroom door, the brown mesas beyond the parking lot and the blue Kaibab plateau in the distance. "From what little I've seen, it's obvious that she wants an exclusive arrangement. You're probably the one to say whether or not that includes marriage."

Matt looked as if he had bitten into something sour. "The woman never stops talking. I took her out to some cliff dwellings last Saturday, and she never shut up the whole time we were there. On the way back—and we saw some splendid things—her whole conversation was about a broken fingernail."

Spider grunted sympathetically, and Matt continued, growing more exasperated with each point, ticking them off on his fingers. "She calls the Anasazi *Anna's Nazi's*. She can't see any difference between their pottery and the Navajo's, and she wants to get an electric Dremel tool to make the ax heads go faster."

"Sounds like the opposite of Linda," Spider said.

"Linda is like...like water to a thirsty man. You don't have to talk to her, you know? When we're out in the canyons, we can hike for hours without saying anything, but when we speak, we're always on the same page. It's like she knows what I'm thinking."

Spider pushed away from the wall. "Except about Tiffany, I think. Why haven't you told her what you just told me?"

"She probably wouldn't listen. She's leaving, you know. Going away."

"Where?"

"I don't know. She left just now because she's got a phone interview. Some other museum will snap her up."

Spider stepped outside and blinked in the sunlight. He turned and spoke to Matt, still standing in the dimness of the storeroom. "Well, if she did spill the beans about the Lincoln letter—and we don't know that she did—I'd better find out from her who—"

At that moment, the phone in Spider's Levi's pocket vibrated and startled him so that he actually jumped sideways. "Hey!" he shouted. He leaned over, searching for the cause, and felt the buzz against his leg again.

"What's the matter?" Matt's voice held concern.

Spider fished the phone out of his pocket, held it up to show Matt, and then moved back into the shade, so he could see the screen. "How do I answer the damn thing?" he muttered.

Matt's hand appeared from over his shoulder and tapped an icon on the screen.

"Thanks." Spider put the phone to his ear.

"Hello? Hello?" Laurie's voice sounded tentative.

"Hello, Darlin'. What's going on?"

"I'm at Jack's office. He's got the next couple hours off, and he wants us to come out to his place for lunch."

Spider's watch said it was half past noon. He looked around the yard and spied Karam and Isaac at the far side by the drill rig. Isaac was making large circular motions with his arms, and Karam was nodding, apparently understanding what Isaac was saying.

"Spider?" Laurie prompted.

"I'm here." Spider wished he had some alternate lunch plans to offer, but he went with the best he could come up with and still be truthful. "I was going to ask Karam to have lunch with us."

"Just a minute." Laurie's muffled voice sounded in the background, and then she spoke into the receiver. "Jack says to bring him, too."

Spider gently scooted a beetle off the sidewalk with the toe of his boot. "All right."

Laurie appeared not to notice the hesitation. "Great," she said. "I'll meet you at the hotel in ten minutes."

Chapter 6

Jack's ranch was at the end of a gravel road that turned north off Highway 89 a few miles east of Kanab on the road to Page. Alfalfa, green and lush, spread out on either side as the Yugo rolled along, a plume of dust hanging in the still air behind them.

"Good looking feed," Spider said, noting the wheeled piping system that irrigated the fields. "Where does he get his water?"

Laurie gazed at the green expanse. "I think he's got a spring up at the head of this canyon, but I'm not sure."

"It'd have to have a pretty good flow to take care of all this acreage."

Karam spoke from the backseat. "Fredonia didn't have a town water supply until 1935. Before then, the people caught rainwater from their roofs and stored it in underground water tanks. I can't remember the name for them."

"Cisterns," Spider supplied.

Laurie turned around. "How do you know that, Karam?"

"Isaac told me. Tomorrow, he's going to take me to look at some of the old houses that still have...cisterns."

He smiled. "Isaac said that when the water got low, sometimes water bugs would come out of the tap."

Laurie grimaced. "Ugh." She faced forward again as they rounded a curve and drove beyond a screen of poplars that hid Jack's ranch. Seeing the house and outbuildings, she whistled under her breath. "Oh, wow."

They passed under a stucco arch with a huge wooden sign spanning the width of the roadway hanging on it. The word *Braces* was carved into it with each letter charred black.

Spider snorted. "Braces? What kind of a name is that for a ranch?"

"It seems very strange." Karam drew imaginary lines from his shoulders to his waist. "Is he talking about things to hold your pants up? Why would he put that over the gate?"

Laurie giggled. "Those are suspenders."

Karam cocked his head. "Really?"

"We call them suspenders; people in England call them braces." Spider traced a line across his bared teeth. "Braces go on your teeth to straighten them."

Karam looked back at the sign. "That doesn't make any more sense than suspenders."

"He's an orthodontist. Braces probably paid for his place," Laurie suggested.

"He must have done a lot of them," Karam said. "This is a very nice place."

Spider slowed the car. "I thought he said it was a straw bale house."

The house rambled in front of them in pueblo style with stucco cubes, cylinders and arches in single and double stories and vigas sticking out at intervals along the top of the flat roofline. A breezeway separated a three car garage from the house.

"It's huge," Laurie said. "It must be three times the size of our place."

"And look at the outbuildings." Spider pointed toward a tall structure in matching architecture set a ways off. It had barn doors with heavy wrought-iron hinges and, on either side, a wing with four horse stalls. "Even his barn is bigger than our house."

The grounds were landscaped with native plants and rock, and a circular driveway made of pavers swept through it. Spider parked the Yugo beside a yellow Mustang with a vanity plate reading *BRACES*. "Figures," he said under his breath.

They got out and stood beside a low, south-facing wall at the edge of the parking area. "This is really beautiful," Laurie said. "Look at the view. I'll bet you can see clear to the Grand Canyon."

"Mighty fine," Spider agreed. He took Laurie's arm and headed toward the house. "Come on, Karam. I hope you like cowboy poetry."

The house had a front veranda, shady and cool, behind a series of arches. They walked across to the massive front door, and when Spider pushed the doorbell, they heard a mellow four-note chime from the interior.

Immediately the door opened, and a short, plump twenty-something in knee-length athletic shorts and flip-flops opened the door. "Welcome," she said, her huge smile doubling the value of the word. "I'm Amy, and I'm going to cook for you."

"Hello, Amy. I'm Laurie. This is my husband, Spider. And this is our friend, Karam."

Amy opened the door wide and stepped back. "Come on in. Jack's out in the garden right now getting corn and cantaloupe. I'll take you to the patio."

Spider took off his hat as they passed through a high-ceilinged entryway to the living room where white plaster walls and windows that let in indirect sunlight gave the room an airy feel. Pausing to look around, he noted the peeled cedar beams, the rounded fireplace on a raised hearth, and the wide staircase and wrought iron banister. When Laurie tugged on his arm he whispered, "Is Amy Jack's wife?"

She shook her head. "Cousin."

"So, she's your cousin, too?"

"No. Come on."

They followed Amy's stocky figure across the terra-cotta-tiled floor of the living room to a bank of glass-paned doors on the opposite wall. Amy opened one of them and let them pass through to a covered patio where a table was set for four.

"Didn't Jack tell you we were bringing a guest?" Laurie asked.

Amy nodded. "I'll be serving you, and then I'm going to eat in my room. I'm writing a symphony, and I take any moment I can to work on it." She pulled out a chair. "If you'll sit, I'll bring you something cold to drink."

The men sat as directed, but Laurie said, "I'll come help, and you can tell me about your symphony." She followed Amy into the kitchen.

Leaning forward, Karam said softly, "What do you suppose she is bringing? I do not drink alcohol."

Spider set his hat on the table. "We don't either. I imagine it'll be lemonade."

Karam sat back and looked around. "This is very nice."

The same terra cotta tiles from the living room extended to the covered terrace and beyond, surrounding a small patch of lawn and stretching to a low stucco wall. Beyond the wall lay a well-tended garden, and Spider could see Jack's tall, gaunt form in the stand of corn at the far end.

Amy appeared with a tray of glasses, and Laurie followed with a pitcher. "Fresh limeade," she announced, pouring a glass and handing it to Karam.

Just then, Jack emerged from the corn patch holding a cardboard box. He stuck it under one arm and waved. "Welcome."

Laurie waved back.

Jack held up the carton and quoted in a loud voice,

> *The fixins in the chuck box*
> *Was gettin' pretty scant,*
> *And all the Bar X punchers*
> *Were lookin' mighty gant.*

Spider pasted on a wooden smile as his host came through the gate and across the lawn, and he stood when Jack reached the tiled margin. Karam stood as well.

Stepping forward, Spider held out his hand. "Nice to see you again, Jack. I'd like to have you meet our friend, Karam."

Jack shook Spider's hand first and then Karam's, continuing with his poem without comment.

The fellas gathered round the pot,
Anticipatin' stew
'Til Cookie lifted up the lid,
Revealin' one old shoe.

Still holding the pitcher, Laurie kissed Jack on the cheek. "I hope you're not planning on feeding us shoe leather."

"Nope. Prime Angus, raised right here on Braces." Jack handed the box to Amy. "Get that corn in the pot right away, and I'll cook the burgers."

Amy smiled. "I've had water boiling for ten minutes already, waiting on you."

"Well, I'm here now." Jack raised the lid of a stainless barbeque unit and turned on the burners.

Spider and Karam sat back down, and Laurie finished pouring limeade. She left the pitcher on the table and followed Amy into the kitchen.

Watching Jack as he pulled hamburger patties out of a drawer in a stainless refrigerator built into the cooking area, Spider searched for some polite comment that wouldn't engender verse. Karam came to his rescue.

"I am not sure I understand about what is a straw bale house. Is it really made of straw?"

Jack closed the stainless lid over the sizzling burgers. "Why sure it is. Come on in here, and let me show you." He opened the door to the living room and waited for Karam to pass through. "You, too, Spencer," he said.

Spider obediently stood and followed.

Jack stepped through and pointed to the casing around the door. "See how thick the walls are? Ever seen a straw bale? That's how thick they are. And lookie here." He lifted a picture off the wall. Underneath, a framed Plexiglas sheet formed a window, allowing a glimpse through the plaster to golden stems packed together.

"That is amazing," Karam said. He stepped back, surveying the wall. "But why?"

Jack frowned. "Why what?"

"Why use straw instead of bricks?" Karam asked. "Will it not fall down?"

"Heck no. The house has a framework of massive beams. The straw bales just fill in the area between."

"It's for insulation," Spider added. "Keeps the house cool in summer, warm in winter."

Karam smiled. "You Americans. You are so inventive. In my country we can build houses that are cool in summer, warm in winter, but we build them out of mud brick. We have been doing it that way for thousands of years."

"Where is your country?" Jack asked. "You from Mexico?" He put one foot forward, held up his hand, and launched in.

> *Way down across the border*
> *Beyond the Rio Grande—*

"Karam's from Gaza," Spider interrupted. Could a guy with that much education be that clueless?

Jack dropped his hand. "Where?"

"Gaza."

Jack looked from Spider to Karam. "Where's that?"

Karam answered. "Right next door to Israel."

"Oh." Jack blinked. "I don't know any poems about that."

"That's all right," Spider assured him, opening the door to the patio. "Those burgers sure smell good."

"That's because it's Braces beef." Jack hurried out, lifted the lid, and shouted, "Amy. I'm turning the burgers."

Spider and Karam sat at the table, and a few moments later Laurie appeared with a tray of condiments followed by Amy with the dishes. By the time the burgers came off the grill, the table was set, and a platter of golden corn steamed in the middle.

All through lunch, Jack retold the story of building the house. Karam ate only corn and cantaloupe, but he listened politely. Now that he had seen the house, Spider listened with more interest and a grudging admiration for all Jack had accomplished.

"You've done a great job," he said as he finished the last of his melon. "The house, the way it's landscaped, your fields, they all look first rate."

Jack's cheeks got rosy, and he looked down at his hands. "Thanks. I've been working at it for a long time.

> *Buildin' up a little place*
> *That I can call my home,*
> *A place to hang my Stetson—*

Jack broke off in the middle of his own verse. "You know, someone else musta liked the looks of it 'cause I got a letter in the mail offering to buy it."

"Is that so?" Spider tried to sound casual. "I don't suppose you were inclined to sell."

Jack snorted. "Shoot, no."

Spider's hand went to his shirt pocket, checking for his notebook. Dang. He really needed to get it back from Laurie. "Do you remember who wrote the letter?"

Jack shook his head. "Tossed it in the garbage. It was no interest to me."

"Huh," Spider grunted. "By the way, where do you get your water?"

"There's a spring up where this canyon intersects with the next one over. That's Martin Taylor's place. We share the water rights."

"I read about water rights as I studied American History," Karam said. "People have been killed here over water rights."

"Well, I'm on pretty good terms with Martin," Jack said. "He rents me his shares since he isn't doing anything with his property. It works out well for both of us."

"Going back to this person who wanted to buy your ranch," Spider said. "Was it someone from St. George? Earnest Endeavors?"

Jack made a flicking motion with his hand. "I didn't even read to the end of the letter. Like I said, I wasn't interested."

Laurie stood and took Spider's plate, stacking it on her own. When she tried to pick up Jack's, he held on. "Leave that be. I want to show you all something down at the barn."

Laurie gave up on Jack's plate and reached for the one Karam handed her. "You fellows go on. I'll help Amy clean up and join you later."

"No!" Jack stopped, seemingly abashed at speaking so forcefully. "I mean, I want *you* to see this."

Laurie continued stacking dishes. "Well, let me at least carry these in." She disappeared through the kitchen door, reappearing a moment later. "Now. What do you want to show us?"

Jack took her elbow and headed across the patio. "It's something I think you'll like."

Spider picked up his hat, and he and Karam followed. As they walked, a breeze from behind stirred the dust and carried a rust-colored puff away. Nearing the first bank of stalls, Spider heard a horse whicker, and a moment later a buckskin's head emerged from the open half door, ears pointed forward.

Laurie stopped and turned to her cousin. "Jack, what have you done?"

Alarmed at how pale his wife had become, Spider stepped up beside her. "What's the matter, Laurie?"

"It's Taffy. Oh Jack, I thought I'd never see her again."

"Taffy?" Spider looked at the mare stretching her neck and pushing against the stall door, his mind trying to work out how Laurie's horse, the one she'd had to sell four years ago when times were so tough, could be here in Jack's barn.

Jack shrugged. "I heard you were selling off your stock, and I knew any horse trained by Laurie Rowland would be worth the price."

"Latham," Spider said. "Laurie Latham."

No one heard him because his three companions were already at the stall door. Laurie had her hands on Taffy's cheeks, and the horse's forehead rubbed against her chest.

Laurie looked back at Spider, and he saw tears streaming down her cheeks. "She remembers me," she said.

He joined her at the stable door. "Of course she does. You had her from before she was weaned."

She sniffed. "Have you got a handkerchief? I need to blow my nose."

Spider felt in his back pocket, but it was empty. "Shoot. I left it with Neva. Here, use this." He looked around to see that Jack and Karam had moved to the next stall before pulling his shirttail out and undoing the bottom buttons. As Laurie bent over to wipe her eyes, he said, "I need to be careful about how many weepy females I come across in a day."

"I guess." Laurie wiped her nose and re-buttoned the shirt for him. "Thank you," she murmured. "You're a good man to have around."

Spider tucked in his shirt and then took her in his arms. "Don't mention it. You all right?"

She nodded. "It was the surprise of seeing her. I'm fine." She gave him a quick hug and then turned to call to Jack. "Could I take her out right now?"

Jack looked at his watch. "We've got time for a short ride." He thought a moment and then pulled out his cell phone. "I think I can get us another half hour. You all start saddling up while I make a call. Spencer, you can ride that bay, and Karam, there's a pinto in the next stall." He took out his phone and walked away, dialing as he went.

Laurie opened Taffy's door and stepped inside. Bending over, she lifted a front hoof and examined it.

"How's it look?" Spider asked.

"Great. She's doing fine." She put down the hoof and patted the buckskin on the neck. Then she let herself out of the stall and opened a door to the left of Taffy's stall. "Here's the tack room."

Karam tugged at Spider's sleeve, his eyes wide. "I do not know how to attach a saddle," he whispered. "I come from the city. This is the closest I have been to a horse."

"Tell you what," Spider said. "Let's run up the canyon and take a look at Martin Taylor's place."

Karam looked down at his shoes. "I am not dressed for running."

Spider's eyes twinkled. "We'll take the car." He turned to Jack, just returning. "Mind if we drive up and look at your spring?"

Jack's eyebrows went up. "You don't want to come with us?"

"Nah. I'd like to see what's up that canyon. What time do you need us back?"

Jack looked at his watch. "How about an hour?"

"You got it." Spider swung by Taffy's stall and looked over the half door at Laurie as she tightened the cinch. "Karam and I are going up to the head of the canyon," he said. "We'll meet you back here."

She smiled and waved assent, and Spider led Karam around the house to the car. They got in, and Spider drove to the access road, turning right instead of left and heading toward the red sandstone cliffs a quarter mile distant. Huge marshmallow clouds boiled up from behind the red mesas, intensifying the blueness of the sky beyond.

"Those look like rain clouds," Karam said.

"Maybe so, maybe not. This is the monsoon season. They generally have cloud buildups like that every day."

The gravel road up to Jack's circular driveway had been well cared for, but approaching the canyon, it deteriorated to a sandy trail. Spider drove as fast as he could to keep from becoming stuck. The car bounced around and shifted from side to side as he tried to accommodate the Yugo's small wheelbase to the ruts made by a pickup.

The road dropped into a dry creek running through a canyon about a half a mile wide with red sandstone mesas rising six hundred feet on each side. Rocks embedded in the sandy bottom gave plenty of traction, but as the valley narrowed, the wash grew deeper. Finally, the track they were following climbed out at a place where the bank, though steep, wasn't straight up and down.

"Hang on," Spider said as he shifted down and mashed on the accelerator.

"I don't think—" Karam grabbed the dash and the door handle and watched, wide eyed, as the little car flew toward the embankment.

They made it halfway up before they lost momentum, and the rear wheels began digging a hole. Spider shifted to reverse, and the tires spun, throwing sand. He kept a steady pressure on the gas, and finally, they rolled back down into the creek bed.

Spider turned off the key, got out, and looked around. All he could see ahead of him was the sandy wall where the dry wash made a turn. Raising his eyes, he scanned the flanks of the nearest mesa rising from the canyon floor and saw a trail traversing to the top. He bent down and looked through the open door at his companion. "Feel like taking a walk?"

Karam unbuckled and got out of the car. Following Spider's pointing finger, he eyed the trail and then turned with raised brows. "Seriously? Now we are climbing mountains?"

"You teach American History," Spider said. "Think of this as a learning experience about westward expansion. It wasn't all flat, you know." He reached into the backseat for a bottle of water and started up the bank. "There's a clump of cottonwoods up the creek. If you want to go sit in the shade, I'll be back in a while."

"No, wait." Karam dove into the back for the other water bottle and became entangled in the seat belt. "I am coming," he called, shaking his right arm to free it. He slammed the door, and with shirt untucked and hair hanging over his brow, he trotted to where Spider stood. "Ready."

Spider smiled. "Good man."

The sandy track angled toward the base of the hill, and they walked in silence. Spider was grateful for the steady breeze that tempered the heat of the afternoon sun and for the scent of sage that drifted up as they brushed against the feathery bushes.

"The sand makes walking extra hard," Karam said, puffing a bit.

"I think the footing will be better once we start uphill."

That proved to be the case, and though they were ascending, the hard packed clay of the trail made walking easier. Halfway up, they took a water break, sitting on a large red-rock slab in the shade of an overhang. Spider scanned the dry creek bed looking for the Yugo and finally spied one orange rear fender. The rest was obscured by the height of the bank. To the left, he could see Jack's place below them, and further on, loping through the sagebrush, the buckskin and the bay.

Spider pointed. "Laurie and Jack. They must be headed to the next canyon."

Karam squinted. "I wonder why they did not come this way. Does this road not lead to the next canyon?"

"Maybe he doesn't like roads."

At that moment they heard the sound of a car coming from the direction of the spring. Spider turned to look, but they had rounded the flank of the hill, and he couldn't see up the canyon.

The sound of the engine grew louder. Curious about who might be coming down the road, Spider leaned against the rock behind him and fixed his eyes on the sandy track below. Soon a burgundy SUV came into view.

"That is a Range Rover," Karam said, untying his shoe.

"Couldn't prove it by me, but I like the color."

"My father has one, only it's black, and not as new as that one."

The Range Rover stopped a ways beyond Spider's car, the driver hidden through the tinted windows. After a moment, the car pulled away and was shielded from view by the bank of the arroyo.

Spider stood. "You ready to push on?"

Karam had his shoe upside down, shaking sand out of it. "It is not the mountains ahead that you have to climb that wear you out, it is the pebble in your shoe," he quoted.

"Is that from the Quran?"

Karam looked up from tying his shoe. "No. Muhammad Ali said it. He was an American boxer."

"I know who Muhammad Ali is," Spider said. "Well, come on. We should catch a breeze at the top."

They followed the trail, scrambling over rectangular sandstone boulders that had fallen from the rocky mesa cap. At last they gained the top.

Spider stood a moment, breathing hard and looking around. Juniper trees dotted the landscape, their powder-blue berries contrasting with the deep green of their foliage. Rabbit brush and sage grew thickly, and here and there orange mallow added a spot of color. "Let's head across," he said. "I don't think it will take very long to get to the other edge of the mesa."

Weaving through the trees, they hiked steadily until, suddenly, another step would have been into thin air. Below, a wide canyon sloped off to the east. "I'll bet this is Martin Taylor's spread," Spider said. "That green place up at the head is where the spring rises."

"Look at the canyon wall on the other side," Karam said.

"Yeah." Spider examined the serpentine crevices and huge, knobby protrusions. "And look at the banding of colors. That's quite a sight."

"Mr. Taylor is a lucky man. If this was mine, I would build a house over there." He pointed to an arched depression in the red rock wall across from them.

Spider nodded. "Good choice. From all the green in that crevice, I'd say there was a spring there, too." He ran his eyes over the landscape, trying to see it as a developer would. With the slope of the canyon away from the spring, a water storage tank adjacent to the source at the head of the canyon would do the job. There'd be no need for pumps, as gravity would take care of everything if it were engineered right. He mentally divided the canyon into two-acre plots and began doing the math, based on what Martin Taylor had been offered for the property.

Karam interrupted his computation. "There's Laurie's horse." He pointed to a place far below where the red, rocky scree gave way to soil and vegetation.

Spider sighted down the angle of Karam's arm and found the buckskin. She seemed to be tethered to a juniper skeleton, and the bay was beside her. Spider's eyes raked the surrounding country, looking for the riders.

"I wonder where Laurie—" Spider didn't finish his sentence because at that moment, he spotted his wife, locked in the embrace of her fourth cousin, Jack.

Chapter 7

◆

Karam was saying something, but Spider's mind, spinning with the image of his wife in another man's arms, wouldn't process the words.

Spider watched Karam's mouth as he repeated the phrase, but he still couldn't make sense of it. He shook his head as if that would erase the picture of Laurie in Jack's embrace.

He turned and looked over the cliff again. His eyes found them instantly, walking to where their horses were tethered. Jack's arm was around Laurie's shoulders, her arm around his waist. They walked as one, as if they were glued together.

Spider turned away as saliva rushed into his mouth, and he felt the Braces beef he had for lunch rising in his gorge. He took a deep breath, forcing himself to regain control. Pulling the water bottle from his pocket, he poured the warm liquid inside the collar of his shirt and closed his eyes as he held out his arms to catch the cooling breeze.

"Do you think we should?" Karam's voice sounded anxious.

Spider opened his eyes. "Should what?"

"Hurry down, so we can go help them."

Spider dropped his arms. "Help them? Why?"

"I just told you. Something is wrong. Jack is in trouble."

Spider turned back around and searched the area below. Maybe it was he, Spider, who was in trouble.

Jack was now on his horse, and Laurie stood on the ground beside him. Spider didn't take his eyes off her, even when his companion spoke again.

"Do we need to go help them?" Karam asked again.

Spider held up his hand. "Wait a minute."

Laurie finally walked to the buckskin. She mounted, and she and Jack started back down the canyon at a lope.

"He looks all right to me," Spider said, "but we'd probably better head back to the house." He began retracing the route they had taken across the mesa, striding through the scrubby trees. He heard a muffled exclamation from Karam and looked back to see that a branch he had pushed aside had swung back and hit him in the face. "Gotta look sharp," he said.

They made it down the hill in a fraction of the time it took to climb it. Spider led all the way, jaw clenched, struggling to keep his mind an empty blackboard and doggedly erasing the recurring picture of Laurie and Jack together.

At the bottom of the hill, Spider paused to take a drink.

"I need to get a hat like yours," Karam said wiping his brow. "The sun is really brutal."

"Doesn't it get this hot in Dubai?"

"Yes. Even hotter, but I work in an air conditioned building."

"Huh." Spider held his water bottle up to check the water level. "This might help," he said and poured the rest of the contents over the head and shoulders of his companion.

"Hey!" Karam sputtered.

"As the water evaporates, it will cool you down."

"You show your concern in interesting ways." Karam wiped his eyes. "Actually, I knew that. A reminder would have sufficed."

"Sorry. You ready to move on?"

Karam dried his hands on his pants. "Yes. Go on."

As they crossed the expanse of sagebrush to the edge of the ravine where the Yugo was parked, Karam called, "Thank you. I'm feeling cooler."

They climbed down the sandy bank into the creek bed, and Spider was pleased to note that the car was sitting in the shade. It was still like an oven when they got in, but he drove at a good clip down the gravel waterway to move air through before he rolled up the windows and tuned on the air conditioning.

"What made you think Jack was in trouble?" he asked.

"He was leaning on Laurie. You didn't see it?"

"No," Spider said, looking sidewise at Karam. He wondered about the cultural customs in his world, this young man who was to marry his cousin to make sure she had a good husband. He wondered how they felt about men and women displaying affection in public. Was Karam too naive to realize what had been going on down there? Or maybe he had it right. Maybe Spider had read too much into what he saw. "Huh," he grunted, pressing a little harder on the accelerator, anxious to get back to Jack's.

They drove the rest of the way in silence and pulled into the circular drive. Spider got out of the car, stretched and walked with Karam to the door.

Karam paused. "Do we knock or just walk in?"

"Knock."

When no one answered, Spider gestured for Karam to open the door. From the entryway they could see Laurie on the patio, so they walked through the living room to the sliding door. Laurie smiled the minute Spider opened it.

"Hello," she said, leaning forward and stretching out a hand.

Spider walked over and brushed her fingers. "Hi. Did you have a nice ride?"

"It was wonderful. I had forgotten what a sweet horse Taffy is."

Spider accepted a cool drink from Laurie and watched the way her eyes rested on her cousin.

"We saw you from up on top of the mesa," he said.

Laurie blinked, looking from Spider to Karam. "Really? How did you get up there?"

Karam answered. "We hiked. It was a hard climb, but the view was wonderful."

"Yeah," Spider took a sip of his limeade. "Sometimes you see things you never would have expected."

"I'm glad you had a good time," she said, her eyes flicking again to Jack.

Her cousin rose. "I've got to get back to the office, but you can stay as long as you like."

"We've got things we need to do, too." Spider held out his hand. "Thanks for lunch."

"Don't mention it." Jack shook Spider's hand and then clapped Karam on the shoulder. "Come any time."

"Thank you." Karam hesitated a moment and, as Spider opened the sliding door for their host, blurted out, "You are well?"

Jack paused halfway through, his eyes moving from Karam to Spider. He smiled, assumed his poetry stance, and began reciting.

> Old age tracks my every move,
> Has been for quite a span.
> I'm slower, but I still do things
> I did as a younger man.

Jack winked at Laurie and stepped through to the living room. He traced invisible lines on the wall with outstretched fingers as he crossed to the entryway and opened the front door. Pausing, he waved to his guests. Then he was gone.

Spider turned to look at Laurie and found her still staring at the closed front door. "You ready to go?" he asked.

She stood. "You go on out. I'll put the limeade in the fridge and stick these glasses in the dishwasher."

"We'll help." Spider handed the pitcher to Karam and picked up Jack's empty tumbler. "Where's Amy?"

Laurie pushed through the kitchen door and spoke over her shoulder. "Someone came by to see her, and they went into town." She smiled. "A fellow. I think he's sweet on her."

Spider followed her in, blinking at the splendor of the kitchen which seemed to have acres of granite counters, stainless steel, and glossy wood. He opened the refrigerator door, so Karam could set the pitcher inside, and then he handed Laurie the two glasses he was carrying.

She put them in the dishwasher. "I think she's in love."

"Amy?"

"Yes. She ran out the door when his car pulled up, so I didn't get to meet him. But he was driving a real nice car."

"The true measure of a man," Spider murmured.

Laurie poked him with a mixing spoon. "Let Karam put his glass in, and then you two can go out to the car. I'll wipe down the counter and be right there."

Karam dropped his tumbler in the rack and followed Spider outside. They got in the Yugo, and by the time Spider had started the engine and adjusted the air conditioning, Laurie was there.

"What a wonderful afternoon," she said as she closed the door.

"Jack was very hospitable," Karam said.

"Yeah." Spider's voice was dry. "Warm and embracing fellow, that one."

Spider felt Laurie's eyes on him, and though he kept his eyes on the road, he knew from her silence they were flinty.

Karam stepped into the breach, leaning forward and clearing his throat. "I am not sure I understand about the light-colored horse."

"I used to own Taffy," Laurie explained. "I raised her and trained her."

"And then we had to sell her." Spider's comment had an edge, and he hadn't meant it that way.

Laurie picked up the narrative. "A friend told Jack that we were selling our horse, and he bought her. That's all."

Nobody spoke as they rattled along the gravel road.

Laurie picked up the thread when they reached the highway, turning around to address Karam. "She has a deformed hoof."

"Excuse me?" Karam looked puzzled.

"Taffy. My—Jack's horse. The buckskin. She has a deformed hoof. The fellow who bred her was going to put her down.

"I do not understand. He was lifting the horse?"

"'Put her down' means he was going to kill her," Spider said over his shoulder.

Karam's mouth opened, and he turned dark eyes to Laurie. "He was going to kill your horse?"

Laurie nodded. "She was the second foal with that deformity out of the mare. He was going to get rid of both the mare and the filly—the baby."

"But you saved them?"

"We were too late to save the mother, but he gave Taffy to me. He made me promise I'd never breed her."

"It's ridiculous," Spider said. "Unless you know what you're looking for, you'd never know there was a problem with that hoof."

"She throws out just a bit when she canters. Jack has a farrier—" Laurie paused to translate for Karam.

"—a horse shoer—who really knows his stuff. He builds custom shoes for her, and I can see that it helps."

They were coming into town, and Spider slowed. "Where to, Karam?"

"I have not been to the Little Hollywood place. Would you care to accompany me there?"

Spider shook his head. "Thanks, but I need to try to connect with Linda Russell."

Laurie's brows went up. "What about?"

"I need to find out about a man by the name of Austin Lee."

Laurie looked like she had another question, but instead of asking it, she pointed out the window at a life-sized plastic horse. "There's your Little Hollywood Museum, Karam. I hope you like cowboys."

"I do," Karam said. "Would you say that Jack is a cowboy?"

"Heck, Laurie's a better cowboy than Jack." Spider pulled into the museum driveway.

"Really?"

Laurie shook her head. "Not better, but I can hold my own."

Karam opened the door. "Thank you so much for a very educational day. I am so glad to have met you."

"We'll see each other again," Spider assured him. "You'll be around a while waiting for your car parts, won't you?"

"Yes." Karam got out and spoke through the open door. "Tomorrow I am with Isaac."

"I'm going to St. George tomorrow, but we'll catch up with you." Spider patted his pocket. "Did I get your cell phone number?"

"Yes, and I have yours. Thank you again." Karam closed the door and waved as they pulled away.

"He's a nice fellow," Laurie said. "Where did you meet him?"

"At the hotel. His first car was a Yugo. It's an instant bond." During their ride back to the Best Western, Spider told her about Karam and how, as a student in England taking Middle Eastern History from a British professor, he decided he would study American History. "He's a sponge," Spider said. "I wish you could have seen him out there with Isaac. He just soaks it up."

"Speaking of the museum, you must have found out something else while I was staying with Martin and Neva. Who is this Austin Lee?"

Spider pulled into a parking spot and turned off the ignition. "I don't know for sure. He appeared about a month ago and started romancing Linda."

"Is that why the engagement is off?"

"I don't think so. I think they broke it off after Matt accused her of leaking word about the Lincoln letter."

Laurie ran her fingers through her hair, lifting it away from her neck. "So, that would be how word got to the Goodman family that the cache was valuable. Did Linda do that?"

"I don't know. I was hoping to talk to her, but she left before I got the chance."

Laurie reached over, turned on the ignition, and rolled down her window. "Let me ask you a question. How many people do you know named Austin?"

Spider rolled his window down, too, and thought a moment. "I don't think I know anyone named Austin.

First real person I've heard with that name is the fellow that I want to talk to Linda about."

"So, is it too much of a coincidence that Amy's boyfriend's name is Austin?"

Spider rubbed his jaw. "Maybe. Did she tell you a last name?"

"No."

"But you said he had a nice car?"

She nodded. "I don't know what kind of car it was, but it was a burgundy color. Nice and shiny."

"SUV?"

"Yeah."

Spider rubbed his jaw again, remembering the Range Rover coming down the wash while he and Karam were up on the mesa. "Huh."

"What are you thinking?"

"Just coming up with more questions. No answers." He drummed his fingers on the steering wheel. "Tell me about Amy."

"What do you want to know?"

"What's she to Jack? Why's she living there with him?"

"She's a cousin. I haven't worked out the connection yet, but she's bipolar."

Spider's brows shot up.

"She's on medication," Laurie went on. "They haven't found the optimum dosage yet, but I think, for the most part, she's stable."

"What does that mean?"

"I don't know for sure. Those are her words. She says she hopes the psychotic episodes are behind her."

Laurie grimaced. "The symphony thing is a symptom, though. In her mind she's writing one, but she's really not. She's got notebooks full of strange marks, but it's not music."

Spider chewed on that for a moment. When he didn't speak, Laurie continued. "She was twenty-one when she was diagnosed—almost through with college. That was four years ago." She shifted in her seat and put an elbow out the window. "Amy's parents are dead. She was living with an aunt and uncle and they thought she was going through a wild phase. Then during Western Legends she put on a long wig and rode in the parade as Lady Godiva."

"Great suffering zot! How long was the wig?"

Laurie chuckled. "Apparently not long enough. I shouldn't laugh because it's really sad. But what a picture!"

"So, why is she at Jack's?"

"She's not well enough to work at a regular job, or even to finish college. Jack has her work for him keeping house and cooking."

"Huh."

"It's hard to think of her having to deal with that." Laurie sighed. "Everyone says she was such a bright, sparkling child, such a smart, outgoing student. And then to have this come upon her. It's a tragedy."

Spider turned on the ignition. "Watch your arm; I'm going to roll up the windows. Shall we go in?"

Laurie got out; he joined her on the sidewalk, and they walked to their room without speaking. Once inside, she took her guitar out of the case. Sitting on the edge of the extra bed by her saddle, she began to tune.

Spider put his hat and keys on the desk. Stuffing hands in his pockets, he leaned against the doorframe and watched the way her auburn hair hung down as she bent her head to listen to each plucked string. Unbidden, the image of her in Jack's embrace came to his mind, and he said, "Don't go out riding tomorrow."

She looked up and blinked. "What?"

"Don't go out riding tomorrow."

She set her guitar on the bed beside her. "Do you have a reason for saying that?"

He spread his hands, palms up. Pushing away from the doorframe, he walked over to look out the sliding glass door, his back to her. "I'd like you to come to St. George with me instead."

"When did you decide that? You've known for a full day that I was planning on going to Inchworm tomorrow."

He turned to face her. "I just don't feel good about you spending the day with Jack."

She didn't answer. She simply stared at Spider.

He recognized the flinty hardness that came into her brown eyes and looked away first.

She stood suddenly, wiped the palms of her hands on her pants, and then clenched them as they hung at her side. "I realize you've just buried your mother," she said. "I've been trying to cut you some slack, but I'm a little tired of the snide comments about Jack."

"There's nothing snide about this. I'm asking you not to go out riding for a full day with another man."

"With my cousin."

"With your handsome, rich, fourth cousin."

Laurie's chin came up. Her mouth compressed in a straight line, and Spider was wishing the whole conversation unsaid.

She clasped her hands in front of her, and her voice had a studied calmness. "You know, Spider, these last eight years have been tough. I didn't mind selling the cattle. I didn't mind when we had to sell my car. I hated selling Taffy, but I was willing because it was going to let us pay our taxes and hang on a little longer."

"I hated it, too." Spider reached out to Laurie, but she seemed not to notice.

"When I saw Taffy in Jack's stable, it was like a tender mercy, as if the good Lord was saying, 'Well done, Laurie. You finished the course.'" Her jaw tightened, and she looked away for a moment.

Turning back, her eyes were bright with unshed tears. "Don't get me wrong. I was glad to have your mother come live with us, even if it meant losing my freedom and spending every waking moment watching that dear woman spiral down into a black, bottomless pit."

Spider opened his mouth to speak, but she held up her hand. "No, let me finish. Last week just about took the cake. Do you know what it's like to have someone's life depend on you, trying to judge the insulin for a body that's no longer taking nourishment? I live every day wondering if something I did may have killed her."

"Oh, Laurie." Again he reached out, and again she forestalled him.

"This ride tomorrow was to be a day of freedom offered to me after two years in Alzheimer's Prison."

A single tear rolled down her cheek, and she dashed it impatiently away. "You've got your undies in a bundle because Jack has a nice house, a herd of Angus, and a stable full of horses, but by the Lord Harry, that's *your* problem. I'm riding tomorrow."

She opened a drawer and took out her pajamas. "I'm going to go take a shower."

Spider watched as she went into the bathroom without another look at him. He stood for a moment and stared at the white decorative panels on the door, wondering if he should burst through, take her in his arms, and apologize. He wanted to, but what would he say? Forgive me for catching you in Jack's arms? I'm sorry there's something going on between you two?

He wanted to pound his fist into the wall or throw something across the room, anything to relieve the pressure inside his chest. The plastic-wrapped glasses and room service brochure on the counter warned him he wasn't on home turf. No wall punching allowed.

His eye fell on the pillows stacked decoratively on the bed holding Laurie's saddle and guitar. He snatched one of the pillows. Holding the open end of the pillowcase, he swung the puffy missile around in an arc and brought it down on the other bed. *Thwack.* He did it again. *Thwack.* That didn't do anything to dissipate the coiled-spring tension inside. He needed to hit something hard.

He spied a wooden armchair in front of the desk and moved in to attack. Swinging the pillow around in a mighty blow, he struck the back of the chair with such force that both the case and the ticking ruptured.

Feathers filled the air, and downy wisps floated on air currents, drifting to the far reaches of the room.

The white feather-storm only tightened the knot in his chest. Tossing the empty pillowcase on the chair, he strode to the door and wrenched it open. Slamming it behind him, he marched to the elevator and stabbed at the button until the lift arrived. When he reached the main floor, he ignored the stares of guests and headed to the Yugo, stiff-arming the swinging doors as he exited the lobby.

Finally in the car and ready to back out of the parking space, he glanced in the rearview mirror and saw what people had been staring at as he had bulldozed his way through the lobby. Tiny white feathers nestled in his hair, hung on his eyebrows, and blanketed his shoulders. He stuck out his bottom lip and blew, dislodging a flurry of fluff that wafted around the interior of the Yugo. "There's no way I'm going to get out of this with any dignity," he muttered. He backed up, put the car in gear, and peeled out of the parking lot.

Turning north, Spider sped along the winding two-lane highway through a dramatic, wind-hewn canyon of red sandstone. The sun, low on the horizon, shadowed cracks and crevices in the towering walls. After ten miles of listening to the whine of the tightly-wound engine, Spider saw a sign pointing left to the Coral Pink Sand Dunes. At the last minute he decided to take the road and turned sharply. The back wheels broke away, and he felt the car skidding. For a moment, he had his hands full, keeping the Yugo on the road and upright.

When he finally had the car straight and heading

west in the right lane of traffic, the corners of his mouth lifted a notch. "Better than punching a hole in the wall," he muttered.

He drove to the state park, pulled into an empty parking lot beside an immense sand dune, and got out. The dune was perhaps a hundred feet high and had obviously been climbed by several people recently. Spider followed their tracks, his feet sinking in with each step as he ascended.

Breathing hard, he finally reached the top. The setting sun intensified the coral color of the dunes, and long shadows etched knife edges onto the tops, creating a crisp-lined black and orange landscape stretching as far as he could see. Spider sat on the ridge and dug his hands into the warm sand beside him.

"Okay," he said aloud. "So what's the problem?"

The problem was that he suspected his wife of teetering on the edge of an affair with Jack. The other side of that problem was that he knew it was impossible. Duplicity was hardly in Laurie's vocabulary, much less in her nature. He picked up a handful of sand and let it drain between his fingers. Karam had likely been right, and he, Spider, should have paid more attention. The result was that Laurie was mad, and the hotel room looked like a herd of molting ducks had passed through.

Spider remembered what Laurie had said about his own feelings about Jack. Was he jealous? Did he covet Jack's ranch and Angus and car? No, he did not. He just didn't want Jack to have them to wave in front of Laurie. All right, maybe he was jealous. Maybe it did sting that he had lost his job when the mines closed, and they had been barely scraping by since then.

The sun had set, but the horizon still had a lavender band around it. Spider dusted off his hands and stood. Time to go face Laurie and apologize. Only this time it would be a real apology. To prove that he was in earnest, he would be kinder to Jack from here on out. He spat on the ground to seal the deal and turned to go.

At the bottom of the dune, he brushed off the remaining feathers before he got in the Yugo. Then he drove back to Kanab, stopping at Big Al's Junction for take-out burgers, sweet potato fries and chocolate shakes. Laurie loved chocolate shakes. He hurried back to the hotel, his apology well-rehearsed.

The room was in semi-darkness, lit only by a shaft of light that fell through the half-open bathroom door. Spider stood for a minute to let his eyes adjust, and then he walked across the room, puffs of white feathers rising each time he placed a foot. He blew a dusting of down away before he set the aromatic sacks from Big Al's on the desk and looked around for Laurie.

What he saw made his heart stop.

The bed they had shared last night was empty. Laurie had pushed the saddle over to the wall on the other bed and was curled up beside it.

He would sleep alone tonight.

Chapter 8

◆

Spider woke the next morning at seven. He turned over to check the other bed.

Empty.

He listened but heard no sound of movement in the room. Lifting up on an elbow, he saw that the saddle had disappeared. Laurie was gone.

The Big Al takeout bag still sat unopened on the desk. Spider wondered if the emptiness in the pit in his stomach was because he hadn't eaten since yesterday noon or because he needed to resolve this thing with Laurie. Probably a little bit of both.

Throwing back the covers, he disturbed a layer of feathers and sent them into the air. He contemplated them from flat on his back. They were a metaphor for his life right now. Scattered. Directionless. When things weren't right with Laurie, nothing made sense. But how to get all those feathers back where they belonged?

This wasn't getting anything solved. Anyway, he couldn't do anything about it until evening when Laurie was home from her ride and he was back from St. George. He got up, showered, shaved, and dressed. After leaving a note saying he was sorry about the pillow and a five-dollar tip for the maid, he tucked the instruction booklet for his phone into his pocket and headed out to breakfast. By eight o'clock he was pushing open the door of Houston's Trail's End Restaurant.

"Hey, Spencer!"

Curiosity, along with a niggle of voice recognition, made Spider look around at the person calling from the adjacent dining room. It was Laurie's cousin.

Jack's smile widened when he caught Spider's eye. "Come on over. Rest your bones in my booth."

Spider took off his hat, threaded his way through tables filled with tourists, and slid into the seat opposite.

Jack raised an eyebrow. "Anything wrong? You look like you've been drug through a knothole backwards."

Spider set his hat on the seat beside him. "I didn't get much sleep last night." He caught the eye of the waitress and raised his hand.

Jack reached over and picked a feather off Spider's shoulder. He set it on the table and chuckled. "Must have been some night."

Spider was grateful the waitress appeared at that moment with a place setting and a glass of water. He ordered ham and eggs over easy and then turned to Jack. "I thought you were riding this morning with Laurie."

"Didn't she tell you? She's going out with Amy. Something came up, and I have to go out of town."

Spider shook his head.

"Too many other things on your mind, I guess." Jack blew the feather off the table and chuckled again.

Spider gritted his teeth and tried to remember that he had committed to himself to be charitable towards Jack. "She was looking forward to going out to Inchworm," he said.

"It's a great ride and a great arch. Big one with a little one right by it. Looks like an inchworm."

"Huh." Spider couldn't think of anything to say.

Jack took a piece of toast and mopped up egg yolk from his plate. "It'll take the greater part of a day to get there and back. She'll be tuckered out when she gets home."

"I'll keep that in mind."

Jack pushed his plate away. "I've got to get going. Sorry I can't stay and chew the fat."

"No problem." Spider watched him slide to the edge of the bench and use his arm to lever himself to a standing position. "You hurt your back out there yesterday?"

"Nah. I just got a hitch in my getalong. Takes a minute to get loosened up after I sit a while."

"Well, take it easy."

"I aim to." Jack gave a half-wave and walked toward the cash register.

Spider stacked the empty dishes at the edge of the table as a busboy came by to pick them up, and then he fished his phone and the instruction booklet out of his pocket. He propped the pamphlet open with his water glass and hunched over the instrument, reading the directions under his breath and then trying to replicate the sequence on the phone. His muttering grew increasingly exasperated, and the taps on the screen gained in force with each failed attempt. "Great suffering zot," he said, sitting back in defeat.

"Excuse me."

Spider looked up to see a young Asian man dressed in a tee shirt and cargo shorts, sporting fashionably square glasses. He bowed slightly and spoke in crisp, well-enunciated English. "May I be of assistance?" He pointed to Spider's phone.

"I'm an old dog," Spider said, poking the phone with his index finger. "I'm not doing too well at learning new tricks."

The young man smiled. "Even an old dog can learn if he has a good teacher. What is it you wish to learn?"

"I'm trying to learn how the GPS works. I can't figure it out from the instructions."

"May I?" The young man pointed at the phone.

"Be my guest. Have a seat." Spider indicated the bench opposite. "My name's Spider Latham."

The young man bowed again and introduced himself as he slid into the booth. "Daisuke Ito."

Spider tried the name on for size. "Dai-su-ke."

"It means 'great helper,'" he explained as he picked up the phone and began pressing buttons with both thumbs.

"The instructions are here." Spider pushed them across the table.

Daisuke didn't look up from his task. His eyes moved back and forth as his thumbs flew, and after a few minutes he shifted from across the table to the bench beside Spider. "I have downloaded a new app. I will teach you how to use it."

"Remember, I'm an old dog," Spider said as he took the phone from Daisuke.

His companion smiled. "Yes, but remember, I am

a good teacher. My advice is, do not over-think it. The program is very intuitive. Now, where do you wish to go?"

Spider took the card that Neva had given him from his wallet and pointed to the address on the bottom. Daisuke walked him through the process, explaining it in a way that was perfectly clear.

"I've got it." Spider grinned. "You are well-named. You're a great helper, Daisuke."

At that moment the waitress arrived with Spider's ham and eggs. Spider turned to the young man. "Will you have breakfast with me?"

He shook his head and slid out of the booth. "I have already eaten, and my companions are waiting for me." He gestured toward two young Asian men standing at the restaurant entrance.

"I've kept them waiting. I'm sorry." Spider stood. "I don't know how to thank you." He offered his hand to Daisuke.

"I was glad to be of help." He shook the proffered hand and then bowed.

Spider wished he could offer more than thanks. "Are you going to be in town for a while?"

"We're on our way to the Grand Canyon," Daisuke said, his eyes crinkling at the corners. "My friends are going to be jealous that I have been talking to a real cowboy."

Spider almost denied that he was a cowboy. Before the words got out, he glanced at Daisuke's friends, standing wide-eyed by the door. Instead of a denial, he picked up his Stetson, put it on, and hooked a thumb in his belt.

"It's been mighty fine talkin' to you this mornin', and I take kindly to your helpin' me out like you did."

Daisuke bowed again and walked toward his companions with a grin on his face.

"Happy trails," Spider called after him and sat down. Happy trails? That sounded like a B movie. Apparently, it didn't ring false, though, for each young man caught Spider's eye and waved through the window as they walked past on the sidewalk.

When the boys had disappeared beyond the frame of the plate glass, Spider attacked his breakfast. The eggs were cold, but his mind was on other things as he ate. He tried to focus on what he wanted to learn in St. George, but he kept returning to the question of why Laurie didn't tell him last night that Jack wasn't riding with her today. With that question still unanswered, he paid his bill and left. Soon he was on his way south to Fredonia. From there it was 75 miles of desert across the Arizona Strip with only the polygamous village of Colorado City before his destination.

Spider ignored the electronic instructions from his cell phone until he got into Hurricane, twenty miles from St. George. Then he started listening. The disembodied voice led him to a tiny, business-on-a-shoestring storefront on North Main Street in St. George, just up the street from the pioneer-era tabernacle.

Spider parked the Yugo and walked half a block to the correct address. There it was on the door, *Earnest Endeavors*. The sign was surrounded with the same floral motif as the one on the business card Spider carried. Wondering what this could have to do with the trouble at the Red Pueblo, he pushed the door open and entered.

Chapter 9

$\blacklozenge$

A MIDDLE-AGED lady with copper-colored hair, thick eyeliner and clumpy black eyelashes sat at a desk in the middle of the room. The desk faced the door, and the nameplate read Leona Rippley. A copy machine was the lonely occupant of the wall beside her, and a scattering of scrapbooking supplies made a sad showing on the opposite one.

As Spider took off his hat and approached, Leona looked up and flashed a wide smile. "How may I help you?"

Spider held up Leona's business card. "Some people over in Kanab got a letter from you offering to buy their property," he said. "They've asked me to come over and talk to you about it."

Leona's smile didn't diminish in size, but it seemed to Spider that it grew rigid. "What was the name?"

"The letter would have been addressed to Martin Taylor."

Leona keyed some information into her computer, her long, boutique nails adding an extra layer of noise to the process. She frowned as her eyes moved across the screen, and she turned to Spider. "What did you say your name was?"

"I didn't. Name's Spider Latham." He put the card in his pocket, pulled out his wallet, and opened it to his badge. "I'm a deputy over in Lincoln County, though I'm not here on county business." He laid the wallet on her desk, so she could get a good look.

The smile was gone now, and Leona had turned so pale that her eyeliner and mascara stood out like black slashes on the white oval of her face. She pointed to a chair with a trembling hand. "Will you bring that over here, please?"

Spider obliged, dragging the chair to the place she indicated by her desk. He picked up his wallet and stuffed it in his back pocket before sitting when she motioned him to do so. He held his Stetson on his lap.

She swiveled her chair around to face him and leaned forward, her knees perhaps two feet away from his. Clasping her hands, she looked into his eyes and said, "I prayed to Jesus."

Someone walked by outside, and Leona grabbed her keys, sprang out of her chair, and went to the door. She locked it and turned the *open* sign around to say *closed*. Then she returned to her chair and assumed the same knee-to-knee, eye-locked position as before.

"I didn't know where to turn," she said. "My son has muscular dystrophy and has such needs."

Spider didn't have any idea where this was leading. He shifted in his chair

"I opened this shop. I do bookkeeping, and I'm a notary. I sell some scrapbooking things, but it's hard when you're a single mom and—" Her eyes welled up.

"—and your son has such needs." It was easy to

finish her sentence because of her obvious desperation, but Spider didn't want to get sucked into something that was going to take time and energy away from today's mission.

"So when he came in, it was like my luck had finally turned."

Spider sat up straighter. "When who came in?"

"I can't tell you that."

"Why not?"

"Because I signed something. I can't talk about any of it. What he asked me to do or what I did or any of it."

"Was it illegal?"

"No."

"But you can't talk about it."

"No."

Spider pointed to her and then to himself. "And yet, you prayed to Jesus, and you've got us here in a conversation position. What are we going to talk about?"

Leona's eyes filled with tears again. She opened the bottom drawer of her desk and pulled out a folded copy of The Spectrum, the local newspaper. She gave it to Spider and pointed to an article. "Read that."

Spider set his hat on her desk and read the suicide story of Mary Defrain, daughter of Frank Defrain, owner of Defrain Construction. Mary had worked in the estimating department of her father's business but had recently been thrown into a depression when they lost a crucial bid that would have saved the overextended development company.

Spider finished the news item and looked at the date at the top of the paper. It was two months ago. "Okay," he said, handing the newspaper back. "I read it. Now are we going to talk?"

Leona cleared her throat. "I think I need to go back to the beginning. You know how, when something is too good to be true, it usually isn't?"

Spider nodded.

"Well, this fellow came in."

"The one you can't talk about?"

"Yeah. He came in and asked me to write letters to people and act as his agent in some transactions. He offered me a really, really good salary for doing that. And," Leona paused, her cheeks growing pink, "he was very suave, very persuasive."

"And you can't tell me his name?"

She shook her head. "He's a lawyer, and he knows how to write a contract that ties you up in knots. I can't tell you his name." She patted a stack of files on her desk, and her hand still trembled.

Spider eyed the stack of files. The label on the top one said *Frank Defrain*.

"When I read about Mary's suicide, I realized that I had a part in it, and I've spent a tough two months." She laughed, a short humorless bark. "I even resorted to prayer, something I haven't done since my son was diagnosed."

"What did you pray for?" Spider's voice was gentle.

"There's a monster loose out there," she said. "I prayed for someone to stop him."

Spider grimaced. "That's a pretty tall order when you won't tell his name."

"I think you're a resourceful man." Leona picked up

her keys."I have to go down the street for about fifteen minutes. Can I ask a favor?"

"You want me to wait here?" Spider eyed the stack of files.

"Yes. Can you mind the shop for me?" She stood. "If anyone wants to make copies, let me show you how it works." She grabbed a paper out of her inbox and walked to the copy machine. After waiting for Spider to join her, she demonstrated. "You can put a whole stack in and it will feed it through. It's very quick." She opened a door at the bottom. "There's plenty of paper. You shouldn't have any problems."

She walked to the door. "I'll be gone fifteen minutes. I'm leaving the place locked, so when you go out, you won't be able to get back in."

"Trust me. I'll take care of everything." Spider waited for Leona to leave, and he watched her walk to the end of the block before he picked up the folders and carried them to the copy area.

Leona was right. The machine was fast. It took him only about five minutes to duplicate the five folders, doing them one at a time and crisscrossing the resultant piles, so he could keep them separate.

When he was finished, he looked at his watch and debated whether to wait for Leona to return, but in thinking about how she had described the door locking behind him, he figured she intended for him to go. He took a moment to make a copy of the newspaper article, gathered up his stack and his hat, and left.

Back in the Yugo, he drove to a Maverick service station and got a thirty-two-ounce Pepsi. He asked the clerk if there was a park nearby and got directions to a cool-looking city block of green with lots of shade trees. Since it was before noon, the thermometer hadn't yet hit a hundred degrees. Spider found a picnic table by a patch of lawn that was still damp from the morning's watering and settled in with his drink and file folders. He spent the next hour reading through the pile and making notes. When he was finished, he pulled out his cell phone and dialed Brick Tremain's number.

Brick picked up on the second ring. "Spider," he boomed. "Good to hear from you. Have you taken care of the problem at the Red Pueblo?"

"Not yet. What I've found out is that Martin Taylor has fallen foul of a developer who preys on landowners. He gets them in a tight box of some sort, so he can buy prime real estate at a distressed price."

"So these lawsuits are bogus?"

"They're to bleed money away, so he'll have to sell the ranch rather than lose the museum."

"Do you know who this developer is?"

"I've got a suspicion; that's all. I wondered if you could have someone in your office do some investigating of a company called Texas Capital Investment, Inc. I need to know who the principal shareholder is."

Brick was obviously writing it down. "How soon do you need this?"

"I'm going to go get some lunch. Could you have something for me in, say, an hour?"

"I don't know. I'll put someone on it right away and call when I have anything."

"Thanks. By the way, you got any businesses in St. George?"

"One or two. Why?"

Spider pulled Leona Rippley's card out of his pocket. "I got some help from a lady here, has a bookkeeping service. This lowlife shyster has been her main client. She's going to need some other work if you could put something her way."

"Got it. Give me her name."

Spider gave him the information and then put the phone and the card in his pocket. He gathered up his papers from the picnic table, carried them to the Yugo, and set them on the backseat. Then he drove down the street, looking for a fast food place.

He had just pulled into a parking space at Smashburger when his phone rang. He let the motor run to keep the air conditioning on as he answered. The voice was unfamiliar, but the woman on the other end identified herself as Wendy, Brick Tremain's assistant. Was Spider ready to receive information?

"Boy, you're fast." Spider pulled out his pen and reached back for a paper off the backseat. "Shoot," he said.

Wendy confirmed his suspicions. The person behind Texas Capital Investments was Austin Lee. "He has an office in St. George," she said. "Would you like me to give you the address?"

Chapter 10

◆

Spider took his notes into the restaurant with him, and as he ate, he pored over them in light of the fact that he was going to be talking to the author of all this misery. What would he say to Austin Lee? According to Leona, what he did wasn't illegal. But how did she know for sure? The so-called accident in the Red Pueblo bathroom smacked of fraud. And the Defrain suicide—what would drive a woman to kill herself if not horrible guilt?

Spider gathered up the remains of his lunch and threw them away on his way out to the Yugo. He started the engine and turned on the air before he reread the newspaper article. Then he sat, tapping his fingers on the steering wheel as he contemplated his next move. His first inclination was to go directly to Austin Lee's office and confront him, but he'd like to know more about how he operated first.

He pulled out his phone and redialed Wendy at Brick Tremain's office, asking her to find an address for Frank Defrain. She obliged, and when he arrived there, it turned out to be an economy retirement subdivision of modular homes.

Spider drove down the narrow lane between the

neatly kept postage-stamp yards looking for Number 375. When he pulled up, a gray-haired slip of a woman was shaking a rug on the front porch. He quickly got out and called, "Mrs. Defrain?"

She stopped flapping the rug and looked first at the Yugo and next at Spider. "Yes?"

He walked around to her sidewalk. "My name is Spider Latham. I'm a deputy sheriff over in Lincoln County, though I'm not here on county business." He pulled out his wallet and opened it to his badge.

The sun was in her eyes, and she squinted at him. "Why'd you say you were a deputy if you're not doing deputy business?"

"I guess to introduce myself. Instill some confidence." Spider pocketed his wallet and moved to a place where she could see him better.

She glanced again at his car and then began rolling up the rug. "Well, it's good you've got the badge because that car doesn't say anything good about you."

Spider smiled wryly. "No, ma'am." He cleared his throat. "Um, would you mind if I talked to you about your daughter?"

Her hands stopped moving, and her eyes met his. "Why?"

Spider moved closer, so his words wouldn't carry to the nearby neighbors. For the first time he noticed the porch had a ramp instead of stairs. "I'd like to talk to you about Austin Lee, see if you think he figures into anything surrounding your daughter's death."

Mrs. Defrain was very still for a moment. "It was definitely suicide," she said.

"So Austin Lee had nothing to do with her death?"

"I didn't say that." She finished rolling up the rug. "You'd better come in."

Spider walked up the ramp and followed her into the house, stepping away, so she could put down the entryway rug. He took off his Stetson and looked around the open area of the kitchen-living-dining room, noting how neat it was and the way the furniture seemed too fine for the economy-model home. Something about the place felt solemn and grave. He took out his phone and put it on vibrate, so nothing could intrude on this meeting.

"Mr. Latham?" The lady was standing in the living room area. "I have a feeling we're going to get to know each other better, so you'd better call me Annie. Come and meet my husband." She held out her hand indicating a recliner facing the TV in the corner.

Spider realized that someone was sitting there so still that he hadn't noticed before. He followed her around, so he was facing Frank Defrain, and he froze at the sight before him.

Though the man's eyes were bright, the left side of his face seemed frozen. The outside point of his left eye, his cheek, and his mouth all drooped like wax that had heated and run. His left arm was slack as well, lying at an awkward angle in his lap.

"Frank," Annie said. "This is Mr. Latham. He's come to talk to us about Mary."

Frank said something unintelligible out of the right side of his mouth and raised his right hand.

Spider shook it, noting the grasp was firm. "Glad to meet you, Mr. Defrain."

Frank asked a question that Spider couldn't decode. He looked questioningly at Annie.

She translated. "What do you want to know?"

Spider ran his thumb across the grosgrain ribbon of his hatband and thought. "I didn't come with any questions. I just need you to tell me the story as you know it. I'm trying to find out if there's anything illegal that Austin Lee did, not just immoral."

Frank gestured to his wife and said something that sounded like a request. She nodded and left the room.

Frank pointed toward an adjoining armchair and said something that Spider interpreted as, "Please sit down."

Spider sat, holding his hat on his knees and trying to think of something to say that wouldn't need an answer. At that moment Annie entered with an envelope in her hand. She pulled a dining room chair with her as she came by, and Spider jumped up to insist that he sit on it, so she could sit in her armchair.

When they were settled, Annie held up the envelope. "This is the note that Mary left. It will answer a lot of questions for you, but first I'd like to tell you the story as we saw it leading up to this."

Spider nodded.

Annie took a deep breath and paused a moment as if marshalling her thoughts. "I think it began when we got a letter from someone here in St. George wanting to buy Defrain Estates." She shot a questioning glance at Frank, and he dipped his head to the right.

"And Defrain Estates is?" Spider asked.

"It's a housing development. Our first try at something

like that. Up until then we had concentrated on our construction company."

Spider took Leona's card from his pocket and held it up. "Was the offer from a place called Earnest Endeavors?"

"Yes." She opened her hands, palms up. "The thing is, with the housing downturn, we were really hurting. We had several units built on spec that were unsold, and the sale of lots was a lot slower than we had anticipated when we set up financing."

Frank slurred something, and Annie nodded agreement, only remembering when Spider raised his brows that he couldn't understand. "It was an upscale development," she said. "A gated community."

Spider leaned back and crossed his legs. "So were you looking to sell?"

Annie and Frank both shook their heads. She answered. "No, because we thought we were going to be all right. The construction company was staying above water, barely. We were set to bid on a huge project. We had an edge, and it was going to save us."

Frank mumbled a short sentence. Spider thought he understood but ran it by Annie. "That's when Austin Lee came on the scene?"

She grimaced. "Yes. I don't know how Mary met him, but they started going out." She touched the name on the envelope with her forefinger. "She wasn't a looker, but there was so much to her. She was smart, so smart. And funny."

Frank added some information, and Annie conveyed it to Spider. "That was about the time we bid on the job. Mary was head of our estimating department, and she worked up the bid herself. It was due at eight o'clock the next morning, and she stayed late working on it." She held up the envelope. "You'll find out when you read this that Austin was there that night with her. She explained the process to him and told him what Defrain was bidding."

Spider looked from Annie to Frank. "I'm afraid I don't understand."

"Austin told our competitor what our numbers were. Their bid was fifty dollars less than ours. They got the job, and we were going under."

"Let me guess," Spider said. "You heard from Earnest Endeavors again. Offering less this time."

"It just about killed me," Annie said. "What we got for the development didn't cover what we owed. We had to close down the construction company and sell off all the equipment."

Frank said something, and Annie reached over to pat his knee. "Yes, Love. It came closer to killing you than me." She pulled the note out of the envelope and gave it to Spider.

He opened it and read.

Dearest Mom and Dad,

By the time you read this I'll be gone. I'm sorry to do this, but you won't need me anymore in the company. What you don't know is, I'm the reason you lost Defrain Estates and Defrain Construction. I was so head over heels in love with Austin that when he asked what we were bidding on the Black Canyon job, I told him. He told the other bidder, and that was that. He left the information as an anonymous tip—he didn't know the people he told, so it wasn't like he did it for a friend. He was only interested in gaining an advantage.

The thing is, he never was interested in me. He was bent on getting our development at a bargain basement price. It doesn't matter whom you think you sold Defrain Estates to; I know in the end, he'll be the one that owns it.

I think I could survive the shame of ruining my family financially. I could probably survive the mortification of being made a fool of by a smooth-talking man. But the two of them coming together are too much to bear.

My one small consolation is that I know he wants our house for himself. He plans to live here, so if I die here, I'll be able to haunt him for the rest of his life. That's my plan.

I'm sorry. I could say it a million times, and it wouldn't be enough. Please don't hate me.

All my love,
Mary

Spider looked up at Annie. "How did she kill herself?"

Frank answered, and Spider understood. "Carbon monoxide."

"So you had a house in Defrain Estates?" Spider handed Mary's note back to her mother.

"Yes. It was beautiful. Up on top of the cliff with windows all along the western side." Tears sprang to her eyes. "I wish I had taken the chance to tell her that the house didn't matter. Defrain Construction didn't matter. She was what really mattered in our lives."

"Was she your only child?" Spider asked gently.

Mary nodded. She pulled a tissue out of her pocket and blew her nose.

"Was Frank's—was it a stroke? Was it tied up in all this?"

Frank took the floor then, explaining what had happened to him. Spider nodded and made conversational noises in what seemed to be the proper places, but in the end, he knew no more than he had at the beginning. "I'm sorry," he said, and he reached over to touch Frank's paralyzed arm.

Looking at Annie, he asked, "Could you give me the address of your house in Defrain Estates? And maybe your phone number here, in case I have some more questions?"

"Certainly." She stood and went to the kitchen. Taking a card from the phone stand, she wrote on the back. "This is one of the business cards for the development," she said. "I'm adding the address and phone number you wanted."

Spider stood as well. "Thank you so much for talking to me. I'm sorry to bring back painful memories."

Frank mumbled something and reached out his hand. Spider grasped it and said, "It was a pleasure to meet you, sir."

Annie stood near the entryway. "I'll see you out."

Carrying his hat, Spider held it up in salute to Frank and then crossed to the door. Annie gave him the card and followed him out, pulling the door shut behind her. "Did you understand the last that Frank told you?"

He shook his head. "Afraid not."

She smiled. "You're very tactful. He was explaining that Austin moved into our house the day of the funeral. It may have been coincidence or not, but when Frank found out about it, it hit him hard. That night he had the stroke."

Spider put on his Stetson. "So, when did all this happen? Was there a span of time between when Mary told Austin about the bid and when she died?"

Annie strolled with Spider down the ramp to the sidewalk. "Yes. It took several months for everything to wind down. Austin stopped calling right after the bid opening, and the combination of losing both him and the project sent Mary into a tailspin. She seemed to obsess about him, and she was constantly angry and depressed. It's almost like—" Annie looked over Spider's shoulder, as if she'd find the phrase she was looking for there. "—like someone had to die to make everything right for her, and she chose to kill herself rather than him." She shook her head. "That sounds so horrible, but that's the way it seemed. At least she's at peace now."

Spider took her hand. "How are *you* doing?"

She shrugged. "Oh, you know. I survive because Frank depends on me." She squeezed his hand. "Thanks for coming by. I hope we've helped."

"You have. I'll be in touch." He walked around to the driver's side.

"I'm sorry for what I said about your car."

He chuckled and waved to say it was okay, but she had already turned and was walking back to the house.

Spider found the address of Texas Capital Investment, Inc. and set out to locate it. As he drove, he played back in his mind the conversation with the Defrains. It might have been a mistake to visit them first. Feelings might run a little high when he finally came face to face with Austin Lee.

Chapter 11

◆

SPIDER DROVE SLOWLY along the St. George arterial, trying to see the numbers on the office buildings clustered around parking lots all along the way. He had tried to work the GPS app on his phone but in the end gave it up, reverting to the old fashioned way—creep and peek. When he spied a number close to the one he wanted, he entered the parking area. Keeping a weather eye out for a parking place, he drove through and read the plaques on the sides of the building. 1342 Nephrology. 1364 Gynecology. 1386 Oncology. This seemed to be a medical complex. A very popular medical complex, as there were no empty spaces.

Ending up at the backside of the third building, Spider could see the neighboring complex and the address he needed. That parking lot was almost full, too, but he spied one empty space. There was no access from this lot to the other, but the curb was low. He saw another car heading toward the single vacant space, and he didn't hesitate. Bumping over the curb, he traversed a sidewalk, a planter well, and another sidewalk before bouncing down onto the pavement and slipping into the parking space just as the other car rounded the corner.

Spider couldn't help smiling at the small triumph. His smile grew broader when he saw a sign in metal letters reading *Texas Capital Investments* on the wall right in front of him. "Dang, I'm good," he muttered.

Spider read the string of other names on the wall. Apparently Austin shared the building with two CPAs and a family counselor. Getting out, he pushed through the office door and entered a reception area with plush carpet and a few chairs in groups. A young woman wearing a headset and a nametag that said *Jennifer* was seated behind a desk. She looked up. "May I help you?"

Spider took off his hat. "I'm here to see Austin Lee."

"Mr. Lee just left for the day." She checked her monitor. "Would you like to make an appointment? He'll be in on Monday."

"Not 'til then?"

"I can give you a ten o'clock." Her fingers hovered above the keyboard as she sent him an inquiring look.

"Sure. Monday, ten o'clock. Name's Spider Latham."

"Spider? Like the...?" She put her hand, spider-like, on her desk.

He nodded, and she entered the name. "Would you like a reminder card?"

Spider noticed a holder with Texas Capital Investments business cards in it. "I'll just take one of these," he said, holding it up between thumb and forefinger. "Thank you very much."

"You're welcome, Mr. Latham. We'll see you on Monday."

Spider strode out of the building, putting on his hat to shade his eyes from the sun. It was mid afternoon, and waves of heat radiated off the blacktop. He got in the Yugo and started it, rolling down all the windows and turning the AC to high. Handling the hot steering wheel gingerly, he backed out of the parking space and started threading his way to the exit.

The light on the street had just changed, and Spider waited behind a Toyota a few years younger than the Yugo as traffic streamed by. Ahead of the Toyota, a yellow Mustang had its nose out, waiting for a gap. One came, and as it turned right, accelerating in a cloud of dust and noise, Spider caught a glimpse of the vanity plate. It read *BRACES.*

Spider was so surprised to see Jack's car pulling out of this parking lot that he put on the brakes and stared. As the Mustang got smaller with distance, the car behind Spider honked. He waved to say *sorry* and concentrated on merging into traffic on the arterial. Jack was momentarily forgotten as he tried to decide what to do next. He didn't intend to wait until Monday to see Austin Lee.

A stretch of road with shade trees lay ahead, and he pulled over in the shadow of one of them. Leaving the motor running, he took the card that Annie had given him and turned it over to look at the address of her former house in Defrain Estates. Acacia Drive. He had no idea where that would be, and he slowly dragged his phone out of his pocket. He needed the help of the GPS but was reluctant to be humiliated again.

He took a deep breath. "Don't over-think it," he muttered to himself, trying to remember how Daisuke had explained it this morning. As he punched icons, suddenly, the window where he was to enter the address popped up, and the rest was easy. Two minutes later he was on I-15 heading south.

Defrain Estates lay on the western edge of town, and Spider saw that one of the selling points would be its quick freeway access. Only one stop light on a busy arterial stood between the freeway off ramp and the road that swept up the side of a mesa to the houses. The gatehouse occupied the middle of the road at the bottom, flanking a huge brickwork sign with palm trees at each end.

He turned on Defrain road and stopped at the gatehouse. It was open but unmanned, so he continued up the curving ascent to the top. Driving through, it looked as if a third of the lots had been developed, and all the houses were large and impressive. Spider read the road signs as he passed, spying Acacia just after the GPS announced it.

Annie Defrain's former home stood alone at the end of a row of four vacant lots. Spider stopped in front of the last house before open territory and walked to the edge of the mesa, thinking he might be able to see the bank of western-facing windows that she'd spoken of. A cinderblock fence surrounded the backyard, but he spied the ladder of a diving board sticking up above the wall. A dirt trail that looked like it had been used by ATVs traversed the flank of the mesa just before the house. Spider walked down the path a ways, pausing by a lone juniper tree and looking back to see the wall of glass. He scanned the western vista that Annie would have awakened to each morning and thought of the little, closed-in modular home she lived in now.

Spider went back to the Yugo and drove the block to

the house. He still didn't have any idea what he was going to say when he confronted Austin Lee, but he pulled into the driveway beside a burgundy SUV and got out of the car. As he approached the front door, he looked at the three garage doors, wondering behind which one Mary Defrain took her last, poisonous breath.

The front door was massive. Leaded glass sidelights pictured red rock arches and plateaus, echoing the sandstone facing that came halfway up the walls. Spider pressed the doorbell and heard rich tones sound inside. He waited, but no one answered. Loath to depart without meeting his quarry, he jabbed at the doorbell again, as if vehemence would make Austin appear.

It worked. Spider heard quick, confident footsteps and then the door opened. He saw the eyes widen slightly, flick over to the Yugo, and flick back. And he saw the corners of the mouth turn ever so slightly down into a quasi-sneer.

Austin Lee was everything that people had been saying about him. Tall and suntanned, with fashionably long, highlighted hair, he wore pressed chinos and a polo shirt that showed off a muscular physique. His eyes moved again to the Yugo and back. "Yes?"

"Afternoon. My name's Spider Latham, and I work for the Red Pueblo Museum."

Austin leaned casually against the doorframe. "And?"

"I've come to serve notice that we're on to you. We know about how you have extorted prime development land from unsuspecting citizens after you have driven them to financial ruin. Not only is it not going to happen to Martin Taylor, but it's not going to happen to anyone else, either."

Austin's sneer became pronounced. "Extort is such a strong word. Using it borders on libel. I would be more careful if I were you."

"You're the one who needs to be careful." Spider took a step back. "By the way, have you been sleeping all right?"

Austin frowned. "What is that to you?"

"I read Mary Defrain's suicide note. She killed herself in this house just so she could haunt you. Did you know that?"

Austin's urbanity deserted him momentarily. "She did it here?"

"Didn't you know? You'd better watch out for the mess you leave behind. It just might trip you up."

Austin stood up straight. "You're the one who needs to watch out. I wouldn't linger in any dark alleys if I were you." He swung the door closed, staring daggers at Spider until he disappeared from view.

"Huh," Spider grunted. He turned and walked back to the Yugo, taking a detour around the SUV to read the logo on the front. Range Rover. It must have been Austin Lee that he and Karam had seen driving down the wash yesterday afternoon. Why would this good-looking slimeball be dating Amy? Did that indicate the marvelous Jack was hiding a dark secret?

Spider got in the car and headed down off the mesa, taking mental inventory as he headed back to Kanab. The trip hadn't turned out too badly. He'd found out enough to ponder on for a while, though not enough to figure out a way to help the Red Pueblo.

Now he needed to see if he could make peace with Laurie.

Chapter 12

◆

SPIDER INTENDED TO drive to the hotel without any other stops, but as he passed the Red Pueblo, he saw Linda's car in the parking lot and turned in. Wearing the usual canvas apron and bandana on her head, she was in the Heritage Yard talking to a visitor. Spider parked beside her car and walked to the gate, letting himself in and strolling up as she finished her conversation.

Though she didn't divert her attention from the museum patron, Spider saw her glance flicker to him and back. He waited several paces away by the dugout.

When Linda was free, she turned to him. "Mr. Latham? Hello. We haven't met."

He offered his hand, appreciating her firm grasp and direct gaze. "Call me Spider."

She smiled. "I wasn't sure I heard your name right. LaJean said you'd probably want to talk to me."

Spider looked around. "Is there a place we can visit without being disturbed?"

She gestured to the small structure built into a hill of dirt. "How about the dugout? I can lock the latch from the inside."

"Sounds good to me." Spider opened the door for

her to enter and followed her in, taking off his hat. Despite the heat of the day, the interior was cool. The room, perhaps ten feet in diameter, had rock walls, a dirt floor, and a single window in the wood panel beside the door. The only furnishings were a cot, a small drop-leaf table, a potbelly stove and a straight back chair. Spider sat on the bed and set his Stetson beside him.

Linda took a wrought iron nail from above the lintel and slipped it through the latch. "This will make it so we can talk without a visitor opening the door." She sat on the chair, clasping her hands in her lap. "What can I tell you?"

Spider figured he'd get right to it. "How about telling me about Austin Lee."

Linda's cheeks blazed, and her eyes dropped to her hands. "The one thing in my life I'd like to forget, and I keep having to relive it."

"Yeah," Spider agreed. "Those are the things we generally have to relive. Tell me about when you first met him."

She hooked her heels on the rung of the chair and leaned forward, elbows on her knees. "Well, the first thing you notice is how he looks." She flashed a smile. "Which is gorgeous. Don't get me wrong. I think Matt is good looking, but Austin almost isn't even real. And there he was, hanging around. Wanting to talk. With me. No one that good looking has ever given me the time of day."

She shook her head, eyes on the floor. "If it hadn't been for the Tiffany thing, it would have just been an interesting anomaly—something nicely strange that happened to me. It would have gone no further, and when he asked me out, I'd have said no."

"Tell me about the Tiffany thing. How did it appear to you?"

"Ha! How did it appear to anyone? Matt fell head over heels for an overly-made-up, show-off-your-money, blonde from California."

"Is that what you think?"

She blinked. "That he fell for her? Have you seen him with her?"

"Well, yes, and at first I thought it was obvious, too. And then..."

"What?" Her clasped hands were under her chin now.

Spider looked away, uncomfortable seeing the raw need in her eyes. "Yesterday morning when he drove away with her, he looked back at you. It was..."

"Yes?"

"I'm trying to find the word. He looked broken."

She stared at Spider a moment and then wiped away a tear with the heel of her hand. "He hates me."

"He doesn't. I talked to him yesterday. He's having a hard time because he thinks you told someone about the Lincoln Letter."

Her mouth dropped open. "Is that what he meant when he said I betrayed him?"

Spider nodded. "The museum is being sued by a descendant of Oscar Goodman. Only a person who knew about the Lincoln letter would know that name was connected to the cache. You're one of the six people who knew about it, and all the rest have kept mum."

Color drained from Linda's face. She covered her mouth with her hands and began to rock forward and back, murmuring, "Oh-dear-oh-dear-oh-dear-oh-dear."

"What's wrong?" Spider asked, though he knew what was wrong.

"I think I told Austin Lee."

"About the letter?"

She folded her arms and held them tight against her midsection. "No, but I was bragging a bit and told him something valuable was found in the cache."

"Not the name?"

She shook her head. "But he knew I was doing research on Oscar Goodman. He could have figured it out." She frowned. "But how did that turn into Alyssa Goodman filing suit?"

"Austin's clever and charismatic. He's also cold blooded and calculating. I imagine he found someone with that surname and convinced her to file." Spider leaned forward and looked Linda in the eye. "I've just come from talking to a mother whose daughter got tangled up with Austin Lee. He ruined the family financially and got their valuable real estate for himself. The daughter felt it was her fault, and she killed herself."

Linda's eyes got wide. "Oh, no!"

"You're not the only young woman he's preyed upon. In fact, I'm going to go talk to another one tomorrow. Now, things look bad for Matt's family, but there's no use in compounding your mistake by breaking and running. That doesn't help anything."

"Even if *that woman* is dangling a quarter million dollars in front of Matt?" She slumped back in her chair.

"Jealousy is just caustic. It's like lye, eating holes in everything it touches. How do you deal with that?"

"You hold tight to love."

"I tried, but it looks like my love is slipping away."

"Is Matt an honorable man?"

"Yes."

"You know that for sure?"

"Yes."

"Then hold on to that." Spider stood. "There's no chance of you doing anything to harm yourself, is there?"

She smiled wryly. "I wouldn't know how. I might be able to do some damage with an Anasazi ax, but it would be easier to hurt someone other than myself."

"Good. We can talk more in a day or two." He picked up his hat. "By then I'll have more of the lay of the land and maybe even a plan."

She stood and pulled the nail from the latch. "Thank you for talking to me. It was good to sit in here with you and talk about Austin. It chased away some ghosts."

"Ghosts?"

She sat down again, fiddling with the nail and compressing her mouth as if to keep her lower lip from trembling. "Yes. The last time Austin was here, I had just finished working with Matt on one of our presentations. Austin said hello to Matt and then put his arm around me and walked me here. We had been in the dugout before, and that time, I let him kiss me."

She looked down at the nail and then laid it on the table. "He took off his shirt and hung it over the window." She gestured at the small pane of glass letting in a meager shaft of light. "I knew what his intentions were, and I think the thought of doing it here, on Matt's territory, so to speak, was what was appealing to him. It didn't have anything to do with him caring for me or wanting me, you know, in that way."

"Is that what you thought at the time, or is that something you've figured out since?"

She met his eyes. "I think I knew it then in my heart, but it hadn't got to my head."

"What did you do?"

"I said no, but that didn't do any good. He was determined. And strong."

"Did he—?" Spider felt his cheeks getting red. Dang. He hadn't blushed since he was seventeen. "Did he succeed?"

She shook her head. "Thankfully, no. Isaac walked by and heard the commotion. He said he thought it was kids wrestling in here, but I'm sure he knew what was going on."

"What did he do?"

"He knocked on the door and told us to stop the horsing around. Then he waited for us to come out. Austin had to put on his shirt, and he buttoned it wrong." She smiled but covered her mouth as if to hide it. "I noticed, but I didn't say anything." With her hand still covering her mouth, she looked away. "The next time he called, I blocked him, and I haven't seen him since."

She sat silently for a moment and then stood, picked up the nail and put it where it belonged. "Now you know everything."

Spider stood as well. "Thanks for talking to me."

"I should thank you. You've given me hope." She

opened the door, stepped into the yard, and walked briskly away.

Spider followed her out of the cool dimness into the blazing afternoon and put on his hat to shade his eyes. He watched her tall, erect form as she strode toward the side door of the museum. She looked back over her shoulder at him, smiled and waved. Raising his hand, he returned the smile.

"Hey, Spider!"

Spider turned toward the parking lot and saw Isaac's SUV pulling into a parking lot. Karam jumped out and waved. "Hey, Spider," he repeated, trotting over to the fence.

Spider met him at the gate. "Afternoon, Karam. Been learning about cisterns?"

"Oh, yes. It has been most fascinating. We were on our way to Kanab when we saw your car. Can I ride back with you? Isaac has to stay here until five."

"Sure. You ready to go right now?" Spider spoke to Karam, but he watched Isaac come limping across the parking lot from where he had parked his car.

"Yes." Karam helped the older man up on the curb. "Thank you, Isaac, for showing me the water system. I enjoyed our day together."

"Don't mention it." Isaac shook Karam's hand and then spoke to Spider. "How's it going?"

Spider opened the gate and stepped through. "I know more today than I did yesterday."

"Not to pressure you or anything," Isaac said, sticking his thumbs in his suspenders, "but the first hearing is the end of next week."

Spider's eyes crinkled. "Ah. Brick mentioned a deadline, but I hadn't heard what it was yet. You coming into the yard?"

Isaac shook his head. "I'm at the front desk."

"Okay." Spider let the gate swing closed. "Then we'll be off. See you tomorrow or the next day, Isaac. How's Martin doing, anyway?"

Isaac grimaced. "He's just not bouncing back. Looks, frail, you know?"

"Well, I hope to have something positive to report in a couple days." Spider pulled out his keys and motioned for Karam to follow.

They got in the Yugo and were soon on the highway going north. Spider adjusted the air, so it was at maximum strength and looked at his companion. "What did you learn today?"

"I learned that these early settlers were very ingenious. Their water catching system was built, so the rain washed the roof first. Only when the roof was clean did the water go into the cistern."

"Is that so? Huh."

"And what did *you* learn today?"

The question surprised Spider, but it had obviously been a serious one, and he thought for a moment. "I learned that jealousy is corrosive, that it eats away at everything it touches."

"How did you learn that?"

"Linda told me. The gal who wears the bandana and apron—have you met her? She was engaged to Matt Taylor, but some rich lady came promising money to the museum, and when Matt started wining and dining her, Linda got jealous."

Karam cocked his head. "A wise man once said that jealousy contains more of self-love than of love."

"Huh." Spider considered the statement. "That another quote from Mohammed Ali?"

"Actually, it's from a seventeenth century French nobleman, Francois de La Rochefoucauld."

Spider sent Karam an appreciative glance. "You pronounced that like a native. Do you speak French?"

"Yes. I speak French, English, Urdu, Hebrew and, of course, Arabic."

"Great suffering zot! What do you do with all those languages?"

"During the summers I work as a researcher."

"You mean when you're not traveling?"

"No, even when I am traveling. I try to spend at least five hours a day at it, but I can work anywhere and anytime. I just need a good Internet connection."

Spider smiled. "Well, I'll be. You just never know." He paused as a thought struck him. "You say you're a professional researcher?"

"Yes."

"What would you charge to do some work for me?"

Karam raised a brow. "Are you serious?"

"Yes. Do you ever do any genealogical research?"

"I do all kinds of historical research. Some of it is genealogical."

"Okay. There's a lady in St. George by the name of Alyssa Goodman. I need to know if she's a blood relative of a man who lived in Kentucky during the Civil War."

Karam nodded. "That will not be too difficult. But let me do one other thing for you as well."

"You want to do something else? What's that?"

"This rich lady who has caused heartache for the lady in the apron—her name is Tiffany?"

Spider nodded.

"I have met her. I do not think she is what she says she is. I do not think she has the money she says she wants to give."

They were nearing Kanab city limits, and Spider stared so long at Karam that the young man cleared his throat and pointed at the highway. Spider pulled the car back into the right hand lane just as a tire hit the rumble strip. "What makes you think that?" he asked.

"My father is an investment banker. We are Palestinians, but we cannot live in our homeland. This has made it so one has to be very careful in judging people. One develops a kind of a sixth sense where money is concerned."

"Yeah, but you're not a banker. You're a teacher.

Karam touched his breast. "I am my father's son. I am an expatriate Palestinian. And this woman is not what she says she is."

"Okay by me," Spider said. "Have at it."

"That means I am to proceed?"

"Yeah. Maybe I should ask what you charge."

"I will do the work for you if you will let me use your car tomorrow afternoon."

"That's all? You sure?" As Spider approached the hotel, he noticed the pickup sitting in the parking lot. Laurie was back, and he'd soon be speaking the apology he'd worn out in rehearsal all day.

Karam apparently didn't notice Spider's distraction, for he went on explaining his need of a car. "Isaac told me about some petroglyphs north of Fredonia that you do not need four wheel drive to reach. The taxi is booked all day tomorrow, so the use of your car would be appreciated. Would you care to accompany me?"

Spider turned into the hotel lot and parked beside the pickup. "What?"

"Would you and Laurie care to go with me to see the petroglyphs tomorrow?"

"No can do. We have to go to Mesquite, but you're welcome to the car." He turned off the engine and reached in the backseat for a piece of paper, checking to make sure he wasn't giving Karam something he was going to need. Turning it over, he wrote everything he remembered being told about Oscar Goodman and Tiffany Wendt.

Karam waited silently, taking the information when Spider handed it to him. "I will get busy right away," he said.

"Let me get my papers, and I'll give you the car keys." Spider got out and opened the back door, stacking the files so he could carry them under one arm.

Karam pointed at the bundle. "You have been doing research, too?"

"Not in the same way as you, but, yeah. I guess I have." Spider locked and closed the door, tossing the keys to Karam. "Have a good time tomorrow."

Karam grinned. "It will be like I am seventeen again, driving my Yugo." He waved and walked toward the side entrance of the hotel.

Spider headed for the lobby, his heart pounding as he practiced what he'd say to Laurie one more time.

Chapter 13

◆

LAURIE WAS IN the bathroom. Spider heard her singing as he entered the hotel room. That was a good sign. Should he let her know he was here?

Setting his papers and his hat on the desk next to a shoebox, he walked to the bathroom door. He paused a moment, the tightness in his chest making it difficult to breathe, and then he tapped lightly on one of the raised white panels. "Laurie?"

The door opened so quickly, he didn't have time to prepare himself. There she stood, dressed in Levi's and an emerald green tee. She had obviously been drying her hair because it had a tousled, dampish look. Her brown eyes sparkled, and her mouth curved in her familiar smile of welcome.

"Hello, Darlin'," he said. Unconsciously, his voice inflected up, so the greeting had a tentative feel. Dang. He didn't want to do that. His mind groped for the words he had practiced all day.

She beat him to it. "I'm sorry I was such a witch last night," she said, sliding her arms under his and around his back and leaning her head against his torso.

He could smell the scent of her shampoo. That, and

the feeling of her body so close, released the knot in his chest and made his voice husky. "I'm sorry for being such a horse's patoot. Forgive me?"

She didn't answer, but she kissed him. The moistness of her open lips, soft on his own, set off fireworks inside. That kind of hunger and desire had been dampened down and pushed away during the last weeks of his mother's illness. Spider cupped her face in his hands as his mouth covered hers, and he leaned in, pressing her against the doorframe.

"Mmmm." Her arms tightened, and her fingernails scraped against his shirt, her breath coming quickly.

Spider swiveled away from the doorway, moving his hands from her face to her shoulders, caressing the bare skin of her arms and feeling her shiver. He reached around to pull her closer and lifted her feet off the floor. It was only two steps to the bed, and she curved her body with his as they lay down on the coverlet. With his mouth still on hers, he fumbled to find the bottom of her tee at the same time a vibration began in his chest.

Laurie pulled away, eyes wide. "What was that?"

"Great suffering zot!" he muttered as the buzzing repeated. "I think it was my phone. How do I turn the damn thing off?" He got up on an elbow, yanked it out of his pocket, and punched a button.

"Spider? Is that you?"

Spider stared at the phone for a moment as Karam repeated his greeting.

"Spider, are you there?"

"Yeah, Karam." Spider held the phone to his ear. "I'm here."

Laughing quietly, Laurie kissed Spider under the ear and disengaged, rolling over to sit on the edge of the bed and run her fingers through her hair.

"I began work on that research right away." Karam sounded excited. "I am glad to report that I have some very interesting findings."

Spider reached over and traced a finger across the small of Laurie's back as he spoke to Karam. "That's great. Tell you what, let's have breakfast together tomorrow, and you can tell Laurie and me both about it."

"Are you all right, Spider? You sound a little out of breath."

"I'm fine. How about we meet at Houston's Trail's End at eight o'clock?"

"Okay near me," Karam said.

It took Spider a moment to process what he was trying to say. "I think you mean okay *by* me."

"Oh. Right. Okay by me." Karam said good-bye and disconnected. Spider put his phone away and lay back on the bed, watching Laurie cross the room. "He really knows how to spoil the moment."

Laurie smiled from over her shoulder. "It's not spoiled, just postponed. Wouldn't you rather wait so we can savor it? So we don't have to worry that someone's going to call or knock on the door?"

Spider shook his head. "Nope."

She slid her feet into a pair of sandals. "Why don't you take a shower and then we can go find a corner booth somewhere to have supper."

"You think I need a shower? Any particular temperature?"

She wrinkled her nose at him. "Go do it. I want to hear about your day, and I want to tell you about mine."

"Nobody's asking me what I want," he muttered, sitting up and pulling off his boots.

Laurie looked up from examining the papers on the desk. "What did you say?"

"Nothing." He unbuttoned his shirt. "While I'm in the shower, why don't you read the top stack. It's about a gal by the name of Dorcas Coleman. She's another one that got tangled up with ol' Austin Lee."

Laurie counted the stacks. "Boy, you have been busy today. Hurry and get ready. I can't wait to hear all about it."

Spider cast one last glance at the depression in the bed and went into the bathroom to shower and change, as requested. He emerged twenty minutes later in fresh Levi's and a short-sleeved shirt but with hair still wet. "I didn't shave," he said.

"I love the scruffy look."

"Well, that's what you've got." Spider pulled on his boots. "Where do you want to eat?"

"Let's just stroll and stop when we see something good." Laurie waited by the door as he put the room key in his pocket and picked up his hat.

They held hands as they rode the elevator down and strolled through the lobby. Outside, the evening was dusky and warm, and they walked toward the center of town.

Spider put his arm around Laurie. "Before you tell me about your ride, let me ask you something. Why didn't you tell me last night, when I was doing my imitation of the north end of a south bound mule, that Jack wasn't going to ride with you?"

"I don't know. I guess it made me mad you were making such a big deal about me going out with him. I mean, Jack? You wouldn't mind me riding with Bud Hefernan, would you?"

"No. It's just—" He didn't know how to put it, so he tried another tack. "Karam said that jealousy is more about self-love than love."

"Well that's an interesting topic for you to be discussing." Laurie paused in front of the Rocking V Restaurant.

"Yeah. But, you know, I think that's right. I didn't want you riding with Jack because he's handsome and educated and successful. It had to do more with self love, or maybe lack of it."

"It had to do with you being silly. Jack can't hold a candle to you in the looks department."

"Yeah?"

Laurie pulled away and looked him up and down. "Yeah. And as far as the successful part, you've been father to two boys that have turned out to be good men. That beats house, money, car, land, cattle, and horses any day."

"All that?" Spider bent forward to examine the menu in the window. "Want to eat here? Food looks all right."

"What looks best to me is that booth at the end of the row where we won't be disturbed."

"You got it." Spider opened the door and let her precede him. When the hostess approached with menus, he pointed to the booth at the back. "Can we sit there?"

"Sure." The young woman led them to the back of the restaurant and stood aside while they slid in, both on the same side. "Are you newlyweds?" she asked, handing each a menu.

Laurie caught Spider's eye. "No. We just like each other."

The waitress left, and Spider tipped his menu toward the light. "Is it kind of dark in here?"

"That's what you get when you want to be alone in a corner booth. Just order a steak. You don't have to see the menu to have that."

"That's a great idea." He put his menu on the edge of the table and propped his chin in his hand as he gazed at his wife. "You're beautiful. I don't say that enough."

Laurie put a finger to her lips. "Shh. You're just saying that because you want to get me in your bed. Tell me about your day."

The waitress returned with water glasses and her order pad and took the order—two steak dinners.

When she had gone again, Spider said. "Let me hear about your day first."

Laurie unrolled her silverware and put the linen napkin in her lap. "It began oddly."

"Oh?"

"When I got to Jack's, I found that Amy had stayed up all night baking cookies. The whole kitchen counter was covered two layers deep, and you remember how much counter space there is in that kitchen."

"What was she doing that for?"

"I guess because she wanted to. She said they're having trouble getting her medication balanced, and she's a little manic." She laughed. "A little. I've never seen so many cookies. I brought a shoebox full back to the hotel with me."

"A shoebox? What are you going to do with that many? And why didn't you offer me one?"

She unrolled his silverware, handing him the napkin and laying the place setting in the proper place. "You had other things on your mind."

"Okay. So was the mountain of cookies the only odd thing about the day?"

"No." Laurie paused while the waitress set down their salads and bread. "When it came time to go riding, Amy made it clear to me that she, not I, would be riding Taffy."

Spider frowned. "Did she know that Taffy was your horse?"

"Apparently. That was why she went out of her way to stress that she was going to ride her. They have a bond, she says. Taffy knows what she's thinking." She shrugged. "I don't remember all the things she said. The end result was that I rode the pinto."

Spider leaned over and kissed the crown of her head. "I'm sorry," he murmured. "I know you were looking forward to a reunion with Taffy."

She touched her palm to his cheek. "It was all right. We didn't go to Inchworm, just wandered around in the canyons. I'm thankful for the smartphone that Mr. Tremain gave me because I used the GPS to track our movements. I wasn't sure Amy would be able to find the way home."

Spider leaned back, his brows raised. "Wait? You figured out how to use the GPS?"

Laurie spread butter on a piece of bread. "Well, yeah. It's very intuitive. A three-year-old could figure it out."

"Huh." Spider picked up his fork and stabbed at a piece of lettuce. "So, did you enjoy the day?"

"I did. It blew away a lot of cobwebs for me."

They took a hiatus from talk and dedicated the time to their salads. When Spider was finished, he pushed his plate away and said, "I have to go to Mesquite tomorrow. Will you come with me?"

"Sure, but what's in Mesquite?"

"It's something I found in the files I brought home. First let me tell you how I got them." He went on to tell Laurie about Leona Rippley and her struggling little business. He explained how she helped him out and what the files revealed. He told her about the visit to Annie and Frank Defrain and then about his visit to Austin Lee.

"No!" Laurie said, eyes wide. "You didn't go visit him!"

"Yeah, I did. There he was, big as life, living in the house he had stolen away from the Defrains."

"What did he say?"

"After I told him I knew what he'd done, he told me not to go hanging around in any dark alleys."

"Did he really say that?"

"Yeah. And I can tell you something else. He is the one that's taking Amy out. Which means he thinks he knows something about Jack that he can use to advantage."

"You think so?"

"Yep. Jack has the land, and land is always the prize. Usually the owner has a precarious financial footing."

Laurie shook her head. "I wouldn't know about that, but I think you need to stop him before he can do anything to Amy or Jack."

"I'm doing my best. Oh, and I stopped to talk to Linda on the way home, too."

"What did she have to say?"

"She said jealousy was like lye, eating away at everything it touched."

Her eyes twinkled. "It looks like you were having philosophical, jealousy-type discussions with everyone. What else did Linda say?"

Spider rubbed his jaw. "You know, I've been thinking about what she said. I don't think she knew much about the second lawsuit, the one about the cache being returned."

Laurie stared into the darkness beyond Spider's shoulder as she processed that. "Let's see. BMW Blonde came on site first. Then Austin Lee came and started making time with Linda, who didn't like the fact that Matt was hanging on every word BMW Blonde said. Relations got strained, especially after they got word about the Goodman lawsuit. Only by then Linda and Matt weren't spending any time together. She might have known they were worried about money because of a second lawsuit, but she might not have known particulars?"

"I think that's right. We can run that by Matt and Neva tomorrow when we get back, but Linda didn't know what Matt meant when he accused her of betraying the museum."

"But did she? Betray the museum?"

Spider grimaced. "She did and she didn't. She was bragging about the museum's importance and said there was something valuable found with the cache that wasn't on display. Then when she was with Austin one time, she let slip that she was researching Oscar Goodman. I don't think he knew about the Lincoln letter, just that there was something valuable—a reason to sue."

"I'll bet she was sick when she realized what she had done."

"Yeah."

The waitress arrived with their dinners, and the rest of their conversation was confined to family matters. For long stretches of time they didn't talk, sitting in easy companionship. When dinner was over, they wandered back to the hotel arm in arm, squeezing through the lobby entrance together and hurrying to catch the elevator before the doors slid closed.

"Want something sweet when we get back to the room?" she asked.

"You're a tease," he said, pulling her close and kissing her.

"I was talking about cookies." Laurie laughed and straightened his Stetson which had been knocked askew.

The door opened, revealing Daisuke Ito and his two friends. Spider disengaged and bowed to the young Japanese. "Good evening."

"Good evening," they said in unison, smiling as they returned the bow.

Spider let Laurie get off and followed, holding the door momentarily, so the young men could enter.

Just as the door was closing, he heard Daisuke call out, "Happy trails."

"I met him this morning," Spider explained as he walked Laurie to their room.

It took him three tries to get the lock to read the key card, but the light finally flashed green, and he pushed the door open. Laurie reached to turn on the light, but he covered her hand. "Leave it," he said.

She turned and put one arm around his neck. Her other hand slid into his breast pocket and pulled out his cell phone. Using her thumb, she pushed the button sequence to turn it off and set it on the desk. "Now," she whispered. "I believe we were talking about something sweet?"

Chapter 14

◆

SPIDER AND LAURIE drove to the restaurant the next morning, figuring to head out of town from there. On the way, they noticed a crew blocking off Main Street on each side of the highway and another crew unloading a truck.

"Looks like they're setting up booths for Western Legends," Laurie said.

Spider drove slowly, observing the activity. "So what exactly is this celebration about?"

"They used to make a lot of movies here. Westerns, mostly. Some of the old movie stars come back each year."

"Huh. I suppose there'll be some cowboy poetry?"

Laurie chuckled. "Tomorrow night. After that there's music. Jack and I are singing at eight o'clock."

"You are? Great. I'll come and listen to you." Spider pulled in the parking lot behind the restaurant, and they went in the back entrance. Karam had been watching the front door from a booth in the dining room, so they surprised him. He stood as they reached his table, a broad smile on his face.

"Laurie! I am so glad to see you. Did you enjoy your ride?"

"Hello, Karam. Yes I did." She slid into the bench opposite and made room for Spider.

When they were all seated, Karam opened a folder. "I have begun work on the Goodman line. I need a little more time on that. It would be good to have the address of Alyssa Goodman, so I make sure I am dealing with the right person on this end. However, I have found the Civil War soldier. The preliminary work I have done looks promising."

"Promising how?"

"He had no issue. No children."

"Wow," Laurie said. "That looks more than promising."

Karam smiled. "If I am correct, it is. As I said, I want to start from this end, from the woman who is bringing suit." He picked up a paper and set it in front of Laurie and Spider. "If I have not missed something, and if her line goes through somebody else, I will give you a copy of what I have discovered, along with this."

Spider looked at the page. "What is it?"

"My credentials," Karam said.

"Great suffering zot." Spider scanned the listing. Karam had a bachelor's degree, two masters' and a doctorate. The list of cases on which he had been expert witness covered half the page. Spider looked up and said, "You better not let people know you'll work for a day's use of a Yugo."

"I don't know," Laurie said. "There aren't many who can offer that."

Spider tapped the paper. "If you are right, then the suit is full of holes. Right? It won't hold water."

Karam's brow furrowed. "Holes? Water? What are you talking about?"

Laurie interpreted. "It means the suit has no merit. Is that what you're saying?"

Karam nodded. "I will give you a correct pedigree chart for Alyssa Goodman and for the soldier Oscar Goodman. That and my credentials should put an end to it."

Laurie reached across the table to give Karam's hand a quick squeeze. "You've saved the Red Pueblo!"

Karam's face was serious. "Not yet. I would not usually say anything without double checking, but I got excited about the other thing and called you too soon."

"What other thing?" Laurie looked from Spider to Karam.

"Karam doesn't think Tiffany is the real deal," Spider said. "He doesn't think she has the money she says she has."

Laurie's eyes got big. "Really?"

"I now know for certain she has not." Karam drew another sheet out of the folder and slid it across the table. "Until recently, she had been working as a caregiver to an elderly gentleman in Modesto, California. The name of the man and his address are in the report. He died two months ago, and the family claims she took off with his car."

Karam paused to check his notes. "She tells people she's staying here with an old high school classmate. That much is true. Most of the rest is fabrication. She is divorced, but her former husband did not have a software company. He was, and is, a truck driver. For the divorce, they split their assets, and her half came to $3,412.52. You will find information about Wendell Wendt, the former husband, in my report as well as a copy of the divorce papers."

Laurie leaned back into the corner. "So she's not going to save the museum?"

Spider picked up the list of Karam's credentials. "Maybe she doesn't have to. With this suit going away, they may not need the donation."

Karam held out his hand. "If you will let me have those papers back, I will give them to you in a folder when I finish. You will get me Alyssa Goodman's address?" He straightened the edges of the papers and put them in his folder.

"I'll call Martin and Neva, but I'll wait 'til after nine, so as not to wake them," Laurie said. "I'll let you know as soon as I do."

"Please, not a word to them about the Goodman issue. I do not want them to get their hopes up before I am certain. On the matter of Tiffany, go ahead and tell them." Karam stood. "I must get back to work."

"You're not going to have breakfast with us?" Laurie asked.

Karam shook his head. "I ate at six. Will I see you either this evening or tomorrow?"

"We'll call on our way back," Laurie said. "Let's have dinner together."

Karam's teeth shone white as he smiled. "I look forward to it." He waved the folder as a good-bye gesture but stopped and took out his phone. "What was that about holy water?"

Spider laughed. "Not holy water. If something is full of holes or won't hold water, it means it isn't based on fact. It's fraudulent."

"Got it. Thanks." Karam tucked his folder under his arm and slowly walked away, both thumbs working as he recorded the idiom.

Moments later the waitress appeared. "I didn't want to interrupt your meeting. Are you ready to look at a menu, or do you want ham and eggs over easy again this morning?"

"You remembered." Spider smiled up at her. "I'll go with that, and my wife will have oatmeal and whole wheat toast." He glanced at Laurie for confirmation.

"And orange juice," Laurie added. "Milk for him."

"Been married a long time?" The waitress stuck her pencil behind her ear.

"A few years." Laurie watched her close her book and walk purposefully toward the kitchen. "Does it show?" she asked Spider.

His eyes twinkled. "Didn't last night."

Laurie blushed. "Shh." Squeezing his leg under the table, she said, "Look at the video monitor." She pointed to a flat-screen above the booth on the opposite wall that showed a group riding horses through country where the red rock had been carved into fantastic shapes by wind and rain. "This country is so unbelievably beautiful," Laurie said. "We were out in stuff like that yesterday."

They watched the changing images with little conversation, even after the waitress brought their orders. "I don't know," Spider said as he finished his breakfast and fished his wallet out of his back pocket. "Don't you feel a little bit disloyal to Lincoln County, raving about how beautiful Kane County is?"

She shook her head as she took the last bite of toast. "It was your folks who settled there, not mine."

Spider paid the tab, and they got in the pickup and headed to Fredonia, turning west toward St. George on the south end of town. As they crossed over Kanab Creek Bridge, Spider said, "Maybe you should make that call to Martin now because we'll lose cell coverage in a few miles."

Laurie pulled out her phone and dialed. Apparently Neva answered, because the conversation proceeded along feminine lines. Laurie said they had some information, but they had to go to St. George today. Spider would come by tomorrow and talk to them about it. What time should he come? She looked up at him and said, "Four o'clock?" and when Spider nodded, relayed confirmation.

"We need some information about the Goodman lawsuit," Laurie said to Neva. "What's the address of Alyssa Goodman, the gal who is suing the museum?" She wrote down what Neva told her and then asked how Martin was doing.

After finding out Martin was perking along pretty well, Laurie dialed Karam and read the address to him. She listened a moment and said, "Oh no! So does that mean you can't work this morning? Okay, I won't keep you. Bye."

"He's lost his Internet," she told Spider. "The front desk says some guy on a backhoe dug up a cable. They hope to have it repaired later today." She put her phone away. "So, where are we going?"

"It's a place called the *V* Bar Ranch in Mesquite." Spider pointed to a folder on the seat between them. "You read the file last night."

"I remember. Dorcas. What's her story?"

"You know as much as I do. That's what we're going to find out. She's young, twenty-five or so. Linda's age."

"Or Amy's. Or Mary Defrain's."

"Yeah. In the file there's a copy of an unlimited power of attorney she gave to our friend Austin."

"That's like letting the fox in the henhouse."

"Yeah. I couldn't find out from the file what he did with it, but I'll bet he's ended up with the ranch."

"How long will it take us to get there?"

"From here? Couple hours or so."

Laurie reached behind the seat and found a travel pillow. "I didn't get much sleep the last two nights. Do you mind if I take a nap?" She put the pillow against the doorpost and leaned her head on it.

Spider patted her leg. "You go on ahead." He smiled over at her as she tucked her hand under her cheek and closed her eyes.

As he continued west across the Arizona Strip, red cliffs marched on his right, and desert landscape gradually fell away on his left until it reached the blue Kaibab Plateau thirty miles away. The fenced rangeland reminded him of his place in Lincoln County, and his idle mind wandered to something his son Bobby had said to him after the funeral on Tuesday. Was that just three days ago?

It was an offhand remark, made as he held his baby son, Spider's grandson, and said good-bye. Bobby had said he'd like to move back to Lincoln County. Because of the nature of his job with the software company, he could live anywhere he wanted and telecommute. He said he'd like his children to grow up there on the ranch.

Spider hadn't had a chance to give the matter much thought. In the flurry of traveling to Kanab and subsequent events, he hadn't even mentioned it to Laurie yet. He glanced at her, but she was apparently asleep.

All the way across the strip, dropping down into Hurricane and on through St. George, he planned the infrastructure upgrade that would have to be done for another house on the property, beginning with a two-inch water line from the artesian well. He didn't come back to the issue of Austin Lee until he was going through the vertical-walled canyon made by the Virgin River twenty miles beyond St. George.

A few miles out of Mesquite, he pulled off the road at a no-services exit and punched in the address of the V-Bar Ranch. What lowdown Austin Lee scheme would he discover there? And what could you do about someone who did bad things but skated within the law?

If Karam was right, they had stopped Austin on this gambit as far as the Red Pueblo was concerned, but what was to prevent him from finding a new way to get Martin's land? Then there was the worrisome detail of his hanging around Amy. And what other worrisome details were hanging out there, ready to bite them? Someone needed to stop this predator, for sure.

Laurie sat up. She blinked, stretched, and dropped her pillow behind the seat. "Are we there yet?" she asked.

Spider chuckled as he pulled onto the freeway. "Are you up for the day?"

She yawned. "I think so."

"I just pulled off to set up the GPS. It says we turn off at the next exit."

The ranch proved to be three miles off the freeway. Half a mile past a new golf course, a gravel road to the ranch branched off the blacktop, crossed a cattle guard and wound another quarter mile to a weathered frame house and outbuildings.

Laurie looked around as they drove in. "Lincoln County looks pretty lush compared to this."

"See it through ol' Austin's eyes. Add a sprinkling system, some houses around the back side of that golf course, maybe some palm trees. It'll look pretty nice."

"Look at the house," Laurie said. "I don't think anyone is home. In fact, the place looks unlived-in."

"Shoot. I hope we haven't come too late."

At that moment, a three-legged dog came running from behind the house, barking furiously. The dog was followed by a tall, big-boned woman in Levi's and worn cowboy boots. She stood, hands on hips, pulling her beat-up straw hat down to keep the sun out of her eyes as she watched them. Spider stopped the pickup in front of the house and turned off the engine.

Chapter 15

◆——————

SPIDER EXAMINED THE red hair curling under the hat brim and the freckled face. "Does she look like she'd be named Dorcas?" he asked.

Laurie opened the door, slid to the ground, and walked to where the woman stood. "Hi. Would you be Dorcas Coleman?"

"I go by Dorrie." She had on leather work gloves and kept one hand on the dog's head.

"I'm Laurie Latham, and this is my husband Spider." She pointed to Spider, just getting out of the pickup.

Spider touched the brim of his hat. "Howdy. We live over in Lincoln County. We've come by to..." He trailed off when Laurie claimed Dorrie's attention by kneeling down and calling the dog to her.

"I ain't never seen anything like that," Dorrie said. "She don't usually take to strangers."

Laurie rubbed the dog behind the ears. "What's her name?"

"Trey."

Laurie smiled. "For three. I see. Was she born like this?"

Dorrie nodded. "The people who owned her were

going to put her down, but I could see she was something special, and I talked them out of it. I went there intending to get a cattle dog, but instead I got a friend."

Laurie looked at the empty pasture beyond the house. "How many head do you have?"

Dorrie looked away and waited so long to answer that Spider thought she might not have heard the question. When she finally faced them again, her eyes were shiny with unshed tears. She flapped her arms against her side as if in frustration and turned away once more. "I'm sorry," she said, not looking at them. "I don't mean to act like a baby." She sniffed. "Truth is, I don't own the ranch anymore."

She sniffed again, and Spider dragged out the fresh handkerchief he had stuck in his pocket that morning. He held it in front of Dorrie where she could see it without looking at him, and she took it with murmured thanks.

She pulled off one of her gloves and stuck it in her back pocket before blowing her nose. "Truth is, I didn't expect to still be here. I put the last of my things in my pickup this morning. I was going to load my horse and leave, but when I hooked up the trailer, something was wrong. I ain't got no lights."

"I could take a look-see, if you'd like," Spider offered. "Where's the trailer?"

She gestured behind her. "Back by the stable."

"Let me get my tools." He walked to his truck, got his gloves and toolbox from behind the seat, and he and Laurie followed Dorrie around the house. In back he found a machine shed, a four-stall stable, and three corrals. The largest of the three held a palomino mare, standing ears pricked forward.

Spider walked toward the trailer parked near the gate. He knelt down and pulled the trailer electrical harness out of the receptacle on the pickup and used his test light to make sure there was power in the hookup. There was, so he turned his attention to the trailer, tracing wires and methodically ruling out problems. It took him fifteen minutes, but he finally found a broken wire at the back of the trailer. He fixed the connection, bound it up with electrical tape, and went to find Dorrie and his wife.

They were in the corral. Laurie was bent over with the palomino's hoof between her knees. The two women had their heads together as Laurie traced the edge of the shoe. As he set his toolbox on the top rail, she looked up. "Guess what? Dorrie has Taffy's sister."

The information took a minute to sink in. He leaned his arms on the railing. "How did you find that out?"

Laurie put down the hoof and straightened up, a big smile on her face. "Dorrie showed me how Goldie would come at a whistle, and I saw her throwing out her hoof the way Taffy does."

"There's not one in a hunnerd would 'a noticed that," Dorrie said. "You got to have a good eye."

Laurie patted the palomino's neck. "Or a horse with the same condition."

Spider frowned. "Having the same condition doesn't mean this is Taffy's sister."

"No, but when I saw it, I asked where she got Goldie."

Dorrie broke in. "Ain't no big coincidence that we both went to Sunrise Ranch when we were looking for a good horse. They're the biggest horse breeder around. Closer to us, but Lincoln County's just a hunnerd miles away."

Laurie picked up the thread. "Remember when the owner told us that Taffy was the second foal with this condition?"

"Yeah."

"Well, Goldie was the first."

"Huh." Spider eyed the palomino. "Sounds like something that belongs in Ripley's Believe it or Not."

"I was just telling her about the farrier Jack uses. Dorrie's got someone that's pretty good, but Jack's guy custom orders shoes that he's able to modify more easily."

Spider picked up his toolbox. "Did you tell Dorrie why we're here?"

Dorrie looked from Laurie to Spider, the smile no longer lighting her face. "No. She didn't."

Spider looked around for some shade. Three cottonwoods towered over a stock tank, casting a large shadow that promised to be a few degrees cooler. "Let me put away my tools, and then let's sit over there and talk. You've got lights now, by the way."

As he walked away, Spider heard Dorrie asking Laurie, "What's this about?"

When he returned, he found them sitting on the wide edge of the huge concrete watering tank, deep in conversation. He hunkered down in front of them, forearm on one knee, and waited for Laurie to finish telling Dorrie how they were called to help out the museum in Fredonia.

Dorrie again looked from one to the other. "But what's that got to do with me?"

"The lawsuits that have been crippling the museum are bogus," Laurie said. "They're made-up, all because someone wants land that the museum owner has. This person is trying to get the museum director in a bad financial position, so he has to sell his land quickly. This person can then pick it up for a song."

Dorrie pushed her heel into the wet earth in front of her. "That sounds a little farfetched, and I still don't see why you're here talking to me."

Spider spoke without thinking. "The person behind the lawsuits was Austin Lee."

Dorrie's freckles stood out as her face went pale. Her eyes and mouth got a bluish tinge around them, and she looked shrunken and defenseless all of a sudden. Spider was immediately sorry he had spoken without preparing her.

Laurie moved closer and put an arm around Dorrie. "Are you all right?" When Dorrie nodded, she went on. "We've found that he's left a trail of broken hearts behind him. He's used the same tactic each time, which is to ingratiate himself with a woman, get her to trust him, maybe fall in love with him, and then use her to get what he wants, which is usually prime real estate at a bargain price."

Dorrie closed her eyes, folded her arms and hunched over. Her breathing became shallow.

"Go get a water bottle," Laurie whispered to Spider.

He got up and trotted back to the pickup, glad Laurie was there to troubleshoot. Give him a car chase or a fistfight. That was easier than watching a good woman go through something like this.

When he returned, Laurie was rinsing his handkerchief in the stock tank. "Can you tell us when you met Austin?" she asked as she bathed Dorrie's brow and the back of her neck. "Tell us how it happened."

Dorrie leaned forward and put elbows on her knees and her face in her hands. "It was over a year ago. He drove in one day saying he was lost."

There was a long pause. Neither Spider nor Laurie prompted her to go on.

Finally Dorrie spoke. "I was the one that was lost, from the moment I saw him." She gave a great, ragged sigh and sat up. "He came back to see me again and again. We rode all over the ranch. He went with me to see my dad at the old folks' home." She laughed, a short, mirthless sound. "He helped me make decisions, and when dad died, he said he'd probate the will for free, since he was a lawyer."

Spider spoke gently. "Did he ask you to sign a power of attorney, so he could do the probate?"

Dorrie nodded. "He said it would be so much easier."

"Then what did he do?" Laurie rubbed Dorrie's broad back.

"As soon as probate was over, he sold the ranch for me."

Spider didn't know whether to give her a break or forge on, but he figured it was like taking off a Band-aid. Better to get it over. "Did he sell it to a company called Texas Capital Investments?"

Dorrie nodded. "How did you know?"

Spider's mouth felt dry. "What did you get for the ranch?"

"A hunnerd thousand dollars."

Spider heard Laurie's intake of breath, and he asked, "For how many acres?"

Dorrie stared at Spider as if that was something he should know. "It's a section—640 acres."

"With good water?" Laurie sounded like she was afraid to hear the answer.

"We've got a spring right about the middle. Sweetest water you'll find."

Laurie let out a sigh. "Oh, Dorrie. I'm so sorry. I don't know if anything can be done."

Dorrie drew her freckled brows together. "About what?"

Laurie swept her hand in an arc, taking in the house, the outbuildings, the rangeland. "Your ranch was worth maybe ten times what you got for it."

Spider grunted. "Right next to this golf course and close to the freeway? And with water? More than that. Way more."

Dorrie blinked. "I don't care about that."

Laurie and Spider spoke together. "You don't?"

Dorrie shook her head. "Nah. I found a little place just south of St. George. It's got stables and an arena and a little trailer house on it. I can board and train horses there. It'll do me just fine."

Laurie put her arm around the larger woman. "Dorrie, listen to me. Austin Lee is building up his personal fortune on the wreckage of other people's lives. He ruined a family in St. George, and after the daughter committed suicide because of what he did, he ended up living in her house."

Dorrie's eyes narrowed. "What was her name?"

"The girl?" Laurie looked to Spider for the answer.

He supplied it. "Mary Defrain. They lost Defrain Estates to Austin Lee."

Dorrie flung her arms out and jumped up. "I won't listen to another word against him. I don't know you people. You come here and say things against Austin, and you got no proof." She reached down, picked up a rock and flung it, hitting the corral fence with a solid thwack. Trey jumped up, whining, and hopped over to stand by Dorrie.

Spider held his hands up, palms out. "Whoa, Dorrie. Easy. We're just trying to figure things out, here. When was the last time you saw Austin?"

Dorrie turned on him, fists clenched, teeth bared. "Why are you asking that? You. Don't. Know. Nothing."

Laurie stepped between Dorrie and Spider, touching her arm and speaking softly. "We'll go now." She looked over her shoulder at him and jerked her head in a way that said *go*.

Spider went. As he walked away, he heard Laurie ask, "Will you tell me the address of where you're going to live?"

He got in the pickup, started it, and turned on the air. Laurie joined him a few minutes later, carrying the water bottle and handkerchief. She climbed in, shut the door, and stashed the water bottle in the cup holder. "Thanks for the AC. I'll bet Mesquite is a good fifteen degrees hotter than Kanab."

"Never mind that. What happened after I left?"

She spread the handkerchief out to dry on the seat beside them. "I asked where she was moving to. She couldn't remember the address, but she said you turn on that big interchange before you get to St. George and go about a mile. Her road is just past a gravel pit. She's a half a mile in."

"Can you write that down? I'll never remember it."

Spider gave her the pen from his shirt pocket, and she picked up the manila folder with *Dorcas Coleman* on the tab. As Laurie scribbled, Spider turned the pickup around and headed back out over the cattle guard. "Was she doing okay when you left her? She seemed really upset."

"She was upset with us. She's very protective of Austin, and she's not going to let anyone paint him as anything but a knight in shining armor. He came and helped her out during a difficult time."

"And he stole her land."

She gave him back his pen. "I don't think that matters. She was shaken up by our news about him at first, but I think that was because she hasn't seen him for a good while. When you're so in love with someone, just hearing his name can make you feel faint."

"Really?"

"Yes. It usually happens when you're in seventh grade, but I don't think Dorrie has had a lot of social experience." Laurie adjusted the vent, so it wasn't blowing right on her. "What's more, she'd probably be glad if you told her that Texas Capital Investments was owned by Austin Lee. She'd be glad to think of him having her ranch."

"That doesn't make sense."

"Love very rarely makes sense."

"You said she hasn't seen him in a great while, but she wouldn't tell us when that was." Spider said that more to himself, and Laurie didn't comment.

They drove in silence until they got back on the freeway heading for St. George. "She's really got an arm," he said. "Did you see her throw that rock?"

"Yeah I did." Laurie laughed. "Do you think she was aiming for that board?"

"I'll bet she was. The Lincoln County Lynx should recruit her for their slow pitch team."

Laurie smiled and nodded in agreement.

Silence again.

"So, how do we convince her?" Spider looked over at Laurie. "What's it gonna take?"

Laurie shot him a puzzled look. "To join the softball team? Why are you even thinking about that?"

"Not the softball team. How do we convince her she's been had?"

Laurie thought a moment. "Why do you have to convince her of anything?"

"Because—"

"No, listen, Spider. What will it accomplish? It won't get the ranch back. It won't make her life better. What it will do is destroy any dreams she's holding onto. She's got a plan about how she's going to go on. Leave her be."

Spider gritted his teeth. "How are we going to get this piece of cow dung held responsible for what he's done to people's lives?"

"I don't think that's your job. You were asked to

come and help the museum. You've made a good start on that."

"Huh." Spider thought about that. "The trick is to make sure he doesn't come back with some other plan. Seems the way to do that would be to get him off the street for good."

"I agree, but there's a more important question to consider right now."

"What's that?"

"Are you going to feed me? I'm hungry. I meant to bring some of Amy's cookies."

"Amy's phantom cookies. You've talked a lot about them, but I've yet to see even one."

"You didn't seem much interested last night." She pointed at an oncoming off ramp. "There's a drive-in. Let's grab a taco or something."

Spider did as she asked, and half an hour later they were back on their way. As they passed through St. George, Spider told Laurie what Bobby had said about raising his kids on the ranch, and they spent most of the way back to Fredonia talking about that possibility.

As they passed the Kaibab Paiute Reservation marker, Laurie looked at her watch. "Do you know where the petroglyphs were that Karam was going to look at?"

"He said they were north of Fredonia, but I got the idea it was on a dirt road." Spider hit the heel of his hand on the steering wheel. "Oh, shoot!"

"What?"

"I forgot to tell Karam about the gas gauge, how it's empty at a quarter tank."

"How much gas was there in the car? Do you remember?"

"A little more than a quarter tank. See if you can get him on the phone."

Laurie dialed, but there was no answer. As they came into Fredonia, they kept a sharp eye out for an orange car pulled off the road. "Should we stop at the museum?" she asked as they drove past.

"Let's go on to the hotel and see if he's there. He may be working and have his phone turned off."

Coming over the hill just after the Utah line, they passed a boarded up restaurant on the left, its flower beds clogged with tumbleweeds. Spider was scanning the area on both sides of the road, and something orange registered in his peripheral vision, just a flash, and it was gone.

Spider braked hard and turned into the vacant parking lot, slinging Laurie against the restraint of her seat belt. She grabbed the panic handle with one hand and pointed with the other. "There's the Yugo behind the building. What's it doing there?"

They bumped over the weed-infested cracks in the parking lot, heading to the rear of the restaurant where the back end of the Yugo stuck out about a foot. The driver's side front door stood open, and Spider had a bad feeling in his gut.

Chapter 16

♦

SPIDER STOPPED THE pickup and opened his door. "Stay here a minute."

"Would he have pulled clear around here if he ran out of gas?"

Spider bailed out of the pickup, not pausing to answer. He approached the car cautiously, scanning the area but seeing no one. When he came in full view of the driver's side, a pair of legs was visible beneath the open door. The crease in the khaki trousers was sharp; the shoes were shined. "Oh, no." Spider muttered. "Karam."

He was around the door in two quick steps, drawing in a sharp breath when he saw his friend lying senseless, sprawled across the bucket seat under the steering wheel.

"What's wrong?" Laurie jumped out of the truck.

"It's Karam. Can you come help me?"

She was there in a moment, covering her mouth with her hands when she saw their young friend so pale and still. "Is he all right?"

"He's got a pulse, but I can't get him to wake up. Help me move him to the backseat."

"That will be too hard in this little bitty car," Laurie

said. "I'll move the pickup into the shade. We can lay him in the bed."

"That'll work."

Spider watched as Laurie climbed in the pickup and deftly maneuvered it into the shadow of the building. He let down the tailgate, and she emerged from the cab with the travel pillow and a fleece blanket she had unearthed from behind the seat. "Good girl," he said, walking back to where Karam lay. "Spread it across the back."

"Want me to help carry him?"

"I think it will be easier if I do it myself." Spider crouched and slid his arms under Karam's thighs and shoulders.

"Lift with your knees," Laurie cautioned.

Spider grunted as he stood, taking care not to knock the unconscious man's head against the steering wheel. He took two steps back and said through gritted teeth, "Close the door."

Laurie gave the door a push and followed Spider to the pickup where he laid Karam's inert form on the fleece with his head on the pillow.

Laurie got the water bottle and handkerchief that she had used to wipe Dorrie's brow earlier. "This isn't very hygienic, but it's better than nothing." She wet the cloth and began bathing Karam's face. "Oh! His eyes are open."

"Hello, Karam," Spider said, looking into the young man's blank eyes.

Karam blinked, his gaze resting first on Spider then on Laurie. "Where am I?" he whispered.

"Right now, we're halfway to Fredonia," she said.

"We found you in the Yugo, parked behind an abandoned restaurant."

Karam stared at Laurie, obviously trying to make sense of her words.

"Don't worry about it now," she said, patting his hand.

Karam closed his eyes again, and Spider turned and looked at the car. There was nothing there to give a clue as to what had happened.

"Somebody tried to put me down," Karam croaked.

Spider turned back. "Say that again."

"Somebody tried to put me down."

Spider and Laurie exchanged quizzical glances. "Because you're a Palestinian?" Laurie asked. "They were calling you names?"

"No. Like your horse. Someone tried to put me down."

Spider worked it out first. "Someone tried to kill him."

Laurie's eyes widened. "Who?"

Karam closed his eyes. "I do not know. I have a headache."

Laurie hovered over him. "Where does it hurt?"

Karam raised his arm and began to touch the base of his skull. "Ouch. I think I have a bump there. What do you call it? A duck egg?"

"A goose egg. Let me see." She slid her hand under his head. "My goodness! No wonder you have a headache. Can you remember what happened?"

Karam spoke with his eyes closed. "I was coming back from seeing the petroglyphs, and the car malfunctioned. It felt like it ran out of gas, but I still had a quarter tank."

"Sorry about that," Spider said.

"I pulled off in an empty parking lot, and someone pulled in behind me. I thought that was just like a friendly westerner." He paused for a moment and then added, "He did not smile when he got out."

"Can you describe him?" Spider asked.

Karam shook his head slightly. "I only saw him for just a moment. He was very large. He spun me around. Got me in a chokehold. Squeezed until I passed out."

Laurie touched the ruby in a ring Karam wore. "If he was trying to rob you, he missed this."

"We'll have him go through his pockets when he feels better," Spider said.

"He said..." Karam's voice was raspy.

Spider leaned down, so he could hear better. "What did he say?"

"I am trying to remember. He said something about the Red Pueblo. Lie down. Lie on. It did not make any sense."

"Did he say *lay off the Red Pueblo*?" Laurie asked.

Karam's eyes were closed. "I do not know. He may have. My ears were ringing, and I was trying to get his arm off my neck." He explored the base of his skull with his fingers. "Why does it hurt here?"

"He must have hit you on the head before he dumped you in the car," Laurie said. "Spider, you've got to call the police."

Karam's eyes opened wide, and he struggled to rise. "No. No police." His face contorted, and he put his hand to the back of his head.

Spider helped him sit up. He had never seen Karam look so grim. "Why not?"

"My interactions with police have not filled me with confidence."

Laurie helped Karam swivel around, so his legs could dangle over the end of the pickup as Spider pulled out his cell phone. "Maybe not in Gaza," he said, "but—"

Karam grabbed Spider's wrist. "If you had skin the color of mine and were Muslim, you would not be so sanguine about the police in America."

Laurie's brows creased. "Surely not!"

Karam looked at her. "You are so good. I know it is hard for you to think badly of anyone. I tell you, if they do not suspect me of being a terrorist, they see my dark skin and think I'm Hispanic. They will think I am an illegal alien." He let go of Spider's wrist.

Spider pocketed his phone and leaned against the tailgate. "I'm a deputy sheriff, Karam. I don't have any jurisdiction here, but certainly my word would stand for something."

"When they bring in Homeland Security, would your word stand for something against them?"

"I think that's a little extreme," Spider said. "But you're the one with a goose egg. We'll do as you say." He drew a card out of his shirt pocket. "However, I am going to make one call."

"Who to?" Laurie asked.

Spider was busy tapping in the number. He held up a hand for silence as he listened to the ringing on the other end. "Hello, Jennifer? This is Spider Latham. I was in to see Austin Lee yesterday. Yes, glad you remembered. Is he in?" There was a brief pause, and then Spider's voice grew hard. "Well, I have a message for you to give him. Do you have a pencil? Good. Here it is. Tell him he needs a better class of goon to do his dirty work. Whoever he sent over here attacked my friend, not me. Tell Austin Lee that I'm coming after him, and I'm going to put him out of business." Spider punched the *off* button and dropped the phone in his shirt pocket.

Laurie frowned up at him. "Was that wise?"

Spider pulled out his wallet again and put the card inside. "I don't know, but it made me feel a whole lot better."

Laurie patted Karam's knee. "Are you doing okay sitting up like that?"

The young man nodded. "If I could get rid of the headache, I think I would be all right."

"I've got Tylenol in the glove box." She headed for the cab and was back moments later with two white capsules.

Karam took them with murmured thanks and downed them with a drink from the water bottle.

Spider held up his hands for attention. "Okay. Here's what we'll do. We'll go back to the hotel. Karam, you'll stay in our room, so we can keep an eye on you."

Karam shook his head then grimaced and put his hand on the sore spot. "I would prefer my own room. It is almost time for *asr*, for late afternoon prayer."

"Are you sure?" Spider sounded doubtful.

"You can check on me all you want. I just need to be in my own room." Karam reached out his hands. "Will you help me down?"

With Spider on one side and Laurie on the other, they supported him as he slid to the ground. Spider walked with him to the passenger side of the pickup and helped him in.

Laurie closed the tailgate and met Spider at the driver's door with the fleece and pillow. Climbing in, she slid across to sit in the middle. As Spider got in and started the truck, she tucked the pillow behind Karam's head as it rested against the doorpost.

"Thank you." Karam's eyes were closed again. "I am sorry I broke your car."

"You didn't break it." Laurie patted his hand. "Spider forgot to tell you the gas gauge doesn't work."

"Ah."

Spider drove across the parking lot and turned north on the highway. "We'll get you settled, and then Laurie and I will come back and pick up the car."

Laurie leaned closer to Spider and spoke in a lowered voice. "We need to go visit Matt and tell him what Karam found out about Tiffany."

The corners of Spider's mouth turned down. "Yeah, I'm really looking forward to that."

Laurie continued in the same lowered voice. "We'll get Karam settled. If he's doing okay, we can run out to the museum and catch Matt. I think he's there 'til closing."

"I will be fine," Karam said.

Spider rubbed his jaw. "We'd probably better let Matt know that Austin Lee reacted to my visit, so they can be on guard. It bothers me that he's turned to violence."

"Especially since he's using hired guns," Laurie

said. "You don't know where the next attack is going to come from."

All the way to the hotel, Spider looked in the rearview mirror, checking to make sure there was no one behind them. When they arrived, Spider walked with Karam to his room and got him settled while Laurie detoured by the Latham's room. She knocked on Karam's door a few minutes later, and Spider let her in.

She entered carrying the box of cookies and some individual milk cartons. "I got these in the gift shop," she said, putting them in the mini fridge. She set the box on the stand next to where Karam lay on the bed. Bending over him, she smoothed back his hair. "Look at me," she said.

After gazing intently at his eyes, she went to the closet and pulled the extra blanket off the top shelf. She covered Karam with it and tucked it around him. "Rest and chocolate chip cookies," she said, patting the box on the bedside stand. "Best medicine there is."

"I will have some in a little while," Karam said. "Thank you." His eyes fluttered and then closed.

"You've got my cell phone number," Spider reminded him. "We're going to go talk to Matt Taylor for a little bit and pick up the Yugo on the way back. Call us if you need anything. We can be back here in fifteen minutes."

Karam's eyes opened. "You can tell him about Tiffany Wendt, but don't say anything yet about the Goodman thing."

"We won't." Laurie pulled the blanket up around his ear. "You just rest."

"I've got your room key." Spider patted his pocket. "We'll check on you when we get back."

Spider rested his hand on Karam's shoulder, and then he and Laurie quietly left. They got in the pickup and stopped at a service station on the way out of town to buy a one-gallon can and fill it with gas. Then they headed south to Fredonia.

Chapter 17

◆

"ARE YOU WORRIED about Karam?" Spider asked Laurie.

"His eyes look okay. You always worry about a bump on the head, though."

Spider grimaced. "I feel so bad that he got pulled into this mess."

Laurie turned toward him. "I tell you what I worry about. I worry that this whole thing is bigger than it seems. What if this is some Mafia-backed real estate grab."

Spider shook his head. "I don't think so. It has the feel of a small-time operator. I think that he's been successful in all these scams, and now when someone is standing up to him, he's resorting to violence."

"But who was the fellow who attacked Karam? Was that Austin Lee?"

"Can't be. He knows what I look like. I think he went to Rent-a-Thug and hired someone to work me over. Austin saw me driving the Yugo, so describing the car was easier than describing me."

"You mean orange roller skate with black flames is easier than tall, dark and handsome?"

Spider smiled. "Something like that." Coming down the hill after crossing into Arizona, he spied the red ochre dots that would grow in size and become the Red Pueblo Museum. "I'm not looking forward to telling Matt that Tiffany was lying to him."

"Working with people is hard on the soul," Laurie observed. "I prefer cattle any day."

"Yeah, well..." Spider didn't finish his thought. The site of the museum fast approaching set his mind to searching for words to tell Matt Taylor that he had been had. Minutes later when he turned into the driveway, he hadn't come up with anything. Matt was on the far side of the Heritage Yard with a wheelbarrow and a shovel.

"Want me to come with you?" Laurie asked.

Spider parked in the shade of a tree and rolled down the windows before turning off the engine. "Probably not. No man wants spectators when he finds out how stupid he's been."

"I'll wait here, then."

Spider got out of the cab and ambled to the gate, passing through and crossing to where Matt was methodically taking out weeds with long strokes of his shovel. "Is this executive work?" he inquired when he got within speaking distance.

Matt leaned on the handle, breathing hard. "We may lose the museum tomorrow, but by golly, it'll look good when we do. You got anything to report?"

Spider pushed the brim of his hat up. "I've got things to report. Whether it's going to help remains to be seen." He cleared his throat. How to begin?

"Well?"

"I went to St. George yesterday, and I visited with several people. I found some answers. Found some questions, too, that I want to talk to you about. But first—"

"Yes?"

Nothing to do but get it over with. "First, I need to tell you that Tiffany Wendt was lying. She doesn't have a quarter million dollars to give to the museum."

Matt didn't move. He stood still as a statue with his hand on the shovel handle, his face growing ashen, eyes never leaving Spider's face.

After waiting for Matt to say something, Spider forged on. "She's divorced, just as she said, but her ex doesn't own a software company. He's a truck driver. The car is essentially stolen, and her net worth seems to be somewhere in the area of three thousand dollars."

Matt's eyes seemed to have sunken into his skull, and there was a blue shadow around his mouth.

Spider took a step forward. "Are you all right? Here, come sit on this timber." He led him to the antique well drilling outfit, and Matt didn't resist the pressure of Spider's hand on his shoulder pushing him down. He leaned forward and let his head hang down, breathing in shallow pants.

After a moment, Matt sat up far enough to prop his arms on his knees and put his forehead on clasped hands. "I am such a fool."

Spider leaned a shoulder against part of the rigging. "You're a good man. You tell the truth, and you expect that others do, too."

Matt shook his head. "I've made such a hash of things."

"You're not the first man to do something stupid where a woman is concerned," Spider said.

Matt sat straight up and looked Spider in the eye. "I wasn't in love with Tiffany, if that's what you mean."

Spider glanced at a pair of museum patrons drifting toward the drill rig and jerked his head toward the far side of the yard. "Let's go over there where we can talk undisturbed." He led the way through the native landscaping, continuing the conversation as they walked. "I never thought you were in love with Tiffany, but I do know you hurt Linda. Drove her to listen when a slick customer came along paying attention to her."

"Guilty." Matt picked up a rock and flung it at a fence post, missing by a hair.

"Did you talk to her about it? Tell her you were sorry for hurting her?"

Matt shook his head, picked up another rock and threw it. This time he hit the post with a resounding crack. "What's the use? She went to Flagstaff to another interview today."

Spider put his hands in his back pockets and examined the toe of his boot. Should he push Matt a little harder to talk to Linda? Somehow he didn't think the younger Taylor's love life was what Brick Tremain meant when he talked about trouble at the Red Pueblo.

Spider moved on to the next order of business. "I went to St. George yesterday. And Laurie and I went to Mesquite today, all on the trail of people who got mixed up with Austin Lee."

"Austin Lee?" Matt frowned. "Why?"

"We found out his visit to the museum and his

dating Linda was all part of a pattern." Spider went on to tell Matt about his visit to Earnest Endeavors, to Annie Defrain, and to Dorrie Coleman. When he talked about Mary Defrain's suicide, Matt gave a sharp intake of breath, and he muttered something that Spider didn't quite catch.

"What was that?"

Matt shook his head. "I'd better not repeat it. If anything happened to Austin, it'd make me a suspect."

"I imagine it fits the situation," Spider said. "Especially when you find out that Austin moved into the Defrain's house after he stole the whole development from them."

"Somebody needs to do something to stop him."

"Up until now, he's been careful to operate within the law, and he's been pretty much unhampered. I let him know we were on to him."

"When was that?"

"Yesterday. Today he sent a thug to beat me up—only he didn't find me. He found a friend who had borrowed my car."

"You're a deputy. Can't you arrest him?"

"I've got no jurisdiction in Utah. Besides, that's not my job. My job is to protect the museum."

"So far, you haven't done much." Matt immediately held up his hands. "I'm sorry. I realize we've been dealing with this turd for months, and we didn't even know who it was until you came."

Spider wished he could tell him what Karam had found about the Goodman genealogy, but he had promised to wait.

Matt flung another rock. "I can't believe he used Linda like that."

"Remember that he got a little help from you and Tiffany." Spider glanced at the pickup and started edging toward the gate. "I gotta go. Laurie and I need to check on Karam."

Matt grabbed Spider's arm. "Wait. Was Karam the one that got beat up?"

Spider nodded. "We think he's going to be all right, but we told him we wouldn't stay away long."

Matt took off his baseball cap and ran his hands through his hair. "This just keeps getting worse and worse."

Spider clapped his hand on Matt's shoulder. "I'll have more to tell you in a couple days."

"I hope you'll tell me that someone has taken Austin Lee out of circulation."

"Forewarned is forearmed," Spider said, opening the gate. "Knowing that Austin was behind the lawsuits, knowing that he's after the ranch—I think that's gonna help keep the museum safe."

"Someone needs to wring that $250,000 he took from my father out of his hide. *That* would keep the museum safe."

"From the accident in the bathroom? I don't think Austin has that money. I imagine he set that up just to weaken your dad's position, make him more vulnerable to a second lawsuit. How is your dad, by the way?"

"He's doing okay."

"I'm going to go see him tomorrow. Pay my respects."

"That's good, because he's at my grandmother's in Orderville tonight," Austin said.

"Sounds good." Spider backed away, touching the brim of his hat as good-bye, and then he turned and strode to the pickup.

"How'd it go?" Laurie asked as he climbed in.

Spider grimaced. "He got a little green around the gills when I told him about Tiffany."

"Was that because of the lost museum donation or because he might have been thinking about marrying her to get the money?"

"Probably a little bit of both." Spider started the engine and backed out.

"What were you talking about when he was hucking rocks at the post?"

"Linda."

"Funny how people want to throw rocks when they realize what fools they've been. Dorrie's got a better arm."

"Think so? They're both lefties."

"Of course, some people don't throw rocks. They destroy pillows."

Spider looked over at her, eyes twinkling. "I didn't think you noticed."

Laurie laughed out loud. "Not notice? When the room looked like something out of *The Snows of Kilimanjaro*?" She undid her seat belt, scooted over and kissed him under the ear. "I love you, Spider Latham."

"Mmmm. Careful, I'm driving." He pulled up the center seat belt and handed it to her. "Buckle up."

They rode to where the Yugo was parked, shoulder to shoulder, thigh to thigh, with Laurie's hand on his knee. When they pulled in, he turned and looked at her, a smile playing around his lips. "So, here's the plan. You take the pickup back to the hotel. I'll bring the Yugo and go by to check on Karam."

"Sounds good so far."

"Then I thought something sweet before dinner would be nice. You got any more of those cookies?"

She kissed him, a lingering, slow promise that left them both a little breathless. "I'll come up with something," she said.

Chapter 18

◆

THE CLICK OF the door closing woke Spider the next morning, and he opened his eyes to a vacant place in the bed beside him. Rising up on one elbow, he saw that the sound was Laurie returning to the room. "Where you been?"

"Good morning," she said. "I was just checking on Karam."

Spider yawned. "Yeah? How's he doing?"

"Pretty well. The lump on his head is gone. The spot is still a little tender, but there's no headache. And he had a good breakfast."

"You took him breakfast?"

"Yep. Oatmeal and toast."

"I wouldn't call that breakfast."

"They're serving pancakes across the street as part of the celebration, so you'd better get up. Karam is going to join us later in the morning, and we're going to wander."

Grumbling about overbearing women, Spider got up, showered and shaved. By nine o'clock they had joined citizens and tourists under an awning on the lawn of the Latter-day Saint chapel across from City Hall.

Jack and Amy were there and joined them in the serving line. Jack was his usual jovial self, but Amy seemed distracted. Her eyes constantly raked the surrounding throngs as if looking for someone, and Spider was pretty sure who it was.

"Do you have a date with Austin Lee today?" he asked.

Amy's head whipped around. "Why do say that?"

Spider shrugged. "You looked like you were expecting someone."

Amy picked up her plate and studied a pile of pancakes in a warming pan. "I may see him today."

"If you do, would you tell him I'm looking for him?"

Amy blinked. "Why would you want to talk to him?"

Spider spooned a pile of scrambled eggs on his plate. "Oh, a little matter of mistaken identity."

Spider became aware that Jack had stopped his conversation with Laurie and was listening to what he was saying to Amy.

Looking at Spider, Jack asked, "Who's Austin?"

"A fellow I've had some dealings with this week. I'll fill you in later."

Jack seemed to accept that, and they carried their plates to a long line of tables clad in butcher paper. During breakfast, Laurie kept up a flow of chatter with both Jack and Amy while Spider listened and watched Amy's darting eyes.

When they were finished, he suggested the ladies go to the bandstand and watch a group of young cloggers. He had something to talk over with Jack. Laurie took Amy's arm and headed across the lawn to the benches set in front of the stage, but Amy kept dragging her feet, glancing over her shoulder with her brows knit.

Spider walked with Jack to the stone steps leading up to the historic old chapel, now a family history center. He climbed halfway up and sat down. The position was away from listening ears and was also a good vantage point for spotting potential trouble, like someone looking to get him in a chokehold.

Jack sat beside him. "What do you need to talk about, Spencer? Are you in some sort of trouble?"

"First, my name's Spider. No, I'm not in trouble. I wanted to ask you the same thing."

Jack drew back and blinked. "You wanted to know if I was in trouble? Whatever gave you that idea?"

"Austin Lee. You're sure you've never had anything to do with him?"

"Positive."

"Well, he was on your property a couple days ago. I caught him driving down from the spring, and from what I know, that's a bad sign. Especially when I find out he's been dating Amy." Spider went on to tell Jack the history, as he knew it, of Austin's mode of operation. When he finished, he added, "I don't want to see Amy hurt."

"Thank you." Jack stood and looked at his watch. "I've got to get to the office. I don't usually work during Western Legends, but a patient broke a wire yesterday, and I need to fix it."

Spider stood as well, his jaw set. Jack was blowing him off. Didn't he realize how dangerous Austin was to someone in Amy's fragile emotional state? "Will you say something to her?" he asked, trying to keep an edge out of his voice.

Jack shook his head. "Amy is an adult. She operates within a different paradigm from lots of folks, but everybody has some sort of flaw. She'll work through it and come out the other side a better person, I don't doubt." He started down the stairs but turned around to say, "I know you mean well. Thanks, Spencer."

"It's Spider." He spoke through clenched teeth as he watched Jack's retreating form. Just beyond, Spider saw Karam coming up the street, scanning the crowd. Jack paused to talk to him, and Spider saw him turn and point out Spider's position. Karam followed his line of sight, spotted Spider, and waved. Spider returned the wave and descended the stairs to meet him.

"How're you doing?" he asked when he met the younger man. "It looks like you got a bit of a shiner."

"Shiner? You will have to translate."

Spider traced an arc under his own eye. "A black eye. Don't worry. It's not real noticeable."

Karam pulled out his cell phone to catalog the idiom, whispering the word as he recorded it. Dropping the phone back in his pocket, he asked, "Where is Laurie?"

"She's over at the stage. Come on."

They joined the ladies just as two actors in cowboy getup were presenting a shootout skit. Spider thought it was overdone, but Karam enjoyed it hugely. When that was over, Laurie led them to one of the booths along Main Street that sold cowboy clothing. She chose a paisley print bandana hanging on a rack and paid the vendor.

"You've got a bruise on your neck," she said to Karam. "Let's tie this around to hide it. The cowboys call it a wild rag."

The young man stood still while Laurie knotted the bandana, and then he touched it. "You are very kind."

"Not at all," Laurie said. "Now, let's plan our day. I want Karam to see the quilt show."

Spider snorted. "Do you think he'll enjoy that as much as the shootout?"

Laurie nodded. "He teaches American History. A lot of the old fashioned quilt patterns grew out of the settlers' need to use up every scrap of material they had. It's part of his education."

"I agree," Karam said. "I would like to see the quilt show. And then, Spider, would you take me to check on my car? I got a call from my mechanic. He said he has good news and bad news for me."

Laurie herded the men across the grass and into the gymnasium of the LDS chapel sitting in the middle of town. The room was awash with colors and patterns, with a hundred quilts hanging on dividers bisecting the room. Two ladies welcomed them, gave them slips of paper, and asked them to vote for best of show.

Karam chuckled. "You Americans vote on everything." He seemed to take the matter seriously, though, and considered each entry carefully as he moved around the room, finally writing the number of his choice in the blank and dropping it into the box.

Spider, who had been observing Karam from a folding chair by the door, got up as he approached. "Have you seen Laurie?" he asked.

"Yes. She is over there." Karam pointed toward a table in the corner underneath a magnificent appliquéd quilt that looked like a painting of the red mesas surrounding Kanab.

Laurie saw them looking at her and smiled, waving three ticket stubs as she joined them. "I entered us all into the drawing for that quilt." She handed them each a ticket. "They're going to give it away tonight right after Jack and I sing."

Spider put his in his pocket. "Do you want to come with Karam and me to see his mechanic?"

Laurie shook her head. "As inviting as that sounds, I'm going to see if Jack wants to practice for tonight. Call me when you get back, and we'll find something nice and greasy for lunch."

"Sounds good to me. Come on, Karam. Let's go see that E-type Jag of yours." As they walked back to the hotel, Spider asked, "How far do we have to go?"

"Not far. On a better day I could have walked."

"We can take the Yugo and gas up on the way back. I was in a hurry to get to the hotel last night, so I didn't stop."

They walked to the hotel parking lot and got the car. Karam directed Spider to a single wide mobile home on the other side of Kanab Creek that had a rambling shop building out back. Spider pulled up in front of a roll-up door, and a wizened fellow in immaculate coveralls stepped out of an adjacent door, hand raised in greeting.

"Come meet my mechanic," Karam said, pulling on the latch.

Spider got out and ambled over to join Karam and

the other man in the shade of the shop building. Karam introduced the older man as Shorty, and Spider shook his hand.

"That's quite a car," Shorty said, nodding toward the Yugo. "Essentially a Fiat 128. Great for basic transportation, but Americans made fun of it."

"So did the Brits. I was in London when I had a Yugo," Karam said. "One of the jokes was that every owner's manual included a bus schedule."

Shorty chuckled. "In 1990, when the Yugo came out with a rear window defroster, people said it was so you could keep your hands warm while you pushed it." He patted the orange-and-flames fender. "But I've always had a soft spot for it. Kind of like the little engine that could. You know NATO bombed the factory during the war in Bosnia, but they're still turning out Yugos. You gotta feel good about that." He stepped to the garage door behind him and rolled it up.

Spider glanced behind Shorty at a low-slung car sitting in the shadows. "Is that the E-type?"

"Yes. Come and see it." Shorty turned on the overhead lights as Karam led Spider inside to where they could view the car from the front.

Spider whistled. His eyes took in the long hood, a full half the length of the car. Painted British racing green, the black canvas top was down, showing off the tan leather seats and walnut steering wheel. The dashboard was all business with rocker switches in a bank across the middle and dials taking up the rest of the space.

Shorty pulled a cloth from his back pocket and

polished a spot on the fender just above one of the recessed headlamps. "In 1960, when Jaguar released the E-type, Enzo Ferrari called it the most beautiful car ever made."

"I believe him," Spider said. "Can I see under the hood?"

"Sure." Karam bent over the cockpit and twisted a chrome hook mounted on the doorpost while Shorty twisted its twin on the passenger side, releasing the latches located up by the windshield. Shorty lifted the hood, swinging it forward on hinges at the front bumper and exposing an expanse of metal and hoses completely filling the engine cavity.

"In the 1970's they changed from a V-6 to a 5.3 liter V-12," Shorty said.

"Wow," Spider said reverently. "I suppose it's got overhead cams?"

"Yep," Shorty said. "It'll produce 241 horsepower."

"Great suffering zot." Spider still spoke in a hushed voice. "What kind of transmission?"

"Manual. It's a four speed synchromesh, not without problems."

"Is that the good news or the bad news?" Karam asked.

Shorty lowered the hood and made sure it was latched. "That's the good news. I've found a rebuilt one in Los Angeles that I can have here in three days."

"And the bad news?"

Shorty jerked his head toward a workbench. "Come over here and I'll show you."

"Can I sit in it?" Spider asked.

"Sure." Karam spoke over his shoulder as he followed Shorty. "Be my visitor."

"Guest," Spider said, opening the door. "Be my guest." Getting in the car took a bit of folding, but when he was finally in the bucket seat, he found he had plenty of leg room. Sitting was surprisingly comfortable, even though he was so low to the ground.

"Go ahead and start it," Shorty said. "There's nothing wrong with the engine."

Spider turned the key, gave it some gas when the engine caught, and was immediately entranced with the throaty rumble enveloping him. He revved the engine and closed his eyes, wearing the throbbing of the powerful engine like a mantle pulled around him. Reluctantly, he turned off the key and looked over at Karam. "I think I'm in love."

Karam grinned. "Careful. She is high maintenance." He held up a small metal part.

Spider climbed out and noted the solid sound as he closed the door. "She's way out of my league." He walked over to join the two men. "Is that the bad news?"

"Yes," Karam said. "I don't understand what it is this does, but the part is essential and unavailable."

"Let me see." Spider held out his hand for the tapered cylinder. He hefted it and ran his thumb over the ridges scored at precise intervals down the length of it. "Couldn't you machine it?" he asked Shorty.

"You could if you had the right lathe and lots of skill. I don't have either one, and neither does anyone else in town."

Spider handed the part back to Shorty. "I can do it."

"You can?" Karam's eyes widened and a smile lit his face.

"Yeah, but not 'til I get back home, and that won't be 'til I'm through with what I'm doing here." Spider watched the smile fade and tried to offer consolation. "You're still looking at two weeks. Wasn't that what you thought it was going to be anyway?"

Karam stuck his hands in his pockets and nodded. He walked back to the car in the driveway, kicking pebbles as he went, leaving Spider to say good-bye to Shorty.

"Glad to have met you," Spider said. "Tell me, how is it that you know so much about E-types?"

Shorty wiped his hands on a rag and stuck it in his back pocket. "I spent thirty years in L.A. working for a Jaguar dealership. I started there the year they made this one." He pointed to Karam's car.

"So, how did you get from L.A. to Kanab?"

"Oh, after I retired, the wife and I bought a motor home. We were going to spend a couple years touring the U.S. of A. We planned to spend a couple weeks here in Kanab." Shorty chuckled. "Been here ten years now."

"So it was a good move?"

"The best." Shorty walked with Spider out to where the Yugo was parked. "The fellows at the garage in town know I'm here, and if something comes along too exotic for them, they send it on up to me. Somehow, word's got around that I know E-types. Every now and then, I get someone bringing one in."

"Are there that many E-types in Kanab?"

Shorty laughed. "No, they come from California and Nevada. Even had one come from Wisconsin. Hey, there

aren't too many of us around that know how they work."
He looked Spider in the eye. "I could take on more work
if I had a good machinist working with me."

Spider held up his hands and took a step back. "I'm
only here for a week or so."

Shorty smiled. "That's what I said ten years ago."

Spider opened his door. "Want me to drop by before
I leave town and see if you still need me to manufacture
that part?"

"That would be great." Shorty cast a glance at
Karam, sitting slump-shouldered in the Yugo. "It's hard
on the young 'un."

"Yeah," Spider agreed. "I'd better get him back to
the festivities, see if we can find something to take his
mind off the bad news."

Shorty looked at his watch. "You'd better scoot.
They'll be closing streets for the parade any time."

Spider touched the brim of his hat. "Thanks. We
will." He got in the car, started the engine, and drove
around the circular drive and back onto the city street,
heading towards the center of town.

Karam let out a big sigh and asked, "Do you believe
in destiny?"

Spider noted the earnest expression on his companion's face. "Does this have anything to do with your car?"

"Actually, it does." Karam looked out the windshield as they dipped down into Kanab Creek Wash and
pointed at a shady spot at the top. "Can you stop there?
This may take a while."

Spider's eyebrows rose, but he pulled over, rolled
down the windows, and turned off the engine. "Okay,
shoot."

Karam looked at his hands for a moment and then he met Spider's questioning gaze. "You know I am Muslim." He waited for Spider to nod assent and went on. "Belief in Allah's power to know and control all things is one of the six articles of faith in Islam. It is called *Qadar*."

"Destiny?"

"A special kind of destiny," Karam said. "A person has the freedom, the choice to do as he wants, but he has no control over the outcome of his choices. It is Allah's will that controls to what destiny that path will lead."

The corners of Spider's mouth lifted ever so slightly. "So what has *qadar* got to do with the E-type sitting in Shorty's garage?"

Karam looked like he was trying not to smile. "You're not saying it right. The R has to come from down in your throat. Ask your question again, but say it right this time."

"I don't know if I can remember it. What does... *qadar*...have to do with the E-type?"

"Excellent, Spider. Well said. Now I will answer. *Qadar* has everything to do with it."

Spider smiled.

"No, I am serious, Spider. Think about it. Ten years ago my father warned me not to buy this kind of car. Instead, he wanted me to have a Yugo. Do you not think it is strange that after I bought the E-type and it left me stranded in a strange land, a friend comes to my aid in a Yugo? Does this not sound like divine destiny?"

"It sounds to me like God has a sense of humor."

Karam looked at his hands. "You said you liked the Jag."

"Well, yeah. What's not to like? It's easy to lose your heart to the sound of the engine."

Karam cleared his throat. "Would you be interested in trading cars?"

Spider's brow creased. Did he hear that right? "You mean the Yugo for the Jaguar? Straight across? That would hardly be fair."

"Oh, but the repairs are paid for. You would not be responsible for any of that cost."

"What I mean is your car is far more valuable than mine, and I can't afford to give you something to boot."

"Why would you give me your boots?"

"Giving something to boot means I'd give you extra money to make the deal fair. I can't do that. In fact, I couldn't even afford to buy the Yugo. It's a hand-me-down car that someone gave me minutes before I met you."

"Someone gave it to you?" Karam paused to think about that. "Do you not see? It is *Qadar*."

Spider shook his head. "I can't take advantage of you. It wouldn't be fair."

Karam smiled. "You would not be taking advantage of me, Spider. You would be doing me a favor. If you feel you need to offer me your boots, you can let me come spend some time with you each summer. That would certainly be extra value to me."

"We'd love to have you come. Stay the whole summer if you like."

"Then are we agreed?"

Spider offered his hand. "Agreed." After a handshake he asked, "When do you want to take care of the details?"

"Right away. Much as I enjoy Kanab, I need to be on my way as quickly as I can."

Spider started the car and pulled back on the road. "So when will you leave?"

"If the hotel has the Internet back up, I will finish the Goodman research today and be on my way tomorrow."

"I'm going to miss you." Spider signaled and turned left on Main Street only to be confronted with a barricade and a sign saying the road was closed. He pulled over to park near the curb. "I think this is as close as we get. They've closed the road for the parade."

"I have not seen an American parade." Karam grinned. "This is great."

Spider checked his watch. "We've got an hour before it starts. Let's go take care of the paperwork and make you the owner of a—" He didn't finish the sentence because he had caught sight of a burgundy SUV making a U turn at the barricade.

Karam tipped his head in the SUV's direction. "Is that the Range Rover we saw coming down the canyon while we were up on the hill at Jack's?"

"Yes, it is. Can you tell how many people are in it?" Spider followed the car in his rearview mirror.

"No. The tinted windows do not let you see in."

"But that's definitely Austin Lee. Ha! He's in town today."

"Who is Austin Lee?"

"He's the fellow behind the trouble at the Red Pueblo." Spider opened his door. "As I was saying, let's go get the paperwork done. We'll make you the legal owner of this car, but before I give you the keys, I'll run by and fill the tank."

Karam got out of the car and closed his door. "That will be my boots."

Spider climbed out, too, and pushed the lock button. "Yeah. That'll be your boots."

Together they walked down the street toward their hotel.

Chapter 19

———◆———

A<small>T FOUR THAT</small> afternoon, Spider sat on the Taylor's well-worn armchair with his Stetson on his lap. Beneath the hat, Karam's finished report lay in a businesslike folder. Neva and Martin sat on the couch opposite.

Spider noted the erectness of Martin's shoulders and the alertness of his eyes. "You're looking better, sir."

Martin leaned back and crossed his legs. "Fine as frog's hair."

Neva smiled at her husband. "Well, maybe not that fine, but he's definitely doing better." She brushed a silver lock away from his brow.

Spider examined the toe of his boot, wondering how to approach the subject of Tiffany Wendt's non-existent fortune. Looking up, he met two pairs of questioning eyes and plunged ahead. "Did Matt tell you anything about the conversation I had with him yesterday afternoon?"

Neva shook her head. "He called to tell us you'd be coming by today and said you had news."

"He sounded pretty grim." Martin uncrossed his legs and sat forward. "Don't be afraid to give it to us straight."

"I have good news, bad news, and just plain information. Let's go over the bad news first." Spider cleared his throat. "Tiffany Wendt isn't going to save the Red Pueblo. She doesn't have a fortune, and she isn't going to give any money to the museum." He paused to gauge their reaction.

Neva let out a sigh. "I'm so glad."

Her husband pulled away and regarded her for a moment. "Because of Mattie?"

She nodded, her eyes misting up. "It's been such a worry. Things have gone bad between him and Linda because he's been paying attention to Tiffany. He's been paying attention to Tiffany to try to save the museum. You can see he's all torn apart." She patted Martin's knee. "Tiffany might have saved the museum, but in the process we could have lost our son."

Martin put an arm around his wife and kissed her cheek. "You're right. It's better this way."

A tear spilled over and ran down Neva's cheek. "Even if we lose the museum?"

Martin was quiet for a moment. He cleared his throat and whispered, "My life's work."

"Your son is your life's work," she murmured.

Silence.

Spider shifted in his chair. "Let's not give up yet." He moved his Stetson from his lap to the coffee table in front of the couch. "I've got some good news for you, but I need to explain the lay of the land and how Austin Lee fits into what's been happening at the Red Pueblo."

Neva's brows drew together. "Austin Lee? Isn't he the good-looking fellow Linda took up with?"

"What's he got to do with the museum?" Martin asked.

Spider explained all he had found out about Austin's land development company, his mode of operation, and how he forced owners to sell prime property to him for fire sale prices.

Neva's hand went to her mouth, and her eyes widened. "Was he behind the first lawsuit? The accident in the bathroom?"

"I'm pretty sure he was," Spider said. "If you'll give me the name of the woman who sued you, I'll talk to her and find out."

"Fabiola De Pra," Neva said. "Who could forget a name like that?"

Spider fished his pen and notebook from his pocket, sounding out the name as he wrote it down. "Where does she live?"

Neva looked at Martin but received no help from him. "I think she lives in St. George."

"I'll see if I can talk to her on Monday." Spider put his notebook away. "Are you ready for good news?"

Neva clasped her hands in front of her chest. "We've been waiting weeks for some good news."

Spider passed the folder to Neva. "I don't think you've met Karam Mansour. He's visited the museum several times, and he was able to help us out. If you'll open the folder to the first page?" He gave them time to read Karam's letter attesting that the report was a true representation of his research and listing his credentials.

"How much did this cost us?" Neva asked. "He sounds like a heavyweight guy."

"It's been covered," Spider said. "Don't worry about it. Now, please turn to the next page."

Neva did as he asked and held the book, so Martin could read it along with her. "What's this? A pedigree chart?"

"Yes. This is the Goodman line for the woman who is bringing suit. You'll see that her line goes back through Jacob Goodman, who entered the United States in 1882 as Jacob Guttman. The immigration official must have changed the spelling when he was processed."

Neva stared at the chart. "Her people came from Germany?"

"Decades after the Civil War," Martin added.

Spider nodded. "Turn the page, please. You can see here that Oscar Goodman, the soldier in the Lincoln Letter, died without any children shortly after the war. Not only that, but he was the last of his line. There is no way that Alyssa Goodman could have any claim on the cache."

Neva looked at Spider, a frown furrowing her brow. "But they submitted a family tree that went from her clear back to Oscar. It was a direct line."

"It was fake. They probably banked on your accepting their official-looking documents. You've got proof in your hand that their suit is without merit."

Martin and Neva looked at each other as if seeking confirmation in the other's eyes.

"It's true," Spider said. "It's over."

"Thank you," Neva said. "I don't want to sound like a worry wart, but what's to keep him from trying some other scheme to disable us and get the ranch?"

"A couple things." Spider leaned forward, marking each point on his fingers. "First, I'm going to talk to him—maybe this weekend, maybe Monday—and make sure he knows we're onto him. Second, we can see if we can prove fraud, especially if he was connected to the bathroom incident. We need to make it so painful for Austin Lee that he will think twice about tangling with the Red Pueblo again."

"Is there any chance—?" Neva stopped and made a *never mind* gesture.

"Go ahead and ask," Spider said. "There are no dumb questions."

"I was wondering. If Austin Lee was behind the bathroom suit—if it was fraudulent and all—is there a chance we could get the money back?"

"You'll have to talk to a lawyer about that one," Spider said. "But I think it's worth exploring."

Martin flicked his hand up. "Now I have a question. Does Mattie know Austin Lee's part in all this?"

Spider picked up his hat. "Pretty much. I told him last night."

Martin's face looked drawn. "What was his reaction?"

"He figures someone needs to put a stop to what he's doing."

Neva put her hand on Martin's knee. "But he's willing to let that someone be you, isn't he?"

Spider looked from one to the other. "Is there something I'm missing? Something you need to tell me?"

Martin lowered his eyes and shook his head, but Neva said, "Mattie's got a temper. Combine that with tunnel vision about the museum and a stubborn nature..." She shrugged. "It's hard to stop him when he's set out to do something he thinks has to be done."

Spider picked up his hat and stood. "Be sure to tell him the latest news about the cache and the Lincoln letter. That should cool him down a degree or two."

Neva stood, too. "We will. Thank you for everything. And tell Mr. Mansour how grateful we are for the research he did." She led the way to the front door and opened it.

Spider stepped out onto the weathered porch and turned to take his leave. "I'll let you know what I find out on Monday." He put on his hat, touched the brim, and then crossed the patchy lawn to the sidewalk.

Why had he thought walking to the Taylors' was a good idea? It was four blocks back to Denny's Wigwam, and he was supposed to meet Karam there in two minutes.

Chapter 20

◆

As PART OF Western Legends, twenty pioneer-era craftsmen had set up displays in the wide concrete expanse in front of Denny's Wigwam, a thriving tourist emporium. Spider found Karam watching a blacksmith make wrought iron nails. Next to the blacksmith, a rope maker coached tourists as they twisted long, coarse fibers into strands of twine. Beyond the rope maker, a saddler worked at his craft, and on the corner, someone had built an ingenious display to show the power of a water wheel.

Karam smiled as Spider approached. "This is a step back in time for most Americans, but I have been in villages in the Middle East where this would be considered modern technology."

"I guess we're not going to wow you with any of these displays, then," Spider said.

"On the contrary. I am enjoying them immensely."

Spider and Karam spent the hours before dusk wandering through the exhibits and talking to the artisans. When people started closing up shop, the two friends drifted to a gravel area behind Parry Lodge where silver-haired men in cowboy boots and large belt buckles tended Dutch ovens set out in ranks over glowing coals.

"That smells delicious," Karam said. "What are they cooking?"

"Looks like fried chicken, potatoes and onions, and biscuits. Let me buy you dinner."

"Will Laurie be meeting us here?"

Spider shook his head as he paid a lady in a sunbonnet and directed Karam to the feeding line. "She's setting up for the program tonight. We'll mosey over after supper, but we have to sit through some cowboy poetry before she sings." He paused a moment as an idea took form. "I haven't taken the Yugo to get it gassed up yet. It's still parked where we left it this morning. Do you want to take some time to do it after supper?"

A concerned look came over Karam's face. "But we'd miss some of the cowboy poetry, wouldn't we?"

Spider picked up two paper plates and handed one to his companion. "Wouldn't want to do that, I guess. Grab a handful of those napkins and stick them in your pocket. We'll need them."

They loaded their plates and found a place to sit at a table in the shadows. The tender chicken oozed juice as they ate it with their fingers. "You know the chicken's done just right when it drips off your elbows," Spider said.

Karam wiped his hands on the last napkin. "I have never tasted anything so good. I'm almost tempted to—" He broke off as he stared out toward the street.

"What?" Spider peered into the dusk, trying to find what Karam was looking at.

"Nothing. I saw Amy. It was a nice experience, seeing a new acquaintance while in a strange place."

"Was she with Jack?"

"No. She was with someone else."

"Tall and blond?"

"Yes."

"Shoot." Spider drummed his fingers on the table. Should he go chasing after them, so he could say what he had to say to Austin Lee? He didn't like the picture of himself dodging around in the dark or the thought of a public confrontation. Let it go for now.

"Is anything wrong?"

Spider looked up to find Karam standing with his plate in his hand. "Nah. Just things on my mind. Are you going for seconds?"

"Do you mean am I having more? Yes. I think I will have more potatoes."

Spider glanced at his watch. He could hear the faint sounds of the loudspeaker at the Pavilion, over behind the museum. "Take your time," he called after Karam's retreating figure. To himself he added, "If we're lucky, we'll miss the cowboy poetry altogether."

As it turned out, they almost did miss it altogether. As they walked into the entrance of the pavilion, they caught the tail end of the last poet. Edging in to join the watchers on the periphery, Spider recognized the man on stage.

Jack stood with his hands at his side, speaking in a quiet voice and looking into the darkness beyond the back row. The audience sat in rapt attention, leaning forward, faces solemn as they listened to the last stanzas of his poem.

Farewell to red rock arches,
Farewell to wonderstone,
Goodbye to sturdy cottonwoods
Shadin' springs I've called my own.

I'm goin', but don't you worry,
I'll be back again.
I'll be in the sage-y fragrance
That follows on the rain.

I'll be in the airy thermals
Carryin' eagles in their flight
And in the purple evening
That eases into night.

I'll be in red dust rising
From some lonely cowboy's trail.
Oh, I'll be back. I may have to go,
But return? I will not fail.

Jack stopped speaking but continued staring into the darkness. Not a person in the audience moved or made a sound until he dropped his eyes and gave a small nod. Then they erupted in applause.

Standing behind Spider, Karam tugged on his sleeve. "That was really good. Will he do another?"

"I don't think so." Spider pointed to Jack walking off the stage. "That looks like the end of the poetry program."

"I shouldn't have gone with seconds for the potatoes."

"Gone for seconds."

"Gone for seconds." Karam pulled out his phone and began keying in the idiom." Oh, look," he said as he pocketed it again. "Laurie is going to sing."

"Let's find a seat." Spider led the way to a bench front and center with two empty places as Laurie and Jack approached the mikes. They both took a moment to check tuning before Jack introduced Laurie. The crowd applauded politely.

"We're going to sing 'Night Herder's Lament,'" Jack announced before he and Laurie swung into a song about an educated, eastern fellow who came west and became a cowboy. They sang about how, on a night when the moon was bright enough to see handwriting, he reread a letter from back home. Laurie took the melody when they hit the refrain.

> *Why do you ride for the money?*
> *Why do you rope for short pay?*

Her clear, soaring voice gave Spider chills, and when she broke into the traditional yodeling passage, the crowd erupted into spontaneous applause that lasted so long she had to wait to begin the next verse.

When the song was over, Karam whispered to Spider, "I think I'm in love with your Laurie."

"You'll have to get in line," he muttered, watching Jack put his arm around Laurie and kiss her cheek. Got to remember not to let that oily versifier get the hackles up.

The emcee thanked Jack and Laurie and announced it was time for the quilt guild drawing. The guild president walked on stage with the prize quilt unfurled and held it up on display while Miss Kane County drew the winning ticket and slowly read the number.

Spider pulled his stub out of his pocket and checked it. "I'm one number away," he told Karam. "Check yours. You may have won a quilt."

"Do you think so?" Karam began searching through his pockets, finding it as the number was being read for the third and final time.

"I've got it," Karam whispered to Spider. "I have the number."

Spider stood and hollered, "Here. We've got a winner." To Karam he said, "You need to take your ticket up and give it to her."

"Well, come on up." The quilt lady's eyes twinkled as she watched Karam approach the stage. She took his stub, checked the numbers, and held up both tickets for all to see. The crowd applauded and whistled until she called for quiet. "What is your name, young man?"

"Karam Mansour."

"And where are you from, Mr. Mansour?"

"Originally I am from Gaza, but I have lived in Dubai since the age of ten."

"My goodness." She blinked. "I'm not sure I even know where Dubai is."

"It is part of the United Arab Emirates, located on the Persian Gulf."

"Well, that's a long way from Kanab. We like to think of a bit of Kanab going halfway around the world, and we hope you'll remember us when you look at it."

Miss Kane County had been folding the quilt, and

she handed it to Karam, smiling brilliantly at the audience as she did so.

"Thank you very much," Karam said. He carried the quilt in front of him like a satin pillow as he descended the steps and returned to his seat, acknowledging congratulations as he went.

"I'd say your *qadar* is working pretty well," Spider said in an undervoice as Karam sat beside him.

"Say it lower in your throat," Karam whispered. He demonstrated the pronunciation and said, "Try again."

"*Qadar*," Spider said obediently.

"Well done."

The emcee got up to announce the final performers would be The Baker Bunch, and Spider looked around for Laurie. He spied her at the side of the stage, conversing with the quilt lady who now held a mandolin. When the lady joined the string band on the stage, Laurie peered at the audience, shading her eyes against the footlights. Spider stood and waved his hat, and she smiled when she spied him.

"Is Laurie coming to sit with us?" Karam sounded like he couldn't believe his good fortune. He stood, too.

Spider moved into the aisle and watched her approach, eyes warm and a half smile on his lips. When she reached him, he dropped a kiss on her lips and whispered, "Well done, Sweetheart." Standing aside, he let her sit next to Karam, and he took the place on the aisle with his arm around her.

The Baker Bunch did a set of traditional numbers, and then the concert was over. Karam applauded enthusiastically and turned a beaming face to Laurie. "The

Baker Bunch was wonderful, but you and Jack were even better."

"Thank you, Karam." Laurie squeezed his hand. "I was so glad you got to hear that song. It's my favorite."

Spider stood. "Shall we get your guitar and head on back to the hotel?"

She shook her head. "The Baker Bunch and some other musicians are going to jam at the Old Barn behind Parry Lodge. Jack and I are going. Why don't you and Karam come, too?"

Spider considered.

"There will probably be some cowboy poets." Though she spoke matter-of-factly, the corners of Laurie's eyes crinkled.

"Nah." Spider put on his hat. "We need to go put gas in the Yugo." He grinned. "If I can remember where I parked it."

Karam patted his pocket. "I wrote it down."

Just then Jack called to Laurie from the stage. He held up her guitar case and jerked his head in a *come on* gesture.

Spider touched Laurie's arm. "Before you go, I need to talk to you about the Yugo. What if I traded it for another car?"

Jack called again, and Laurie waved to show she heard him. "Does the other car have flames on the front?"

"No. It's a good-looking car."

"Then it's a no-brainer. Gotta go." She waved to both of them and worked her way through the exiting crowd to join Jack on the steps to the stage.

"You did not mention to her that the other car

isn't running right now," Karam said as they joined the stream leaving the pavilion.

"It will be in two weeks."

They walked through the downtown area and turned on Main Street where, according to Karam, the Yugo was sitting. He carried his prize under his arm, and other concert-goers called congratulations to him as they passed, heading to their own cars.

"So, where is Laurie going? She said something about jelly."

"She said she was going to jam. It's where the musicians get together and play for fun."

"Oh." Karam sounded wistful.

To the north, a flash of lightning momentarily lit the sky, and several long seconds later a dull rumbling reached them. "Might have some rain tonight," Spider said. "I'm glad it put off until after the concert."

They arrived at the Yugo, sitting alone in the shadows mid-way between two widely spaced street lights. Spider had to feel around under the door handle to fit the key in to unlock it. Remembering Karam's wistful tone, he asked, "Did you want to go with Laurie? You can do that, and I'll go fill up with gas."

"Would that be all right?"

"Sure. Come by the hotel room when you get back. What time are you leaving tomorrow?"

"I will probably leave early."

"Then we'll say our good-byes when I give you the keys." Spider opened the door. "Want me to take the quilt, so you don't have to carry it around with you?"

"Oh. Yes." Karam handed over his prize, and Spider

tossed it through the door, got in, and put the key in the ignition.

Karam backed away. "Where will Laurie be?"

"It's there where we had supper. Behind Parry Lodge. A big barn."

"Thank you." He pulled out his cell phone as he turned away and began keying something as he walked.

Spider closed the door and pushed the quilt out of the way with his elbow.

"Hey, Spider." Karam stood under the street light, looking back at the car.

Spider rolled down the window. "Yeah? What d'ya need?" He put his hand on the key, ready to start the engine.

"Was it jelly or jam?"

"Jam," Spider called. "It's called a jam session."

He turned the key in the ignition, and all hell broke loose.

Chapter 21

◆

SPIDER HEARD A hissing sound first, followed a nano-second later by a detonation that seemed to play out in slow motion—a flash of light just before an ear-shattering boom. The dash turned into plastic shrapnel, and flames shot past his shoulder. For a moment, gravity seemed suspended, and then something hit him, making fireworks explode inside his skull. After that, it was like a series of clanging knife gates came down, shutting off sound first, then light, then feeling. All that was left was silent, utter darkness.

And then even that was gone.

◆ ◆ ◆

Sound came back first. It came in baby sound bites with long, vacant gaps in between. Little snippets of words. The clink of metal against metal. A short whirring sound.

Spider floated up from one of the inky voids and became aware of a continuity of sound, a low-voiced conversation going on in the dark quite near him. It was a conversation he had heard before, and for a moment he was disoriented, wondering if he had been thrust back in time to relive something he hadn't got right.

"He took off his shirt and hung it over the window," the person was saying in almost-whispered tones. "I knew what his intentions were, and I think the thought of doing it there, on your territory, turned him on."

"Wait," another voice interrupted, no longer hushed. "Wait. This happened in the dugout?"

"That's what I'm telling you. You were talking to Tiffany, and he just took my hand and led me over there. You didn't even notice."

Spider turned his head toward the speakers, peering through the blackness, trying to see where they were, but it was as if his eyes were glued shut, and he couldn't open them. He knew now that Linda was taking the opportunity to clear the air with Matt. Should he say something, let them know he was privy to their conversation?

"So, what happened?" Matt's voice had a ragged edge to it.

"He locked the door and came on to me. I said no."

"That's all?" Apparently she didn't answer because Matt asked again, "Is that all that happened?"

"No. He tried to force the issue. He...he was very strong."

"The swine! Did he—?"

"Would it make a difference?"

Spider was relieved when there was no answer. The silence stretched out, and he realized someone else was in the room. He heard small noises beside him, and then an unfamiliar female voice asked, "Has he wakened yet?"

Linda answered. "No."

"His vitals are good. We're keeping a close eye on him that way, but call me if he wakes up."

"We will."

The silence surged back, and Spider worked to unravel the meaning behind the stranger's words. Whose vitals was she talking about? Where was he? Why didn't someone turn a light on?

Linda and Matt resumed their conversation, but things were becoming fuzzy around the edges. He could no longer track what they were saying. Something was wrong, though, and he fought through the fog to define what it was. Just before he let go of the last wisp of consciousness, it came to him. Laurie wasn't here. Where was Laurie?

◆ ◆ ◆

A brisk voice hailed Spider into consciousness. "Good morning, Mr. Latham. Shall we take these bandages off and see what we've got?"

Spider felt pressure against his temple and heard the sound of scissors.

"There wasn't any damage to your eyes, but the wound was near enough to one of 'em that Dr. Timms didn't use tape. He ran the bandages clear around, figuring you wouldn't have any need to see before morning."

He heard the last snip and then the clink of scissors being set down on the table.

"Close your eyes," the brisk voice warned. "The light's gonna hurt at first."

Spider did as he was told. He felt the bandages come off and raised his lids cautiously a millimeter at a time, squinting at the brightness. He blinked and found a round, middle-aged face peering down at him through rimless glasses. "Hello," he croaked.

"Hello." She lifted a gauze pad and cocked her head as she examined what lay beneath. "You're a lucky son-of-a-gun. That's all I got to say. Just an inch difference, and they'd be calling you One Eye." She took a roll of tape from her pocket and tacked two corners of the pad to his forehead. "That'll hold it until the doctor gets a chance to look at it."

Spider touched her hand. "What happened? And where's Laurie?"

"Is that the lady that's been sitting with you? She'll be back—oh here she is now. And by the way, the sheriff is on his way over to see you." She picked up the bandages, folded them inside one of her latex gloves as she pulled them off, and dropped them in the garbage on her way out the door.

Spider turned his head to welcome his wife, but it was Linda who came in, not Laurie. She had a worried expression on her face, but her brow cleared when she saw him.

"Oh, Spider! It's good to see you awake." She pulled her chair over and set it between the bed and the window. "I was so worried about you."

"What happened, Linda? How'd I get in here?"

She sat down. "You don't remember? Somebody set off a bomb in your car."

Something flashed through Spider's mind, so fleeting it was just a blip on the memory screen—his hand turning the key. He stared at Linda, trying to remember more but gave it up and turned to more important things. "Where's Laurie?" he said. "Is she all right?"

"She's fine. She stayed here until they said you were going to be okay. After that, she said that Karam needed her more. She called Taylors, and Neva sent Matt and me to sit with you, so Laurie could go to the sheriff's office."

Spider looked around. "Where is Matt?"

Linda looked down at her hands. "I don't know. I dozed off in the middle of the night, and when I woke, he was gone."

Spider put his hand to his forehead. There was something else he wanted to ask, and he finally succeeded at pulling it back from memory. "Why did Laurie go to the sheriff's office?"

"Because they've got Karam in jail."

"What?" Spider sat up in bed, but the room began to spin. Immediately sorry for his hasty action, he lay back down. "Why is Karam in jail?"

"I've talked to Laurie a couple times, and as near as I can figure, they think he's a terrorist. They claim he planted the bomb in your car."

"That's ridiculous."

"You know it, and I know it, but there's a local fellow who swears he saw him detonate the bomb with a cell phone."

All of a sudden Spider's memory reappeared. He remembered Karam standing in the light of the street lamp, entering the latest idiom into his list. He remembered turning on the key, remembered the blast of the detonation. "It couldn't have been Karam," he said.

Linda glanced out the window. "Well, you'll get a chance to tell that to the sheriff in just a few minutes. He just pulled up."

Spider looked around the room. "I don't suppose there's a mirror you could find, so I can see the damage?"

"There's one in the tray table." She got up and swung the tray over his bed. I'm going to raise your head a bit." She pressed the remote control. "Tell me when to stop."

Spider lifted his hand when he was on a comfortable incline and then had her raise his knees. "That's good. Thanks." He lifted the hinged area of the table and regarded himself in the mirror.

What he saw wasn't as bad as the amount of bandages the nurse took off might indicate, though an impressive maroon area circled his right eye and bled over onto the area below his left. He lifted the gauze bandage stuck on his temple above his right eyebrow and examined the raw meat beneath.

Linda sucked in a breath. "That's an ugly looking wound."

"It's not deep, though. Lucky I have such a thick skull." He turned his head, keeping his eyes on the mirror. "Can't see any other damage."

"You have a bruise on your arm."

Spider felt around the darkened place. "It's a little tender, but not bad." Pushing the tray away, he flung back the covers and swung his legs around. "I don't know why they've got me in here. There's really nothing—"

Linda stepped closer, pushing against his shoulders to keep him from falling off the bed. "You're white as a sheet. Please stay where you are, at least until the sheriff's gone."

Spider let her help him lie back and get his feet back on the bed. He fought the wave of nausea sweeping over him and hoped he wouldn't disgrace himself by vomiting. He closed his eyes and took deep breaths. After a few moments, things settled down enough that he could open his eyes. "Thank you," he said to Linda. "I'll wait for the sheriff right here."

She looked toward the door and then at her watch. "There he is. Look, Spider, I've got to go. I'm afraid—well, never mind." She pulled up the covers and patted his hand. She nodded to the uniformed man as he walked in and stood in front of Spider's bed, and then she left.

Spider watched her go and then turned to examine the officer, noting that he was a deputy, not the sheriff. Of moderate height, muscular and fit, he was dressed in a tan uniform with knife-sharp creases and shiny black leather at his waist. He looked to be in his mid-thirties.

"Mr. Latham?" The deputy's voice was respectful.

"Yes, sir."

"I'm Deputy Toby Flint. It's good to see you looking better. With that head wound, you were bleeding like a stuck pig."

"Glad to see you." Spider pointed to the chair. "Have a seat."

Deputy Flint sat down and cleared his throat. "I know you're a deputy sheriff over in Nevada, and I've met Mrs. Latham."

"I heard she's at the sheriff's office." Spider smiled. "How're you all getting along?"

The deputy shook his head. "She's quite a lady. Says she's not leaving until this Mansour fellow can come with her."

"Why is Karam in jail, anyway?"

"Your car was blown up by a bomb. I've got a citizen who saw Mr. Mansour with his cell phone out at the moment of detonation."

"Did you round up all the people with cell phones out at the moment of detonation?"

Deputy Flint paused before answering. "No. Mr. Mansour is the only Palestinian in town."

"Which proves what?"

"It would indicate that he's much more familiar with bombs than any local citizens."

Spider smoothed the wrinkles out of the sheet. "You know, Deputy, Thursday afternoon, Karam was driving my car—it's a distinctive looking car, wouldn't you say?" He paused, half smiling, waiting for a response. When the deputy nodded, he went on. "He pulled over at the state line and got out of the car, and someone pulled in afterward and attacked him." Spider held up a hand when it looked like the deputy was going to speak. "Let me finish. When his attacker left, and just before he knocked him cold, he gave Karam a message that was obviously intended for me."

"Did he report the attack?" Deputy Flint asked. "Which side of the border was it on?"

"It was in your territory. I wanted to call it in, but Karam wouldn't let me. He said that his experience with police didn't give him any confidence. In fact, he was afraid to report it."

"Well, I can understand that. Police where he comes from are probably corrupt."

"He wasn't talking about police in the Middle East. He was talking about American police and racial profiling."

Deputy Flint looked at his shoe tips, obviously digesting the information. Looking up, he asked, "How do you know about this attack?"

"I had loaned him my car while Laurie and I went to St. George in the pickup. On the way home, we found the car parked behind a building with him unconscious inside it."

"I see. And he didn't want you to call the police?"

"He said you'd either think he was a terrorist..." Spider let the word hang for a moment. "...or, because of the color of his skin, you'd suspect him of being an illegal Hispanic."

Deputy Flint grimaced and scratched the back of his head. "Okay. Let's start again. You obviously don't think he had anything to do with the bomb in your car. Why not?"

"Well, first because he's a friend. Second, because he didn't have opportunity. Or motive. Third, because—do you have his cell phone?"

"Yes."

"Do you know what time the bomb went off? It was about nine-thirty, wasn't it?"

"Yes."

"Well, if you look in the notes section on Karam's phone, he was jotting down the definition of jam at the precise time of detonation."

"Jam? Like strawberry preserves?"

Spider shook his head. "Like a bunch of musicians getting together to play. He was heading over to the Old Barn for the jam session. Karam teaches American History." Spider smiled as he saw the deputy's eyebrows rise. "He gathers idioms and puts them in a list in his cell. That's what this citizen saw him doing."

Deputy Flint again looked at the shiny toes of his shoes, as if a decision could be read there. Apparently it could. He looked up and said, "I've got a man that can examine the cell phone. If that checks out, I'll release him into Mrs. Latham's custody."

"It'll check out."

"The FBI is coming in to go over the car. Mr. Mansour is not to leave the area until we've given permission."

"He can't leave. That was his car that blew up."

Deputy Flint blinked. "I thought you said it was your car."

"It was, but just yesterday morning I traded the Yugo for his broken-down E-type Jaguar."

"That was his car? Over at Shorty's?" The deputy put his elbows on the chair arms and leaned in. "Now it's yours? I was over there last week looking at it. What a beauty." He cocked his head. "Why would he trade it for—no offence—a little orange box with wheels?"

"And flames. Don't forget the flames."

"I wasn't forgetting them."

Spider smiled. "It's a long story. Short version is that he needs to get on his way, and the Yugo would be a ride out of town. He had one when he was young. Might have been a bit of nostalgia there."

Deputy Flint stood. "We called in the FBI because this had the look of a terrorist bombing, but even if it's not, I'll be glad to have their people looking at the evidence around the car. When they get here, I'll tell them about the assault on Mr. Mansour yesterday. Most probably the two incidents are related. Do you have any enemies, anyone who would want to hurt you?"

"Well, yes." Spider pointed at the chair. "Sit down, Deputy. This may take a while."

Chapter 22

◆

LAURIE AND KARAM, still wearing Laurie's gift around his neck, arrived about the time the patient was released from the hospital.

Spider left with a gauze pad taped to his forehead and an admonition to lie low for twenty-four hours. He grumbled at being taken out in a wheelchair but ended up accepting a boost from Karam to get up in the pickup. Laurie drove back to the hotel, and the trip from the parking lot to their room turned Spider into a dishrag. He gratefully lay down on the bed, and when Laurie covered him with a blanket, he kissed her hand.

She and Karam took up residence in the only two chairs in the room, opening books and quietly reading. Their silent presence weighed on Spider, and he felt like he needed to make conversation or entertain them in some way. He raised his head and said, "You don't have to stay here. I'll be fine."

Laurie smiled. "I wouldn't feel good about leaving you alone."

Spider put his head down and closed his eyes, but he couldn't relax. Each time he heard a page turn, he waited for the sound of the next. He raised up on an elbow. "Really. I want you to go. Take Karam and do something wonderful. He'll be leaving soon. Go see the sand dunes or run up to Zion National Park. I can't rest with you here."

Laurie put down her book. "Oh. I didn't realize that. Do you want something to eat before we go?"

He shook his head. "Right now, I just want to sleep."

"You got it." Laurie kissed him and motioned to Karam. Still in quiet mode, they tiptoed out of the room and pulled the door softly shut.

◆ ◆ ◆

By mid-afternoon Laurie must have forgotten about quiet mode. She breezed in, letting the door bang shut behind her. "Wake up, sleepyhead. I've got take-out from Big Al's."

Spider surfaced. It took a moment to figure out where he was and the chain of events that brought him to this moment. Then he got up and crept over to sit in the chair. He took the paper bag she handed him and looked inside it. "No chocolate shake?"

Laurie shook her head. "It's so hot out, I was afraid it would melt before we got home."

Spider pulled the corners of his mouth down.

"Don't pout. We brought you some sweet potato fries, and Karam's gone to the vending machine to get you a Pepsi."

Karam came in on cue with the soda and handed it to Spider.

"Thanks." Spider pulled out a burger and unwrapped it. "Where you been?"

Karam flashed a wide smile. "We went riding."

"Riding? I thought you didn't do horses, Karam." Spider fished the bag of fries out of the sack.

"I never have before, but Laurie assured me that Scout would be very tame."

"It's the pinto that I rode the other day," Laurie said. "I knew he'd do fine on her."

Spider flattened the sack on his lap as a makeshift tray. "Did Jack or Amy ride with you?"

Laurie snitched one of his fries. "Nope. They weren't home."

"Did they go to church?"

"I don't think so. The pickup and horse trailer were gone, and Taffy wasn't in her stall. He must have taken her somewhere."

"Huh," Spider grunted. "So you just stole a couple of his horses and went joyriding?"

"He told me I could come out and ride anytime. It was great. There was a hard rain last night—did you hear it?"

"I don't think I was conscious at the time."

"Well, there was quite a bit of water running in the arroyos still, and the rocks were deep red."

Karam added, "Yes, and the air smelled so good."

"That's great." Spider put his half-eaten burger down on the flattened paper bag and jerked his head toward a chair. "Sit down, Karam. Let's talk about the car situation."

As Karam took the other chair, Laurie sank down on the bed. "What car situation?"

Spider answered her question with another.

"Remember when I mentioned trading the Yugo for another car?"

Laurie wrinkled her forehead. "Last night? Vaguely. A lot has happened since then."

"Well, I traded it to Karam for the car he has in the shop. He was going to leave early this morning in the Yugo."

Laurie looked from Spider to Karam. "I'm trying to figure out which of you has more completely lost his mind."

Karam leaned forward, his face serious. "If you knew all the factors involved, you would understand that it is a very good solution."

Spider held up a fry. "*Was* a very good solution."

"So what are we going to do?" Laurie asked.

Karam pointed first at Laurie and then at Spider. "You do not need to worry. The Yugo was my car. I had insurance coverage on it."

Laurie laughed out loud, and Spider shook his head. "I doubt you'll get anything for it."

"And how are you going to get where you're going?" Laurie added. "Can't you wait however long it is until your other car is fixed?"

"It is not my car. It is yours."

Laurie's eyes grew wide. "You can't think we'd hold you to that bargain."

Karam laughed. "Spider can tell you there is more to the bargain than transportation. If you will take me to the airport in St. George, tomorrow, I will be in your debt."

"Sure," Spider said, offering the bag of fries to

Karam. "No matter what Deputy Flint says, he can't keep you from leaving. We'll take you."

Karam ate a couple of fries and then accepted the napkin Spider proffered. He wiped his hands and stood. "I think I will go back to my room and finish packing."

Laurie stood, too. "What time do you need to be in St. George tomorrow?

"I have reservations to fly out at noon."

"How about we leave at nine? I think I can make sure Spider's up and dressed by then." Laurie walked Karam to the door, accepted his thanks for a pleasant day, and closed the door after him.

Spider crumpled up the takeout bag and tossed it into the wastebasket. "I may have to take another nap."

"Me too." She yawned. "I didn't get much sleep last night."

Spider chuckled as he got up and made his way to the bed. "Ol' Toby Flint says you're quite a lady."

She pulled the covers back for him. "What does he mean by that?"

"Well, I think you had him buffaloed. He's probably never had someone occupy his office in protest." He sat on the bed and lay back on the pillows, uttering a sigh. "That plumb wore me out."

"You may have to stay here tomorrow and let me take Karam over by myself."

He pulled up the covers and turned on his side. "The doctor said I should be better tomorrow. I wonder when we're going to hear anything from the FBI."

Laurie lifted the spread and lay down, spooning next to him even though he was between the sheets, and she wasn't. "I hope not for a couple of hours."

Spider clasped the hand that she put around him. He heard her sigh and moments later heard the regular breathing of sleep. He matched his breathing to hers and soon drifted off himself.

◆ ◆ ◆

Laurie got her wish. Deputy Toby Flint rapped on the door at six o'clock in the evening. Spider reflexively threw back the covers and sat up, but Laurie was out of bed and heading for the door before he had even figured out where he was.

At the sound of Laurie's sleepy voice and Deputy Flint's official one, Spider stood and walked to the armchair. He got there just as she stepped back to admit their visitor.

"We were grabbing a nap," Spider said. "Forgive the bed hair."

"No problem, Deputy Latham."

"I'm not in Kanab as a deputy. Call me Spider."

Laurie pushed the side chair closer to Spider's. "Have you got news for us?" She sat on the nearby bed.

"Some." Deputy Flint dropped a plastic garbage bag on the floor and took the proffered chair. Spider noticed he had dark circles under his eyes, and his shoes no longer had a mirror polish.

The deputy apparently was doing his own assessing of Spider as he pulled a notebook and pen from his pocket. "Your black eye is purple this afternoon," he said. "It was more of a liver color this morning. How does your head feel?"

"Pain pills are a wonderful thing. It doesn't hurt a bit, and I've slept the day away."

"Okay." Deputy Flint took out a pair of reading glasses and put them on to consult his notes. "The FBI got here this morning, just after I left you. They brought a whole herd of people and a mobile lab. I guess anything that smells of terrorism is pretty high priority."

"Were they disappointed?" Laurie asked. "I mean, when it turned out not to be?"

The deputy glanced at her over his glasses. "I'll get to that in a minute. First, let's talk about your Mr. Mansour." He shifted in his chair. "It turns out that he's the son of a very well respected, very wealthy, businessman and—" He paused as if practicing the word mentally before trying it aloud. "—philanthropist." Again he looked over his glasses at Laurie. "Why didn't you tell me that last night?"

"Would it have made any difference?" She spoke in a light, matter-of-fact tone. "It looked to me like a lot of people had made up their minds that because he was a Muslim, he set off the bomb."

Spider broke in. "As a matter of fact, she couldn't tell you because we didn't know anything about his father. I'm as surprised as you are. But I'll tell you something. That's one fine young man."

"Right." Deputy Flint drew a line through the first item on his list. "He's free to leave town anytime he wishes."

Laurie smiled. "I was confident you'd see it that way."

"Were you? Good." He picked up the black garbage

bag and handed it to Spider. "The FBI gave me this to give to you."

"What is it?" Spider reached inside and pulled out Karam's quilt. The back side was charred in places, but as he opened it up, the side with the appliquéd picture was undamaged.

Laurie whistled under her breath. "Isn't that something? Where was it?"

Spider turned it over and looked at the burned patches. "It was right by the driver's seat. I remember pushing it out of the way with my elbow." He touched a place where heat had burned away the backing and melted through the inside fill. "That would have been me if it hadn't been there. Karam would call that *qadar*."

Deputy Flint leaned toward Spider. "You got something wrong with your throat?"

Laurie laughed. "No, he doesn't. He was giving the word an Arabic pronunciation." She patted Spider's hand. "We're suitably impressed. Now, what does the word mean?"

Spider smiled at her and translated. "Fate."

Deputy Flint's mouth turned down as he drew a line through the second item. "Now, for the bomb." He cleared his throat. "Even if we hadn't ruled out Mr. Mansour for other reasons, the FBI says that this was the work of—" The deputy's eyes fell to his notes. "—an inept, domestic terrorist wannabe."

"How do they know?"

"Several ways." The deputy counted them on his fingers. "The type of black powder used, the type of detonator, the container that the bomb was in." He chuckled.

"They say they've never seen one like this. It was in a stainless steel thermos."

Spider sat up. "A thermos? I've never heard of that."

"Neither had they. They thought maybe this guy wasn't the brightest tool in the drawer and had heard about bombs being made from pressure cookers. Maybe he thought a thermos would work as well. Who knows?"

"Well, it seems to have worked," Laurie said.

"Yes and no." The deputy glanced at his notes. "It did go off and do some damage, but the stopper was made of plastic and gave way sooner than the casing. It made it a kind of a rocket. It tore through the engine compartment and firewall. Tore up both the front and then the backseat as it went through." He grimaced. "If the seat had deflected it to where, ah, Spider was sitting, he probably wouldn't be here."

Laurie shivered.

Spider winked at her. "Lucky for me that Yugo seats aren't rocket-proof."

"They slowed it down enough that it couldn't break through the back end, and it rattled around in the trunk for a bit. It was pretty beat up, but the FBI managed to find some useable prints on it."

"Really?" Laurie sat up straighter. "Do they know whose fingerprints they were?"

Spider leaned over to where he could see Deputy Flint's notebook. "Not so fast, Darlin'. He's got one more item before fingerprints."

The deputy cleared his throat, and Spider wondered why a blush was spreading up his neck. "Don't you, Deputy Flint?"

The officer grimaced. "I, ah, wasn't going to mention that item. It was more a comment made by one of the agents, not part of the official paperwork."

Spider leaned back and crossed his legs. "If it's information, let's have it." He looked expectantly at the policeman.

The deputy sighed. "It was their opinion that this copycat terrorist did you a favor. They said that was the ugliest car they had ever seen."

Spider threw back his head and laughed. "Thank you, Deputy. You just made my day. Cross that one off and let's get on to fingerprints."

"All right. Fingerprints. I wonder—" Deputy Flint looked from Laurie to Spider. "—would it be possible to have Mr. Mansour join us? I've got some pictures I'd like to have him look at."

"Sure." Laurie scooted up the bed to the phone on the bedside stand and dialed Karam's room. She explained the situation, listened, and hung up the phone. "He's on his way."

"While he's coming, I can tell you about the fingerprints." Deputy Flint glanced at his notes. "They belong to a known felon, fellow by the name of Aldo De Pra."

Spider blinked. "De Pra?"

The deputy turned the page toward Spider so he could see it. "I think I pronounced it right."

"I'm sure you did. I've heard that name before. But where?" Spider rubbed his jaw.

A knock on the door signaled Karam's arrival, and Laurie went to open it. "Come on in. You'll have to sit by me on the bed," she told him.

Deputy Flint stood as Karam came in, and he offered his hand. "Mr. Mansour. Thank you for coming. I apologize for the earlier problems."

Karam smiled, shook the deputy's hand, and then took a seat beside Laurie. "Tell me how I can be of service."

The officer took out his phone and went through a series of menus before pulling up a photo. "The FBI identified the person who planted the bomb by his fingerprints. We think the bomb and the attack on you the day before—"

Spider raised a hand to interrupt. "I told him about that, Karam. In light of the bomb, I thought I should."

"Of course, Spider." Karam looked at Toby. "Please go on."

"As I was saying, we think the two incidents are linked. I'm going to show you six photos, and I want you to tell me if one of them is the man that attacked you." He touched the screen and held it so Karam could see. "Here's the first."

Karam shook his head.

"Here's the second."

Karam shook his head at the third and fourth photos, but at number five, he jabbed a finger at the screen. "That is the one. I have still got the marks on my throat." He pulled off Laurie's scarf and pointed to the purple bruises.

"Take a look at the last picture just to be sure." Toby held up the screen again.

Karam shook his head. "I am sure. The picture before this one is the man who knocked me out."

Toby showed the screen to Laurie too. "That is Aldo De Pra. He's the one that set the bomb. He's also the person who assaulted Karam."

Leaning over to catch a glimpse, Spider scratched his head. "I'm sure I've heard that name. I just can't remember where."

"He gave Karam a message about the Red Pueblo," Laurie said. "That should tie him to Austin Lee, shouldn't it?"

Spider raised his arms above his head and shouted, "Bingo!"

All heads turned toward him.

"I remember where I've heard that name. Guess the name of the woman who sued the Red Pueblo about the accident in the bathroom."

Laurie looked mystified. "I don't think I ever heard her name."

"Her name was Fabiola De Pra. What are the odds of finding two unrelated people with that same last name? There's got to be a connection."

Karam's brow furrowed. "I do not understand."

"Me neither." Deputy Flint stowed his phone in his pocket and took his notebook back out.

"You both know about the lawsuit about ownership of the cache." Spider nodded toward Karam. "You helped us show that it was a fraudulent suit with Austin Lee behind it. He was trying to put Martin Taylor in a position that he'd have to sell his property for whatever he could get out of it."

"I understand that," said Karam.

Spider went on. "The lawsuit about the cache was

Austin's second try. The first try was someone who said she fell in the bathroom and was hurt. Martin settled out of court for a quarter million dollars."

Toby whistled. "And the woman in the bathroom was Fabiola De Pra?"

Spider nodded. "I was going to go see her tomorrow and talk to her about that suit, but I imagine Deputy Flint will be going there instead."

"I'm interested in finding out who Aldo is," Laurie said. "Is he Fabiola's father?" Her cell phone rang, and she stood and went to the corner of the room to answer it.

Karam picked up the thread. "Or her brother?"

Toby put an emphatic period on the sentence he had been writing. "Or her husband? We'll know tomorrow."

"Just a suggestion," Spider said to the deputy. "Talk to Martin and Neva before you head over to St. George. They can fill you in on that first lawsuit."

Laurie rejoined them, pocketing her cell. "That was Neva calling just now. They wanted to know if they could come see how Spider's doing."

"What did you tell them?" Spider asked.

A knock sounded at the door, and Laurie pointed to it. "They were in the lobby. I told them to come on up."

She opened the door and ushered in Neva, Martin, Linda and Matt. Toby greeted them and gave up his seat, hunkering cowboy-style next to Spider's chair. Karam moved from the bed to the floor. As soon as everyone had a place to perch, Laurie sat in the chair Toby had vacated. She patted Spider's arm.

He took the cue. "I'm glad you all came. There have

been some developments in the Red Pueblo affair that you all need to know about." He looked at Neva and Martin, holding hands as they sat at the end of the bed. He looked at Linda, sitting cross-legged on the floor by Karam and at Matt, hugging his knees as he sat by Toby.

"This has moved from the area of a civil affair to a criminal one," he went on. "Toby's now in charge. He can explain where we're at and where the investigation is going."

Toby took out his notebook and repeated what he had gone over with Spider and Laurie, leaving out the FBI's commentary on the Yugo. When he was finished, Neva and Martin told him details of the first suit, pausing at intervals for him to jot down his notes.

At eight o'clock Laurie finally called a halt. "Spider thinks he's going to St. George tomorrow to see Karam off, so we need to let him get to bed."

That caused a flurry of good-byes. Toby shook hands all around and left first. Neva hugged Karam, telling him thank you again for his work on the Goodman suit. Martin told him to come back next summer, promising to take him out in the hills and canyons and show him aboriginal wonders. Linda and Matt filed out last, eyes on the floor, both saying a subdued farewell.

Laurie closed the door behind their guests and leaned against it. "Are you worn out?"

Spider held out his hand to her. "Not bad. Come sit a minute. Tell me what you think."

She crossed the room and sat in the chair, taking the hand he offered. "About what?"

"About the whole affair."

"Well, I think you need to call Brick Tremain and tell him about the Yugo."

Spider grinned. "He'll likely give me a bonus for getting rid of it so spectacularly."

"And, he'd probably appreciate an update."

"I'll do that tomorrow before we leave."

Laurie squeezed his hand. "And—" She paused, brow furrowed and lips pursed.

Spider chuckled. "Now that's a face! What were you going to say?"

Laurie shook her head "I can't put it in words, but something is dreadfully wrong between Linda and Matt. Did you watch them while they were here?"

Spider absently stroked the fingers of the hand he held with his thumb. "Yeah. Her eyes kept wandering over to him, but he wouldn't look at her. Not once."

"But it wasn't a look of desire she was sending out. It was more like when someone has a fever, and you're worried about them."

"Or if they've been victims of a bombing? Like that?"

"Yes." She stood and pulled him to his feet. "Not desire. Just concern. Let's get you to bed."

He put his arms around her, drawing her close and kissing her. "You sure about that?" he murmured, nuzzling into her neck.

"Mmm. About what?" She put her hands on his hips. "You must be feeling better."

"Must be." He wound the fingers of one hand through her auburn mane. As the other hand slid to the small of her back, holding her close, he felt her arms encircle him.

Her mouth found his again and then she pulled away, letting her fingernails scrape across the back of his pajamas as she did so. "I was talking about concern," she said. "Look into my eyes. You'll see I'm concerned about getting you to bed."

He cupped her cheek, stroking the high cheekbone with his thumb. "Was that *to* bed or *in* bed?"

She started unbuttoning her shirt. "Don't get hung up on semantics."

Chapter 23

◆

AT TWO THE following afternoon, after dropping off Karam at the airport and going by Frank and Annie Defrain's to give them a report, Spider and Laurie walked out of the Maverick station on the south side of St. George carrying large soft drinks.

"I can't believe I let you talk me into this," Laurie said. "Thirty-two ounces is a quart. I'm going to be floating by the time we get to Colorado City."

"I put a bit of cherry Coke in it. I know you like that."

"Well, yes, but not in such quantity." She handed him her drink to hold while she got in the pickup.

Spider gave her back her cup and then walked around and got in, setting his own drink in the cup holder and fastening his seatbelt.

"I've been meaning to ask you," Laurie said. "What did Karam mean last night when we were talking about the car trade? He said something about—" She paused to think about it. "—there was more to the bargain than transportation."

Spider checked the rearview mirror before pulling out of his parking space. "Well, there are a couple of things that make it about more than transportation.

First, when he was younger and wanting his first car, he tried to get his dad to get him an E-type Jaguar."

"A new one? What did his father say?"

"Well, by then they had quit making them. The car would have been at least twenty years old. His father bought him a brand new Yugo instead."

"So, buying this Jaguar was the accomplishment of a dream?"

"That's what he thought when he bought it. Turned out to be more of a nightmare. He said it was *qadar*. Kind of Allah-directed fate."

"So his logic was, if you traded him the Yugo, it would be like he was acknowledging the wisdom of his father?" Laurie took a long drink of her soda.

"I guess. Anyway, he thought there was some kind of cosmic balance that could be restored if I let him have the Yugo."

"I like this with the hint of cherry in it. Thanks."

Spider merged onto the freeway. "No problem."

"So what was the second thing that made it more than transportation?"

"Karam wants to be able to spend part of his summers with us."

"No, really?" Laurie's smile was huge. "I would love to have him visit. You could take him up to the mines. You could show him how the farmers irrigate. Take him to the square dance. We could do lots of things that would help him with American History."

Spider's phone rang, and he checked his rearview mirror before taking it out of his pocket.

Laurie swallowed the Pepsi in her mouth. "You're not supposed to drive and talk."

Spider didn't pay any attention to her. "Hello. Oh, Hi, Toby." He listened for a moment, his face becoming grim. "Five minutes, max," he said and pocketed the phone.

"What was that about?"

"It was Toby. He's at Austin Lee's house, and he wants us to come by."

"Oh? Why?"

"He's dead. Has been since some time yesterday morning." Spider checked lanes and moved over to the exit lane.

"I presume you mean Austin's dead, not Toby. Did he say anything else?"

Spider shook his head. "He said he'd fill us in when we got there. We're only about a mile from Defrain Estates."

They made it through the only stop light on green and were soon turning on the road to the top of the mesa. The gate attendant was an extremely obese senior citizen. Spider gave him Austin's address.

The attendant spent several moments staring at the dimpled roof of Spider's pickup. "You coming in to do yard work?" he asked.

Spider showed his deputy's badge. "I've been asked to come by the local police."

The attendant winked. "You're in deep cover. I get it." He logged in the information. "I suppose the bandage and black eye are part of the disguise. What's going on up there, anyway? There's been a whole slew of police up and down for the last couple hours."

"It's top secret," Spider said. "They'd have my job if I said anything."

"Mum's the word." The rotund attendant waved him on.

Spider drove the rest of the way up the hill and easily found his way to Austin Lee's house. A half-dozen official cars were parked nearby, including an aid car and a Kane County sheriff's pickup. Spider parked in the same place as his first visit and looked at Laurie. "Coming in?"

She shook her head. "They don't need me tripping around, contaminating the crime scene. Or is it a crime scene? I just assumed someone had murdered him."

"I'm not sure. I'll know in a minute. There's Toby. He must have been watching for us."

"Don't be too long," she warned. "That quart of Pepsi you gave me is a ticking time bomb."

Spider's eyes twinkled. "Um, I'm a little sensitive about the mention of bombs."

"I guess you would be," Laurie said. "Roll down the windows, will you? There's a bit of a breeze coming up over the mesa."

Spider did as she asked and then got out and headed for the house. Toby walked to meet him and handed him a pair of paper covers for his boots. As soon as those were on, he took Spider inside and introduced him to the St. George Police team.

"So this wasn't suicide?" Spider asked as he followed the deputy into the living room.

"Not unless he had the power to beat himself in the back of the head after he was already unconscious," Toby said grimly. "They're just about ready to take the body away, but I wanted you to see it."

"Why me?"

"You're the one who's been aware of Austin Lee's activities. You know more about him than anyone else. The St. George Police want you in the loop."

The body was on a gurney with uniformed people standing by. One of them raised the sheet, and Spider sucked in a breath. Austin Lee's handsome, broad forehead had a wound similar to Spider's above his right eye. A dark maroon circle marked where blood had pooled and coated his brow as it rested against the floor.

Toby pointed to the scar on the temple. "That's the one that felled him, but this is what killed him." Leaning over, Toby shone a flashlight on the back of Austin's head.

Spider squatted down and looked where Toby was pointing the light. At first, all he could see was dried blood caking the artfully-cut blond hair. Then he saw the multiple lines where the scalp had parted, revealing what looked like jerky underneath. "So that's what a blunt instrument injury looks like," he muttered.

"You're only seeing part of 'em," Toby said. "The back of his head looks like hamburger. This was a crime of passion." Toby stared at Spider a moment. "You all right? You look a little green around the gills."

"I could do with some fresh air," Spider admitted.

"Come this way." Toby led him out through the kitchen and open garage and around the corner where they could stand in the shade and catch the breeze.

"Doing better?" Toby asked.

Spider nodded. He leaned his back against the rockwork on the garage, rested his heel on the stem wall, and hooked his thumbs in his pockets. Out of the corner of his eye, he saw movement, and he looked toward the edge of the mesa. Laurie was walking back toward the pickup. She must have gone over for a look-see.

Toby followed where Spider was looking. "Mrs. Latham didn't want to come in?"

"Not her thing," Spider said. "So, when do they think ol' Austin died? Do they know yet?"

"Preliminary guess is yesterday morning."

"Huh."

"You got any ideas who might have done this?"

Spider considered the question. "I've met several with motive but none that I can picture doing the deed."

"Yeah." Toby scratched the back of his head. "They're going over the records from the gatehouse. The city has surveillance on the stop light at the intersection, too, and they're going to try and get that footage. They may ask you to come and look at some of it, since you're familiar with lots of the players."

"I can do that." Spider watched as they wheeled the stretcher out to the aid truck. "So, who found him?"

Toby kicked a rock off the driveway. "I did." He shrugged. "Well, me and a St. George officer."

"Yeah? How'd that happen?"

"I talked with the local folks about Aldo De Pra, and we had a joint force go pick him up and bring him in. Me and some St. George guys. We no more than got him down to the police station than he started singing like a canary. Told about the scam with the accident in the bathroom. That was his wife, by the way." Toby joined Spider with his back against the wall, his hands in his pockets. "De Pra told how Austin hired him to intimidate you and how he was supposed to put you out of commission. Austin didn't tell him to use a bomb, but he made it plain he wanted you hurt."

"Well, De Pra wasn't a complete washout," Spider said. "Any chance he was the one that did this?" He indicated the house with his thumb.

"Maybe." Toby scratched the back of his head. "Maybe the tune he was singing was to cover his tracks." He grimaced. "Somehow I don't think so."

Spider glanced toward the pickup and was surprised to see Laurie hanging her soft drink cup out the window, waving it gently back and forth. He cleared his throat and pushed away from the wall. "I need to be on my way, Toby. Thanks for keeping me in the loop." He offered his hand. "Anything you want me to do, just call."

Toby shook hands with Spider. "It's a pleasure to work with you. Say hi to Mrs. Latham."

Backing away, Spider said, "I'm sure she'd rather you call her Laurie."

Toby smiled. "All right. Say hi to Laurie, then."

"I will." Spider turned and trotted back to the pickup, asking as he climbed in, "Is the bomb about ready to detonate?"

"Pretty soon. I was getting ready to call you on the phone."

Spider started the truck and pulled away from the curb. "Your semaphore with the cup worked pretty well."

"After about five minutes."

"There's a gas station just around the corner. Hang on. We'll get there." Spider slowed and waved at the gatehouse attendant. "What were you doing over at the edge of the mesa?"

"I was looking for a clump of trees. There was a

scrub juniper just over the top of the mesa, but nothing else all the way down."

"That's a pretty high-class area to be squatting in the woods. Are you aiming to embarrass me?"

"Me embarrass you? You're the one wearing little paper bootees." She laughed as Spider leaned over and glanced at his feet. "And besides, you're the one that fed me a thirty-two ounce soda." Laurie unlatched her door as he turned into the station parking lot. As soon as he pulled into a parking space, she was out and sprinting for the restroom.

Spider pulled off the paper foot covering, put them in the litter bag, and then leaned back to wait for Laurie. Visual flashbacks of the ugly blunt trauma marks on Austin's head kept flipping through his mind. Trying to divert his thoughts, he pictured Austin as he had last seen him, standing in the doorway, a sneer on his handsome face as he looked beyond Spider to the little orange car he was driving.

"Dang," he said to himself. "I wish the Yugo would have survived.'"

Laurie opened her door. "Are you talking to yourself?"

Spider smiled. "Yeah. Austin didn't like my choice of car. I was wishing it had survived."

"So you could drive up to his house and say *neener-neener*?"

"Something like that."

Laurie climbed in, closed the door, and buckled her seat belt. "Okay. Now I can concentrate. Tell me what Toby said, starting with when we pulled up, and he came to meet you. Don't leave anything out."

Chapter 24

◆

SPIDER AND LAURIE drove to the museum the following morning. They had called Neva to tell her they had news, and she told them to come at ten when everyone could be there and hear it at the same time.

Cumulous clouds boiled up from behind the mesas to the north. Spider watched them in his rearview mirror. "I wouldn't be surprised if we didn't get another rain this afternoon."

When they reached the museum, the only cars in the parking lot belonged to staff. Spider was glad of that. They had no idea the type of news he was bearing, and a houseful of patrons would be awkward.

He parked by Linda's beat-up Kia. They got out, and as he and Laurie walked toward the building, his cell phone rang. Checking to see who was calling, he stood aside to let Laurie precede him through the entrance. "Hi, Toby. How goes the fight?"

He paused, listening to the deputy's request. He checked his watch. "We can be there in two, two and a half hours. All right. See you then."

Laurie was already greeting Martin and Neva, and he joined her in the lobby.

Isaac and LaJean came in from the Heritage Yard. "We heard you got something to tell us," she said, eyeing Spider. "Hope the news is better than you look."

Isaac frowned at her. "Mother! What kind of a thing is that to say?"

"Well, look at him. He's got a shiner that won't quit. How're you doing, by the way?"

"Much better, thanks."

Isaac clapped Spider on the shoulder. "I heard you stood up for Karam. That's one fine fellow."

"We took him to the airport yesterday," Laurie said. "He said to tell you all good bye and that he'll see you next summer."

Isaac hooked his thumb in his suspenders. "I'll look forward to that. So, Spider. Good news, you say?"

"I'll let you be the judge of that," Spider said, looking around. "How about Linda and Matt? Are they here?"

"They're coming," Isaac said. "They're getting ready for a tour bus we got coming in at ten-thirty."

Spider looked through the window into the office. "Can we all fit in there?"

"I'll grab a couple more chairs." Isaac picked up the two folding chairs that sat behind the reception desk. "There are already four in there."

As Isaac carried the chairs into the office Linda came through the door from the yard and greeted Spider and Laurie.

"Is Matt coming?" Spider asked.

Linda looked behind her. "He was on his way, but don't wait for him. He'll be right here, I'm sure."

"Let's all come into the office." Spider made a

herding gesture with his arms, and everyone moved into the room behind the lobby and took one of the seats Isaac had arranged.

"I'll stand, and Matt can stand when he comes in," Spider said, looking around at the attentive faces turned to him. "Isaac and LaJean, I presume that you've been kept abreast of the events as they've happened."

They nodded.

Spider leaned over, so he could see the door to the yard, checking to see if Matt was coming.

"Spider?"

He looked at Linda, eyebrows raised. "Yes?"

"While we're waiting for Matt, I have some news."

Spider stepped away from the front of the room. "Be my guest."

Linda drew a folded piece of paper from her Levi's pocket as she rose. "I was going to share this with Matt this morning, but I haven't had a chance to..." She glanced through the window, too, obviously wondering where Matt was.

"What is it you have to share, dear?" Neva's voice gently brought her back.

Linda came to the front of the room. "It's an email. I don't know if you know, but I went to the museum in Flagstaff for an interview last—" She wrinkled her brow. "I can't remember when it was. It seems so long ago." She dismissed the calendar problem with an impatient gesture. "Anyway, I was telling them what we had been doing here and about the cache. This morning I got this email asking if we'd be willing to let the cache go on tour. They'd negotiate the price with us, but what they're offering is pretty substantial." She handed the paper to Martin. "I got to thinking, if we let it go on tour for a couple years, we could end up with the money we need, and the museum would be in the black again."

Linda's eyes moved to the door and back, and Spider followed her glance. Matt had entered the room and stood silently at the back, behind his father.

Matt spoke, and his voice had an edge to it. "Did you tell them about the Lincoln Letter? Is that why they were interested in the display?"

Color rose in Linda's cheeks, but she kept her voice calm. "No, I didn't tell them about the Lincoln Letter. It would certainly enhance the exhibit and probably affect the price we—you—could ask, but I left that for you to disclose."

Spider smiled as he moved to the front of the group again. "Thanks, Linda. I think all here would judge that to be good news." He cleared his throat and waited for her to sit down. "Okay. So my news is that the bathroom injury suit was a fraud. Austin Lee was definitely behind it."

There was an instant flurry of murmuring and sounds of surprise. Spider waited for the comments to subside and went on. "I know you're wondering if you can get the money back. I don't know. You'll have to get some legal advice on that. The police have sworn testimony about it, so that should help. You'll have to make a claim against Austin Lee's estate."

"His estate?" Martin and Isaac spoke together.

Matt was quiet, his face paper white.

Linda, too, went pale.

"Yes," Spider said. "That's the second part of what we're here to tell you. Austin Lee is dead."

Isaac, LaJean, Neva and Martin all erupted with questions. How did Spider know? When did he find out? How did Austin die? Both Matt and Linda sat stone still and quiet.

Spider held up his hands. "Austin Lee was murdered. Someone beat in his skull with a blunt instrument."

"When?" Neva asked.

"They figure it was sometime Sunday morning."

Martin raised his hand then asked the question without being called upon. "Do they have any idea who did it?"

Spider didn't answer. Instead he watched as Martin's son's eyes rolled up in their sockets, and he slid down the wall, ending up in a heap on the floor.

The room erupted into chaos. Neva sat against the wall and watched the men bending over Matt, asking, "What's the matter with him?" It was a question no one could answer. Linda joined her there and took her hand.

Martin loosened Matt's collar, and LaJean scooted over closer, took off her oxygen tubing, and handed it to him. Martin fixed it around Matt's face.

"There. He's starting to get some color back," Martin said.

"His eyes are open," Isaac added. "Mattie. Mattie. You gave us a scare."

Matt looked blankly from his dad to Isaac. He blinked and then turned his gaze on the other people in the room, ending up with Spider. "What happened?"

"You passed out," his dad said.

Matt struggled to rise, but Martin held his shoulders down. "Wait a few minutes."

Spider felt something against his leg and looked down to see LaJean sagging against him. "We have another crisis," he said, grabbing hold of her substantial shoulders. "I think she needs her oxygen back."

Matt ripped the tubing off his face and handed it to Isaac who put it on his wife's face. Moments later, LaJean's eyes opened. "Sorry about that," she said. "It came on too fast to say anything."

Linda stood. "The bus is here. You all take care of Matt and LaJean. I'll go out and start the tour."

Matt got to his feet. "I don't need to be taken care of. I can help with the tour."

LaJean held out her hand to her husband and, with his aid, struggled to stand. "Me too. I'm ready."

"Okay," Spider said. "It looks like we're done here. We got a call from Toby. He wants us to come over to St. George to look at some CCTV footage, so we need to be on our way."

"Thanks for coming by," Neva said. "The fact that someone killed Austin is awful. Just awful. But I don't think any of us will mourn his passing."

LaJean seemed to be back in operational mode. "We're glad your brush with him wasn't any worse than it was. You're doing okay?"

Spider patted her on the arm. "I look a lot worse than I feel." He caught Laurie's eye. "Are you ready to go?"

Laurie nodded and said a quick good-bye to Neva and Linda. On the way to the door, she whispered, "What's going on?"

"I guess we'll know when we get to St. George." He held the door for Laurie and then relinquished it to the bus driver, who propped it open for his tour group.

When they were clear of the tourists, Laurie said, "I meant what's going on in there? Why do you suppose Matt passed out?"

"I don't know. You know the old saying, be careful what you wish for. Maybe he realized all of a sudden that he hadn't been careful about what he'd been wishing for."

Spider held the pickup door for Laurie, got in, himself, and they were soon on their way across the Arizona Strip, heading for St. George.

◆ ◆ ◆

An hour and a half later, they met Toby in the lobby of the St. George police station. He ushered them into a small room where a technician sat at a computer in a dimly-lit room. Toby introduced him as Sam.

Spider took off his sunglasses and smiled inwardly at the way Sam avoided looking at the massive bruising around his eyes. "Glad to meet you," he told the technician. To Toby, he said, "What's going on?"

"That's what we want you to help us figure out," the deputy replied. "We've got gaps in the times that the gate was manned. The city has a web cam on that main intersection, and we're going to check the download."

"What for?" Laurie asked.

Toby pulled a side chair over in front of the computer and motioned for the tech to do the same. "To see if any of the people with a connection to Austin Lee came through it."

Spider set his hat on a nearby table and pointed to the chairs. "You want us here?"

"Yes, please." Toby pulled up a chair for himself, and they all clustered around the monitor. "I've never done this," he admitted. "I guess we just watch and say *stop* if we see a car or passenger that we recognize. Right, Sam?"

Sam nodded, and with a few keystrokes, he set the footage rolling.

"So, what time is this?" Spider asked.

"We've started at nine o'clock," Sam replied. "The gatehouse has an active log for this time, but I thought we should cover the window of time they've set for the murder. They said between nine and noon."

Images of cars queuing up at a stop light and then spilling through the intersection ran in a continuous, monotonous thread. Spider had to keep blinking and squirming in his chair to stay awake. Surreptitiously, he checked his watch. Had it only been ten minutes since they started?

Laurie jumped up. "Stop." She sat back down. "Can you go back a ways?"

Spider squinted at the screen as traffic reversed in a whir of grainy images. "What was it?"

"There." Laurie stabbed a finger at the screen. "Hold it right there."

Toby took his notebook out of his pocket and squinted at the screen. "That's Dr. Houghton's pickup and horse trailer."

"I see now," Spider said. "The horse trailer's got *Braces* painted on the front. Huh."

"We're not looking for just anyone you might know." Toby put his notebook back in his pocket. "We're looking for people who have a connection to Austin Lee. Roll it, Sam."

"Well, as to that—" Spider didn't get his thought finished because Laurie jumped up again.

"Stop. Go back a bit." She bent over and stared at the screen. "It's hard because we don't have color to help out, but look at that pickup. The one with a rack of lights on top?"

Spider whistled under his breath. "Matt Taylor."

"We've got him signed in with the gatehouse," Toby said.

Spider frowned at Toby. "You didn't mention you had him on the gatehouse log."

"Didn't I?" Toby scratched the back of his head. "Well, we do. We only have him logged in, not out. Go ahead, Sam."

Spider leaned forward, eyes on the monitor as traffic skittered across it in double time. He blinked periodically to rest his eyes but returned his gaze to the screen each time until he started to feel a dull ache at the back of his head. The ache morphed into a vise that was attached just behind the ears, exerting steadily mounting pressure. Closing his eyes eased that pressure somewhat, and he found himself giving in to the relief he found that way.

"Wait." Laurie put her hand on his knee. "Was that Linda's car?"

Spider opened his eyes. "I didn't see."

"Back up. Back up. There." Laurie leaned forward and touched the screen. "See? Her SUV is tan, and the front bumper is turned down a bit, like a frown. I'm sure that's her."

"Well, well, well." Toby peered at the screen and scribbled in his notebook. "So, Matt Taylor comes through, and twenty minutes later, when Linda comes through, Matt is still there."

"Wherever 'there' is," Spider said. "This road leads lots of places."

Toby put his notebook away. "But we've got Matt in the gate log. Don't forget that."

Spider rubbed the back of his neck. He didn't feel like trying to argue. He clasped his hands, rested his elbows on his knees, and tried to ignore the tightening of the vise. He was being no help. Laurie was, though. And since he brought Laurie, he was a help, after all. He closed his eyes, felt the pressure ease, and decided to keep them closed.

Spider didn't know how long he drifted in darkness. He may even have dozed, but Laurie's elbow nudging his arm brought him back. "Linda again."

"Stop," Toby said to Sam. "Back up and let's get a look at that. Yep. You're right. She's going back the other direction." Out came the notebook.

Spider sat up and blinked. His headache was better, but when the images began racing across the screen again, he closed his eyes. How long was this going to go on?

"Boom." It was Toby who nudged Spider this time. "There's Matt, five minutes after Linda goes through."

He wrote furiously for a moment, closed the notebook with a flourish, and stood. "Thank you all for coming over. Laurie, you were a great help. I knew you would be." He turned to the technician. "Thank you, Sam."

Spider reached for his hat. "So, have we watched the whole time frame that you were given for the murder to have been committed?"

Toby scratched the back of his head. "Not the entire window. You think we ought to do that?"

Spider set his hat back down. "That depends on if you've got your mind made up about who did this or not."

"I've got an open mind," Toby said. "Okay. We've got another ten minutes or so to watch. Let's get to it." He nodded to the technician. "Roll 'em, Sam."

Sam rolled 'em. Toby sat down, and Spider tightened his jaw as he leaned forward again, elbows on knees. They could have been out of here if he'd kept his mouth shut.

He watched for as long as he could before the pressure at the back of his head forced his eyelids closed. It seemed forever before Toby said, "That's it, then. Looks like we didn't learn anything more out of this last bit of footage."

Spider stood and picked up his hat. "Yeah, but you feel good because you exercised due diligence."

Laurie put her hand through Spider's arm and pinched him, at the same time asking Toby, "Is that all you need us for?"

"Yes. Thanks for coming over." Toby busied himself rolling one of the chairs back to its place.

"Glad to meet you, Sam." Spider raised his hat in salute and walked Laurie out into the lobby. He blinked at the brightness and put on his hat and sunglasses as he headed for the entrance doors. Once outside, he took a deep breath. "I'm glad to be out of there. Ol' Toby Flint was wearing mighty thin."

"He's nice," Laurie said.

"He's willing to learn, but he's a lightweight. Come on. Let's go find a place to buy a Pepsi."

"As long as it's not thirty-two ounces, I'm with you."

They walked to the pickup and drove with the windows down and the air conditioning on until they got to a drive-through. Spider ordered soft drinks and gave Laurie hers with a questioning glance. It was half the size of yesterday's, and she took it with a smile.

Spider put the change in the ashtray. "Any other place you want to go, or shall we head home?"

Laurie's eyes twinkled. "By home, I assume you mean Kanab? No, I don't have anywhere else to go."

Spider pulled out of the drive-in and got on the arterial that would lead to the freeway. Laurie sat silently sipping her drink, apparently lost in thought. She surfaced about the time he spied I-15 in the distance.

"Which way do you turn to get to Defrain Estates?" she asked.

"South. Why?"

"Um, I think I'd like to go there."

Spider shot her a quizzical look. "Whatever for?"

"I'll tell you when we get there. There's something I want to show you."

Spider moved over to the right lane. "They won't let

us in the house. Probably not even the yard. It's a crime scene."

She raised her hand in a dismissive gesture. "It's not near the house. I'll show you when we get there."

Spider glanced at Laurie. She leaned her head against the window, the soft-drink straw in her mouth. But she wasn't drinking. She was staring straight ahead.

It didn't take long to come to the off-ramp, and they soon passed through the intersection they had been watching all morning. "You just had your picture took," Spider commented. He was rewarded with a faint smile from Laurie.

The gatehouse was uninhabited, so they drove up to the top of the mesa without stopping. When they turned onto Acacia Street, Laurie sat up and pointed. "Pull over where you parked yesterday."

Spider did as he was directed. "Okay. What do you want to show me?"

"We have to get out." Laurie opened her door.

Mystified, Spider turned off the ignition and climbed out of the cab. Laurie waited for him to join her, and he followed her across the vacant lot toward the edge of the mesa, repressing the urge to ask again what she had to show him.

She led him to the beginning of the primitive road that dropped down the slope to the bottom. "Notice anything?" she asked.

Spider stood with his hands on his hips and examined the lane. Not quite wide enough for a sedan to negotiate comfortably, it had obviously been used by dirt bikes and ATVs. Made mostly of clay soil, the grade was steep, and at one place rain had washed away part of the far edge. At the bottom, the track cut across a vacant field to an electrical substation sitting a couple hundred feet away from a paved road. Spider turned to Laurie and shrugged. "It's a way to get off the mesa. It'd be hard in a sedan, but not impossible."

"Well, that, too. But look here." She pointed to horse tracks coming up the road to the place where a scrub juniper grew at the top. "I noticed these when I was checking for a bush I could use yesterday. Something about them didn't register until we were watching the video this morning."

Spider hunkered down and traced around one of the horseshoe prints. "You mean it registered when you saw Jack's horse trailer?"

Laurie squatted beside him. "Yeah. That's Taffy's hoofprint. I'm sure of it."

"Huh." Spider stared at the track, his mind working. "What makes you so sure?"

"It's the special shoes that Jack's farrier uses." She pointed to two places on the imprint. "The nail holes are placed differently from a regular shoe."

"So you're saying this is Taffy?"

Laurie sighed. "I'd stake my life on it."

Spider stood and offered his hand to help Laurie up. Neither spoke, and when Spider walked away from the tree, eyes on the ground, Laurie followed.

"I don't see any boot tracks," Spider said.

"There's one heel mark here," Laurie said, pointing to it. "Up there on top, the soil's sandier. You sink in farther, and the top falls in on it. It doesn't keep a print."

Head down, Spider scanned the area around the tree. "Here's one that isn't too bad."

Laurie examined the print. "What size would you say that was? Man or woman?"

"Hard to say. It looks like the boot slid in the track. You think it could have been Amy?"

"I have a hard time thinking it could be Jack. Except—" She got a stricken look on her face. "Oh, dear."

"That sounds bad."

She sank to the ground in the shade of the tree and hugged her knees. "I think it may be."

"You'll get your bottom all dusty," Spider warned, hunkering down beside her.

"In the great scheme of things, a dusty bottom is nothing." She patted the place beside her. "Sit down. I've got something to tell you."

Spider was tempted to make a joke about Laurie wanting the chance to dust off his rear end, but the look on her face stopped him. He sat with boot heels dug into the dirt and knees slightly bent. "Okay. Shoot."

"It's about Jack." She picked up a stick and started drawing circles in the area between them. "I don't know if you remember that day we had lunch at his place."

Again Spider suppressed a flippant reply. Of course he remembered. It was a terrible, heart-wrenching day for him, the day he caught his wife in the arms of another man. "I remember," he said.

"Well, we rode around to Goblin Valley. There's a small cave there with a spring in it where white salamanders live. We got off the horses and were walking to where the cave was, and he got real dizzy. I had to hold him up—it seemed like forever. He wouldn't let me help him sit down. Said he was like an old horse. He had to stay on his feet or he'd die."

The sun went behind a cloud, and Laurie paused to look at the sky. A breeze sprang up, blowing her hair away from her face. She ran her hands through it and then continued her narrative.

"After a while he got over the dizzy spell. We gave up on the cave and went and got our horses. I had to give him a boost up on his horse, but he was able to ride home. On the way, he told me that he had cancer three years ago. They treated him but said he could expect it to come galloping back some day. He thought maybe that was the day."

"Was that why he didn't go riding with you?"

Laurie nodded. "He went to St. George to the clinic."

"Huh. I saw him that day. He was pulling out of the parking lot where Austin has his office."

Laurie grimaced. "That doesn't look good. He told me, when we were rehearsing for Western Legends, that the doctor gave him six weeks or less." She paused, looking up as the iron-gray clouds bulldozed in front of the sun. "He said he was busy getting loose ends tied up. Said he wanted things to be better for people after he was gone."

"Farewell to red rock arches, farewell to wonderstone," Spider murmured.

"Yeah." A tear slid down Laurie's cheek.

Spider put his arm around her.

She sniffed. "That's why it's been so hard to have you sniping at him all the time."

"Well, it looked to me like he was in love with you, and that day it looked like you might be leaning toward reciprocating."

Laurie's eyes widened and she pulled away. "Spider! How could you think that?"

"Last week, when Karam and I were up on the mesa, I saw you down there in a long embrace. How was I to know he was feeling poorly at the moment? He's always trying to sneak an arm around you."

"That's just his way. He honestly loves people but not in that way. He's never been interested in girls."

"Great suffering zot, do you mean he's gay?"

"No. Maybe. I don't know. He told me when we were teenagers that he would never marry. Said he didn't feel for girls what he thought he was supposed to. I think he loved me because it didn't change the way I thought about him."

"Well, that sure puts a new face on everything."

"That's what I mean. You've been so jealous you couldn't see what a good man he is. He's dying, and he's trying to make things better for other people."

Spider cleared his throat. "That sounds really great until you think of what happened in that house over yonder."

"I can't believe that he did it."

"Even in the face of that?" Spider indicated the tracks with his thumb.

Laurie was silent for a moment, and then she nodded. "Yes. Even in the face of that. I think Jack doesn't have the capacity."

Spider smoothed out the dirt, erasing the circles

Laurie had drawn. "Have you remembered that there are two horses with misshapen hoofs?"

"Do you think I haven't been thinking about that? But it won't work. Dorrie's farrier modified regular shoes, just like our man did. I saw the tracks just last week. They're not the same."

"So, we're back to Amy."

"Aggh! How do you deal with this kind of stuff all the time?" Laurie got to her feet and brushed off her pant legs.

"Give me a hand." Spider reached up, so Laurie could help him stand. "I don't often meet this kind of a situation, either."

"Well, I've told you what I know. It's yours to deal with. I'm not going to think about it anymore."

Spider looked at the sky. "What if it rains tonight?"

Laurie's auburn hair cascaded down her back as she looked up, too. "It would destroy the evidence. I think I'll pray for rain."

"Yeah, that's what I'm thinking."

"You're going to pray, too?"

Spider smiled. "No. I'm going to preserve the evidence. Come on. Where can we get some plaster of Paris?"

Chapter 25

◆

SPIDER AND LAURIE were having a silent breakfast at Parry Lodge the next morning. He wore sunglasses at the table, so the public didn't have to look at the bruising around his eyes. When his phone rang, he raised them to read the ID of the caller and answered, "Hi, Martin."

Laurie looked up from the French toast she'd been pushing around her plate.

Spider frowned as he listened. "Do you think you'd better have a lawyer there when they come?" He listened, looked at his watch, and said, "We'll be there."

"What is it?" she asked when he stowed his phone in his pocket.

Spider smeared some jam on his toast. "Martin says Toby's on his way to the museum. Says he wants to talk to everyone there. He's bringing a St. George policeman and the Fredonia Marshal. It's going to be Cop City at the Red Pueblo."

"Why did you suggest he have a lawyer?"

"Because Toby's hot on the trail of arresting Matt, and possibly Linda too, for Austin's murder."

"How do you know that?"

Spider didn't answer. He took a bite of toast and gave a half smile as he chewed.

"Okay," she said. "I know the answer to that. We all saw Matt heading to Austin's house. What did Martin say? About the lawyer?"

"He didn't see the need, and besides, he says he can't afford one." Spider pointed his fork at her plate. "You haven't eaten a bite."

"I'm not hungry. I've been all tied up in knots ever since yesterday afternoon." She set her fork on her plate. "Do you really think Toby will arrest Matt on the strength of the video footage?"

Spider shrugged. "Maybe the forensic team found something at the house."

"If Matt did it, that means that Jack didn't, and that's good," Laurie said. "But I can't believe that Matt had anything to do with it, either."

"Well, we'll know what Toby knows in just a bit. Want to head on down, since all you're going to do is worry that French toast to death?"

Laurie smiled and laid her napkin beside her plate. "Yes. Let's go. Do you think you need to prepare them, just in case?"

"I don't think they need preparing. I think they've been on edge about what Matt's volatile temper might cause him to do."

Laurie stood. "Do you think Matt did it?"

Spider picked up his hat and stood as well. "Don't look so hopeful, Darlin'. I don't think anything yet. Like Toby Flint, I'm keeping an open mind."

◆ ◆ ◆

Half an hour later, they pulled into the Red Pueblo parking lot. Linda's SUV was missing, but everyone else seemed to be clustered in the lobby, watching Spider and Laurie walk up the sidewalk.

They all offered a subdued greeting as Spider pushed open the entrance door. Matt, who had been squatting down, arranging things in the bottom of the glass display case, stood. He closed the case and locked it, pocketing the key. "Mornin', Spider." He cleared his throat. "I wonder, would you come out into the yard for a minute? I'd like to talk to you."

Spider briefly met Laurie's troubled eyes. He saw the same fearful look mirrored in Neva's and LaJean's eyes. "Sure, Matt," he said. He walked to the side door and held it open for the younger Taylor.

By silent accord, they walked past the log cabin to the timber drill rig. Matt sat down on the cross beam, and Spider rested a boot on a horizontal wheel spoke. "Whatcha got on your mind?" he asked.

Matt cleared his throat. "I didn't get a chance to tell you. I had a talk with Tiffany."

"Oh? How'd it go?"

Matt spoke through clenched teeth. "I'm not good at stuff like that. I didn't know what to say." He reached down and picked up a rock. "I was going to have to call her a liar. That's a hard thing to do."

"But, how did it go?"

Matt balled the rock in his fist. "She did most of the talking. Said she wanted to help so bad that the promise just came out. She didn't mean to lie."

"Do you believe her?"

Matt dropped the rock. "Almost." He turned and squinted into the sun as a St. George police cruiser pulled into the parking lot followed by the Fredonia marshal's rig. "They're here."

"Yeah, we'll go see them in a minute. So, what's Tiffany going to do?"

Matt looked down as he ground a boot heel into the soil. "She says she's going to travel on. She mentioned St. George and asked about Austin Lee, about whether he was still interested in Linda."

"You didn't tell her he was dead?" Dang, why hadn't he watched the stop light footage better? Did they miss a red BMW convertible?

"I talked to her on Saturday morning. He wasn't dead then."

"Huh." Spider rubbed his jaw and looked at the toe of his boot. Where did this new bit of information fit into the puzzle?

"There's Isaac, waving us in." Matt wiped the dust from his hands onto his pant legs.

Spider looked up to see the older man in the parking lot, limping toward the entrance. "Looks like he's closed the gate, so we won't be disturbed." Spider began walking with Matt across the Heritage Yard. "I asked your dad if he didn't think you all should have a lawyer present. He said no."

"I agree," Matt said. "We've got nothing to hide."

"I wish you thought differently about that, but there you go." Spider held the side door open for Matt to precede him into the lobby.

The three officers of the law turned their heads in

unison at their approach. Toby was again shined and creased, standing with his thumbs inside his glossy black leather duty belt. Next to him stood Sergeant Whipple, a tall, thin, uniformed officer from St. George that Spider remembered being introduced to at the crime scene. The third man was middle aged with thinning hair, a wiry build, and a hawk nose. He wore a blue uniform, and Toby introduced him as Marshal Thayne.

Spider stood by Matt. He took off his hat and nodded a greeting as each officer was introduced.

Sergeant Whipple murmured something to Toby, who said, "Could you remove your sunglasses, please, Mr. Latham?"

As Spider took them off, Toby took a step back. "Oh, geez! I forgot about the black eyes. Sorry, Spider. Geez. Put 'em back on."

"No, that's fine." Spider parked the glasses on top of his head. "I'm more comfortable without them." He looked around. "So, how long is this going to take? Do we need to find a place for people to sit? We need chairs for Isaac and LaJean at least."

"And my parents," Matt added. "I'll get chairs out of the office."

Marshal Thayne silently followed him and helped carry chairs from the office into the lobby. He wheeled the office chair in and placed it beside the others Matt had lined up. He gestured for Laurie to sit, then stood at the back of the room with his hands clasped behind him.

Spider set his hat on the glass display case and joined the rest of the museum personnel, leaning a shoulder against the archway that divided the exhibit room from the lobby. He tried not to smile, watching Toby's discomfort as he operated under the gaze of the metropolitan policeman.

Deputy Flint pulled his notebook from his pocket. "Though Sergeant Whipple is senior to me, since I'm a reserve officer in the Coconino County Sheriff's Office and thus am certified to work here in Fredonia, I'm taking charge of this—we'll call it a meeting, for now." He glanced at the silent, uniformed man at the back of the room. "We've asked Marshal Thayne to be here as a courtesy, to keep him in the loop."

The deputy's gaze swept the room. Nobody spoke.

"Right." Toby took out his pen and clicked the point down. "Pushing on, I guess you all know that Austin Lee was murdered last Sunday. He was beaten to death with a blunt instrument. We're checking on people who had a beef with him—"

"Of whom there are many," Spider murmured.

Toby shot a glance at Spider but went on. "—who had a beef with him who were in the vicinity on that day." He blinked and looked around the room again. "Where is Linda Russell?"

"She's not here," Neva said.

Toby clicked his pen several times. "Why not? I specifically asked that she be here."

Neva shrugged. "I called her cell phone and left a message. That was the best I could do on short notice."

Toby stood still, his thumb furiously working the button on his pen. He shot a look at Sergeant Whipple. "Right. We'll talk with her separately, I guess. Okay. Austin Lee. I understand that he had been causing the museum some trouble?"

The statement hung as an interrogatory, but no one volunteered to tackle answering it. They all stared with blank faces at the deputy.

Finally Matt, who had one hip perched on the guest book table, stood. "What do you want us to say? You know what he was up to. Do you also know that his fraudulent lawsuits, his greed for land, especially land that had been extorted from families who had held it for over a hundred years, his weaseling and sliming around, forcing people against their will—" Matt stopped. He cleared his throat and started again. "He put my father in the hospital. Do you have that in your notebook?"

Toby clicked his pen. "No. When was this?"

Neva answered. "It was a week ago yesterday."

As Toby wrote down Neva's information, Spider watched Sergeant Whipple move past Isaac to the glass display case in front of the reception desk. He squatted down and began to look at the artifacts that were for sale, the little white tags turned so the price was visible.

"What other doings did you have with Austin Lee?"

LaJean spoke up. "Some of us had some interaction with him, but none of it amounted to a hill of beans. What do you want to know?"

Toby glanced over at Sergeant Whipple. "Anything you can remember."

"Well, he leaned on that glass counter and told me he loved seeing senior citizens overcoming disabilities to be of service. It sounds patronizing now, but when he said it, it sounded right pretty."

Isaac said, "Ha! Salting the cow to get the calf."

"What do you mean by that?" Toby stood poised to

write, but his eyes cut over to the sergeant still crouching in front of the glass.

Isaac answered Toby's question, but he was watching Sergeant Whipple, too. "He was fixing on Linda. She wasn't paying him any attention, so he figgered if he got LaJean on his side, the conquest would be easier."

A half smile lifted the corners of Spider's mouth as he watched Toby scribbling Isaac's words, obviously oblivious to the fact that the tall St. George officer had stood and silently made his way to stand next to him. When Whipple bent down to murmur something in the deputy's ear, Toby was so startled that his hands flew up, and the pen went flying.

Spider grabbed the missile as it flew by him and waited until Sergeant Whipple had finished before handing Toby his pen back.

Toby took the pen without a thank you and cleared his throat. "I'm going to turn the time over to Sergeant Whipple. He's got something to bring up."

The tall officer walked to the front of the room and did a military about face. Spider almost expected him to click his heels. Whipple's eyes swept the room. "We appreciate your being here this morning. We appreciate your cooperation." He pasted on a wooden smile, as if he were reading from a script and obeying instructions in parentheses. "We wonder if you would mind if we examined the contents of this case?"

"What do you mean by that?" Martin looked from Matt to Neva and then to Spider. "What does he mean by that?"

"He wants to do some searching without a search warrant," Spider said. "You can say no."

Sergeant Whipple made a steeple of his fingertips. "That will simply delay the inevitable. We can get a court order by phone in half an hour."

"Maybe," Spider said. "Maybe not. Depends on the judge. Depends on your reasons for asking." He met Marshal Thayne's eyes, and the other officer gave a tiny nod.

Matt took a step forward. "Here's what I say. Let them look through the display case. We've got nothing to hide. Anything to get this prissy clown out of here sooner."

Toby held up a hand. "Easy, easy. No need to get personal."

Sergeant Whipple strode toward the entrance. "I'm going to go get my kit," he said as he passed Toby.

Toby looked after the tall, retreating figure. "What kit?" Receiving no answer, he stared at the closing door for a moment then turned back to the staff. He cleared his throat and again took out his notebook and pen. "All right. Going on, I need to ask Matt something."

Matt again rested against the table. "Go ahead. Shoot your best shot."

"Your name is in the Defrain Estates gatehouse log book on Sunday morning. Can you tell us why you were there?"

"I was thinking about buying a house."

"That sounds a little farfetched. Isn't it true that you drove up on that mesa to confront Austin Lee?"

"About what?"

"About defrauding your father of a quarter million dollars with the scurrilous bathroom injury lawsuit."

When Sergeant Whipple entered with a backpack, Toby's arms fell to his sides, notebook in one hand, pen in the other.

The sergeant set his kit down by the glass case. "I need the key, please."

"I've got it." Matt tossed the key to Isaac who handed it to Whipple. "About that lawsuit," Matt said to Toby. "I didn't know that Austin was behind it until Sunday evening."

Toby rolled the pen in his fingers. "Well then, you went to confront him because he tried to defraud the family again in a second lawsuit that had to do with the Goodman cache."

Matt shook his head. "There was no need. I knew the Goodman lawsuit was a nonstarter."

"Well then, why did you go to Austin Lee's house?"

Matt didn't answer. In the silence, as everyone waited to see what he would say, Sergeant Whipple slid the door of the display case open. Every head swiveled, and each person watched as he unzipped his backpack.

Even Toby was silent, moving forward to watch as Sergeant Whipple put on a pair of latex gloves and took a plastic bag of Q-tips and a vial of liquid out of the backpack. The St. George officer picked up the first Anasazi reproduction ax in the line of four, wet a Q-tip from the vial, and began swabbing the pointed bottom of the weapon. He bent over and poked the saturated cotton end down into the crack where the stone was attached to the haft. "Ha!" he said, holding up the now-pink swab.

"Ha what?" Toby came nearer. "What are you saying?"

"There's blood on this ax."

Matt strode to the display case, leaned against the *Don't lean on the glass* sign, and jutted out his jaw. "You're crazy."

Sergeant Whipple dropped the ax into a plastic bag. "We'll see who's crazy when we get this to the lab."

Matt's hands were balled into fists. "You're not taking that ax anywhere."

"'Fraid so." Whipple stuffed it in his backpack and stood. "We're taking you, too."

Spider pushed away from the archway where he had been leaning with arms folded. "What's the charge?"

"Murder. The murder of Austin Lee. Read him his rights, Flint."

Toby came closer, leaned over the glass case, and in a whisper that all could hear said, "Can we talk about this before you charge him?"

"I'm senior to you." Even at a murmur, Sergeant Whipple's voice had a hard edge to it. "The crime was committed in my jurisdiction. We're taking him in."

While the two Utah officers continued talking in heated undertones, Spider turned to Marshal Thayne. "What do you say? Can two Utah officers come into Arizona and drag someone across the state line?"

The marshal's mouth turned down as he nodded. "Yep, they can. That's 'cause Deputy Barney Fife over there is an Arizona reserve officer."

A smile touched the corner of Spider's lips. "Deputy Flint, you mean?"

Marshal Thayne's face remained impassive, but his eyes twinkled. "Did I get his name wrong? Must have been a slip of the tongue. They'll take Matt to the shiny new county jail just across the border and hold him until he can see an Arizona judge."

Spider turned his attention back to Toby. His body was rigid, and the hand that clutched his pen had the knuckles showing white. "I'm telling you, you don't need the cuffs," he hissed. "Not on my territory, not with these people."

"It's regulations, but have it your way." Whipple's voice had a petulant tinge to it. "I'm not going to be responsible for a lost prisoner."

Toby turned to say something to the museum staff, and Spider watched as his eyes shifted from one attentive face to the other. A blush crept up his neck and suffused his cheeks as he realized that everyone had heard his interchange with Sergeant Whipple. He looked at the ground for a moment and then methodically closed his notebook and stowed it and his pen in his pocket. When he looked up, he spoke quietly. "Matt Taylor, I am arresting you for the murder of Austin Lee." He proceeded to tell Matt his rights under the law and then asked if he understood.

"Yes." Matt's voice was raspy as he turned to Spider. "I don't know how blood got on that ax."

"I hear you," Spider said. "They've got a ways to go to make a case. Could have been a false positive."

"Could be some animal's blood," Isaac added. "That's one of the rocks I picked up for you. Maybe some coyote killed a rabbit there."

"I'll make sure I get a copy of the lab results," Marshal Thayne said, shooting a glance at Sergeant Whipple. "We'll keep them honest."

"Flint!" Sergeant Whipple's voice cracked like a whip. "It's time to be going."

Reluctance showed in every line of Toby's body. He stood aside and said, "Matt, you'll have to come with us."

Matt cast a pleading look at Spider.

Spider ground his teeth. This is why he had pushed to have a lawyer present. "Better go on with them," he said, looking to Marshal Thayne for confirmation.

The Marshal nodded. "No good will come from resistin'. We can get this sorted out peaceable like."

"Come on, then." Toby took Matt by the arm.

Matt shook himself out of Toby's grasp and strode after the tall form of Sergeant Whipple. Toby raised his hands in a no-harm-no-foul gesture and followed them out of the museum.

Chapter 26

◆

EVERYONE DRIFTED TO the window to watch Matt get in the back of the police cruiser. Neva and LaJean were weeping, and their husbands comforted them as best they could. Laurie stood by Spider, and he looked down to see that her eyes were shiny, too. He put an arm around her and pulled her close. "This isn't the end of anything," he said.

Marshal Thayne took a card out of his pocket. "I think I'll follow them up to the jailhouse. If you need me, my phone number's on here."

Spider took the card and glanced at it. "Thanks."

"Send me a text or call me, so I'll have your number." Hat in hand, the marshal took a step backwards toward the door as he addressed Matt's folks and the Bakers. "I'll keep an eye on things, let you know what's happening."

Neva wiped her eyes with a tissue. "Thanks, Marshal."

The officer turned and strode to the door, putting on his hat as he walked toward his pickup. He stopped with his hand on the door as Linda's car sped down the highway and turned into the parking lot. The marshal waited for her to get out and then said something to her, pointing to the group assembled in front of the window.

Linda nodded and trotted toward the entrance stiff-arming the doors as she reached them. "Martin? Neva? What's happened?" The red bandana she wore on her head accented the pallor of her face. Her eyes had the look of a frightened animal.

At the sight of Linda, Neva broke down sobbing. LaJean shouldered her canvas oxygen tote and put an arm around her friend, leading her to one of the chairs. "Let Spider talk to her, Martin," she advised over her shoulder. "You need to be over here with your wife."

Linda turned to Spider. "Tell me!"

"Toby and a police sergeant from St. George were just here and arrested Matt for Austin Lee's murder."

Linda's mouth dropped open. She stared at Spider for a long moment and then asked, "How could they do that? What evidence do they have?"

"They found blood on one of the Anasazi axes in the display case. I think they think it's the murder weapon."

Linda's face, already pale, suddenly became ashen. She closed her eyes and whispered something to herself.

Spider dragged one of the chairs over to where they stood. "You look ill. Please sit down."

She sagged into the chair. "I don't understand." She spoke in a voice barely above a whisper. "Why Matt?"

"He was at Defrain Estates on Sunday morning at the time Austin was murdered. That's a pretty big coincidence. He's publically said that he'd like to kill whoever it was that was doing this to the Taylors. I heard him myself."

"How do they know he was at Austin's house?"

"He signed in at the gatehouse. Also, he's on camera at the main intersection just off the freeway."

"You're on it, too," Laurie said to Linda.

Linda turned blank eyes to Laurie. She seemed not to be able to process what she said. "I'm on what?"

"On the video footage. We saw you coming through after Matt, but you weren't in the gatehouse ledger."

Linda swallowed. "So, they have evidence that Matt went to Austin's house?"

"They have evidence he was in the area. I don't know if they have been able to place him in the house with fingerprints. This Whipple character is annoying, but I've got to hand it to him, he's pretty sharp. He could see that the edge of that ax was the same size and shape as the wounds on Austin's head."

"He tested it for blood and found some," Laurie added.

Linda looked from Laurie to Spider. "Is it Austin's blood for sure?"

Spider answered. "They don't know yet, but Sergeant Whipple's taken it away to send to the lab."

Linda closed her eyes again and pressed her fingers against her forehead.

Laurie touched her arm. "Are you all right?"

Lids still closed, Linda nodded. Moments later, she opened her eyes and spoke in a firm voice. "I need to talk to Spider. Alone."

Spider blinked at the change in Linda. "Okay." He glanced at the office to see if it was available.

"No, let's go to the dugout." Without waiting for him to agree, she strode towards the door to the yard.

Spider paused to give Marshal Thayne's card to Laurie and ask her to text him their phone numbers. Then he followed Linda out to the dugout. When he entered, he found her seated on the bed with her hands folded in her lap.

"I want to confess to the murder of Austin Lee," she said. "I killed him."

"Whoa there. Let's go back to the beginning." Spider sat on the chair. "Why'd you go to St. George that morning?"

She chewed on her lip for a moment, eyes on the floor. Then she looked up. "I went to talk to Austin. I was going to tell him it was all over between us. I never wanted to see him again."

Spider rubbed his jaw and then sighed. "Linda," he said. "This isn't going to help Matt. The way you can help Matt is to tell me everything that happened—the truth—from the time Neva sent you to sit with me in the hospital early Sunday morning until you got back from St. George."

"Why don't you think I'm telling the truth now?"

"Well, first, because there never was much between you and Austin. Second, the little there was between you was over quite a while before Sunday." Spider leaned back and crossed his legs. "And third, there's no way you could have killed Austin Lee."

"What do you mean? Why not?"

"Because whoever struck that first blow was left handed."

Linda sat still as a statue. She looked as if she was seeing something inward, examining a memory as it played through her mind. When the mental movie was over, she slumped and put her hands over her face, asking in a muffled voice, "What can I do to help Matt?"

"Tell me everything."

"Everything?" She let out a mirthless little laugh and then took a deep breath. "Okay, here goes." But she didn't speak.

"Take your time," Spider said.

"All right. Saturday night Matt asked if I wanted to walk around Western Legends with him. He said you had talked some sense into his head. He was still moody, but a lot of that was blaming himself for how things had gone wrong between us. He told me about Tiffany not having any money, and he said that made him feel like a bigger fool. I told him I knew now that he was doing it for the museum."

"So things were better between you?"

She nodded. "We went to his house afterwards and were sitting out back visiting with his folks when Laurie called. She told us about the bomb and asked for someone to come sit with you while she went to help Karam. Matt and I offered to do it."

"I appreciated it, too. I woke up during the night and heard you talking."

"Oh? What were we talking about?"

"You were telling him about you and Austin and the incident here in the dugout."

"I should have kept my mouth shut." There was a bitter edge to her voice.

"Why do you say that?"

She scooted back on the bed and leaned against the

rocky back wall. Her feet stuck out over the edge of the bed, and she looked like a little girl to Spider. A lost little girl.

"Things were going so well. He told me about Tiffany, and we got the air cleared about that. I thought if I talked about Austin, we could clear that up and be back to where we were." She pulled the bandana off her head and laid it in her lap. "But it didn't work out that way."

"What happened?"

"When I told him that Austin tried to—"

"—rape you. You might as well call it what it was."

"It's such an ugly word. But yes, when I told Matt, he was so angry. Not with me, and not with Austin so much as with himself. He realized he just stood there as Austin walked over here with me, and it was going on when he wasn't a hundred feet away. He blamed himself."

"And because he was so angry at himself, he wanted to rearrange Austin's features?"

"I think so." She smoothed the red handkerchief in her lap and then looked up. "But that's different from killing someone."

"I agree. Go on with your story."

"By then it was about four in the morning. I fell asleep in the chair, and when I woke up, he was gone."

"What time was that? I remember talking to you just before Toby showed up. Around eight?"

"Yes. I hadn't been up very long. I'd been trying to reach his phone, but he wasn't answering. I went by the house, but his folks hadn't seen him. He wasn't at the museum, so I headed on over to St. George."

"Why did you go to St. George?"

Her chin quivered. She cleared her throat. "Because I just knew that's where he went."

"Did you see him there?"

Her head rolled back and forth over the rocky wall in a forlorn negative. "I know you said he was there, but I didn't see him."

Spider uncrossed his legs and leaned forward, arms on his knees. "Okay. Let's go over what you did when you got there."

"I drove to his house. Austin's house."

"How did you know where he lived?"

Linda grimaced. "He took me there one afternoon. I think he was showing off."

"Okay. Then what?"

As Linda talked, she methodically gathered the red fabric up into a tight ball and enclosed it in one clenched fist. "I knocked on the door, but there wasn't any answer. When I knocked again, the door swung open a bit. I pushed it halfway open and called Austin's name, but nobody answered. I was just ready to pull the door shut and leave when I saw his feet sticking through the door to the living room."

"What did you think?"

"I thought the worst, that Matt had come and beat him up."

"So you went in. What did you find?"

Linda's chin began to quiver again, and she covered her mouth with the wadded-up bandana. Her eyes widened, as if she were seeing the horror again, and she spoke from behind the cloth. "I don't know if I can describe it."

"Give it a try, please."

She put her hands in her lap and started twisting the handkerchief. "He was face down. Dead. I knew he was dead before I knew anything else."

"Go on."

"Somebody had bashed him over and over with—" She swallowed. "—with an Anasazi ax. It was the one he bought on that first day I met him."

"The ax was there?"

"Yes. It was lying on the floor over by the kitchen door, like somebody flung it away when they got done."

"Is that how the ax got in the display case? Did you put it there?"

She nodded. "I took it home and washed the blood off it. I let it dry in the sun and brought it in early and put it in the case."

"When did you do that?"

"Sunday afternoon."

"So, when you and Matt came to see me Sunday evening, you thought he had killed Austin Lee?"

She shook her head, more vigorously this time. "I don't think I thought he had killed him. Matt might have knocked him out, but he wouldn't have pounded his skull to hamburger."

"But you knew Austin was dead?"

"Yes."

"That explains why you were so quiet. What about Matt? You were both keeping your distance."

"I think he was still working through the rape thing."

Spider sat a minute, pondering. In his mind's eye, he tried to picture the group when he had told them yesterday morning about Austin Lee's death. He re-membered Linda's unsurprised expression, and he remembered Matt's eyes rolling to the back of his head before he fainted and landed in a heap on the floor.

"Did Matt know you went to St. George on Sunday?"

Linda's hands, which had been worrying the fabric, stilled. She looked at Spider and then beyond his shoulder, apparently searching her memory. "He could have. Martin and Neva showed up at the museum just after I put the ax in the display case. They asked where I'd been, and I told them I'd had some errands in St. George. They asked me to come to supper that evening."

"So they could have mentioned it to Matt?"

"They could have." She frowned. "But why would he think that I was going to see Austin?"

"But you did go to see Austin."

"Yes, but only because I was afraid Matt was going to go see him."

Spider took a deep breath. "Okay, Linda. Let's talk about something else. You're an educated girl. Did you never think, through all of this, that you were doing something wrong by tampering with evidence? That you might be committing a crime?"

"While it was happening? No. Since then, yes. I've lost a lot of sleep over it."

"Well, you're apt to lose a little more. This is a seri-ous thing you've done. Don't do anything, though, until we get you a lawyer." He stood. "Let's go in and talk to Martin and Neva. They need to get a lawyer for Matt, too, and hang the cost."

Chapter 27

HALF AN HOUR later, as Spider and Laurie crossed the state line on their way to the county jail, Spider was finishing a conversation with Brick Tremain.

Laurie glanced over. "What did he say when you told him that Martin was thinking of selling the Lincoln letter, so he could hire a lawyer?"

"This is mixed company. I can't repeat what he said." Spider pocketed the phone. "He's going to call Martin right back and tell him it's a bad idea. He'll also have a few pithy words about him not getting a lawyer in the first place. He had some for me not pushing it harder."

They turned off the highway onto the gravel road to the dump, also the road that led to an impressive, state-of-the-art jail. Built with an eye toward housing over-flow from state prisons, the facility had an occupancy rate higher than even the most successful hotels in town.

Pulling into the parking lot, Spider said, "Tell me again what Marshal Thayne said when he called?"

"He said Matt seems to listen to you, and you need to come talk some sense into him."

"I wonder what that means." Spider turned off the engine. "You coming in?"

"They have a nice waiting room. I'll come in and sit where it's cool."

"I forgot you already have a history with this place. There's Marshal Thayne. Looks like he's been watching for us." Spider got out and waved. He waited for Laurie and followed her up the sidewalk to the door. The Fredonia lawman greeted them and then escorted them inside.

"Mrs. Latham, you can wait in here." The marshal opened the door to a glass-walled room off the lobby. "There's magazines or a TV. I don't think anyone will come bother you here."

"I'll be fine." She smiled and waved at a woman at a desk next door. If I need anything, I'll ask Connie."

Leaving Laurie in the waiting room, Spider took off his hat and followed Marshal Thayne down the hall. They passed through a manned and locked door to another lobby with an officer sitting at a desk. The marshal spoke to him, and he directed them to a small, sparely furnished room with a large glass window looking onto the lobby.

"Go on in," Marshal Thayne said to Spider, "I'll wait outside. I don't want to get in the way of anything he might say to you."

"Thanks for doing this," Spider said.

The marshal held up his hand. "Don't thank me. I like young Taylor. He's a bit prickly, but years of roaming the canyons alone will do that to you. He's made of good stuff, and I hate to see him mixed up in something like this." He opened the door. "Go in. Have a seat. They'll bring him down in a minute."

Spider went in and sat on one of the two straight back chairs. He put his Stetson on the small table and looked around at the shiny, utilitarian interior. He checked the clock and wondered how long he'd have to wait.

As it turned out, it wasn't long. A guard accompanied an orange jumpsuited Matt to the door, let him in, and stood in the corner.

Matt looked at the guard. "Does he have to stay in here?"

"Apparently so. Sit down. We probably have a limited amount of time, so let's get to it."

"To what?"

"Marshal Thayne thought you might have something to say to me."

Matt shrugged. "What would I have to say?"

Spider leaned back in his chair and regarded the younger man. "Let's get one thing straight. Linda didn't have anything to do with the murder of Austin Lee. If you think you're protecting her, you're wrong."

"How did you know—?" Matt stopped himself and shifted gears. "Why would I think that she had anything to do with it?"

"Because you saw her in St. George and figured she had gone to see Austin. But you're wrong. She was there because of you."

"Because of me? Why?"

"She was afraid you'd gone over to clean Austin's clock because he tried to rape her. Was she right?"

Matt looked down at his hands. "Yeah."

"So, tell me what happened Sunday morning. Start

at the time you left the hospital. By the way, thanks for coming and staying with me."

"No problem," Matt muttered. He ran a hand through his hair. "Okay. I left the hospital and I drove up Hog Canyon, up to the antennas. I needed to get away, clear my head. I watched the sunrise. Thought about what Linda had told me. Decided I needed to go tell Austin Lee what I thought of him. Yes, and maybe give him a sock in the jaw."

"Okay," Spider said. "What time did you get to St. George?"

"I don't know. After I watched the sunrise, I drove back down the canyon and had breakfast at Nedra's. That would put me leaving town somewhere around eight or eight-thirty."

"Which puts you at Defrain Estates around nine-thirty or ten?"

"Probably. I practiced what I was going to say all the way over. I called him some pretty creative names. They all had to do with someone who has to force his attention on women. I think I planned on making him take a swing at me, so I'd have an excuse to take him on."

"And then what happened?"

"The biggest anticlimax of the century. Nothing. He wasn't home." Matt paused and thought a moment. "From what the police say, I guess he was home, just not able to answer the door because he was, you know, dead."

"Did you knock or use the doorbell?"

Matt's brows drew together. "What kind of a question is that?"

"A fairly crucial one. Can you answer it?"

"I don't know." Matt rubbed his forehead with his fingers. "I used the doorbell. I remember now. It was set in some sandstone rockwork."

"All right. Then what did you do?"

"I got in the pickup and drove away."

Spider leaned back and folded his arms. "When you came up into the subdivision, you checked in at the gatehouse. Why didn't you check out when you went back through?"

"Nobody was there."

"Okay. Where did you go after you came down off the mesa?"

"There's a gas station down towards the stop light. I went there to get gas." Matt glanced at the guard. "While I was filling up, I saw Linda drive by."

"What did you think when you saw her?"

"You want the completely honest answer?"

Spider cocked his head. "I hope you've been completely honest all along."

Matt waved a hand as if to indicate that hadn't been important. "That was easy to be honest about. This one is hard."

"All right. Let's hear the hard honest answer." Spider waited. Saw Matt's Adam's apple dip. Waited some more.

"I thought—" Matt ran his hand through his hair again. "I thought she was going up to see him because she wasn't over him yet. Hell, he's handsome, has lots of money, big car, clothes that look like the labels would be hard to pronounce. What've I got besides a track record that's got Tiffany Wendt written all over it?"

"So you didn't follow her up to his house?"

He shook his head. "I was too chicken."

Spider sighed and shook his head. "Son, when we're done with this, I want you to grow some self-confidence and start believing in yourself and in Linda. She loves you. If you'da followed her, she'da told you so at Austin's doorstep, and you'da both left. When the police came around, the murder weapon would have been right where it was tossed after the murderer mashed Austin's skull in."

Matt drew back, frowning. "I don't understand."

"Linda knocked on the door, and it swung open. Whoever went out of it last didn't pull it tight. That's why I asked if you used the doorbell or knocked."

The color drained from Matt's face. "So when the door opened, she went in and saw Austin's dead body? And she thought I did it?"

Spider unfolded his arms and leaned forward. "Yes. And to protect you, just about an hour ago, she confessed to the murder."

"No," Matt whispered.

"Don't worry. The confession was to me, nobody else. I told her why I knew she couldn't have done it, and she agreed to tell me the truth about what she did on Sunday."

Matt's eyes dropped to his hands, obviously processing all Spider had told him. He raised his head and looked at him with narrowed eyes. "Is that how the ax got in the display case? Did Linda bring it and put it there?"

"Yep. She thought she was protecting you, hiding it

in plain sight. But an overzealous cop playing a hunch undid that plan."

Matt put his face in his hands. "You know, just once I'd like to do something right. What a mess!"

"You've done a lot of things right. We'll get you through this some way. Mind you, Linda won't get away with carrying off evidence, but any education costs something. If you two learn to trust one another, the price you pay will be worth it."

The officer in the room looked at his watch and held up two fingers. "Two more minutes."

Spider nodded to the guard and turned back to Matt. "All right. One last question. What did you do after you saw Linda go by on her way to Austin's?"

"I spent a miserable twenty minutes waiting for her to come back. When she finally did, I drove home and went hiking in the hills until suppertime. I spent the whole time picturing them together, and it just about did me in."

"But you said he wasn't home—or at least you thought he wasn't."

"I knew he wouldn't answer the door to me. I thought he probably answered when she came to the door."

"Oh, Matt. You're almost a lost cause."

"Yeah. And when I got home at suppertime, she was there."

"Yes, and remember, she thought you had killed Austin."

"No wonder she wouldn't look at me. I thought it was because she and Austin had made up."

The officer gave the high sign, so Spider picked up his hat and stood. "You've got lots to think about. I know you didn't kill Austin. Brick Tremain and your dad are working on getting a lawyer for you, and Marshal Thayne and I are going to see what we can do about proving you didn't do it."

Matt stood, too. He grabbed Spider's hand and shook it. "Thank you. I don't know how to repay you."

"Learn the lesson. Grow some confidence. And, you might tell Linda you love her."

Matt grimaced. "You're asking a lot."

"You told me once she was like water to a thirsty man. Can you tell her that?"

Matt looked at the floor. "I'll do my best."

Spider watched the guard walk Matt out the door and down the hall. Stepping out of the room, he spied Marshal Thayne standing by the exit door and joined him there.

On the way out, as they walked through the locked and guarded door, Spider reported on his conversation with Matt. Arriving at the lobby, he said, "I wonder if you could do a couple things for me."

"What do you need?"

"Could you get a copy of the gatehouse log, beginning the day before, say four in the afternoon?"

The marshal raised an eyebrow. "You think maybe someone came and stayed the night?"

"Could be. And here's another thing. I need a line on a truck driver, name of Wendell Wendt. He lives in Modesto California."

The marshal had his phone out, tapping in notes. "Yeah? What do you need to know?"

"I need to know if he was working last Sunday. And I need to know if he's left handed."

Chapter 28

LATER THAT DAY at a picnic table outside the Subway shop, Laurie unwrapped her sandwich. "Tell me again why you're sure Matt didn't kill Austin Lee?"

Spider adjusted the umbrella to maximize the late afternoon shade and then sat down opposite. "Several reasons. First, he didn't deny it until I told him there was no way that Linda could have killed Austin."

"I don't understand. Why is that a reason to believe him?"

Spider took out his sandwich. "He thought she did it. He was trying to protect her by letting them blame him. He couldn't have done it if he believed she did it."

Laurie cast her eyes up as she chewed, obviously going through his logic. "Okay. But why did he believe she did it?"

"Because he knew she had gone to Austin's house the morning he was murdered. Remember when I told them Austin was dead?"

"Yeah. He passed out. I thought that was kind of wussy." Laurie licked some mayonnaise off her fingers.

"He had just put two and two together. Austin was dead, and she had been to his house the morning he died.

Boom, over he goes. Add to that the murder weapon appearing at the museum, and he knows he didn't put it there."

"So, he thinks she did it, and she thinks he did it?"

"Yeah. She knew he was mad as hell when he found out that Austin tried to rape her."

Laurie almost choked on a bite of sandwich. "What? I didn't know about that. How do you know it?"

"She told me. That's when she called it quits. Austin didn't dump her; she dumped him."

"So how did Matt find out that Austin tried to rape her?"

Spider finished chewing before he answered. "When they were sitting with me Sunday morning, he told her he was sorry about the Tiffany thing and that he was a dope. Since they were clearing the air, she told him about Austin. He didn't take it well."

"I don't imagine he did. So he went to St. George to give Austin a knuckle sandwich, and she followed him there?"

"Yeah." Spider opened a bag of chips. "She didn't see Matt in St. George, but she was pretty sure that was where he went. So when she went into Austin's house and found the body, she thought he did it. Especially since the weapon was an Anasazi ax."

"How do you know she couldn't have done it?"

"Whoever hit Austin that first blow was left handed."

Laurie was silent a moment. Then she sighed. "Is Jack right or left handed?"

Spider crunched one of his chips. "I don't know. What hand did he flip the hamburgers with?"

"I can't remember. What about Amy?" Laurie considered. "Is she big enough? She's stout but not very tall."

"She'd need the element of surprise for the blow to the temple," Spider said. "After that, he'd be down, so it wouldn't matter what size someone was while they were bashing in his skull."

"What about Tiffany?"

"Motivation?"

"I don't know."

Laurie wrapped up the second half of her sandwich. "I can't eat this right now. Let's go up to Jack's and get the whole thing out in the open."

"All right." Spider loosely rolled his sandwich in waxed paper and picked up his soft drink. "You drive. You may not be able to eat right now, but I'm hungry."

They got in the pickup, and Laurie drove while Spider finished his sandwich. He crumpled up the paper and put it in the litter bag as she pulled in beside Jack's yellow Mustang parked in front of the house.

"Looks like he's home," Spider said. He took a hasty swig from his Pepsi, got out, and waited for Laurie. They walked together to the front door, and Spider rang the bell. There was no answer, and they could hear no movement inside.

"Maybe he went somewhere in the pickup," Laurie said.

"Maybe he hasn't come home from wherever he went on Sunday."

Laurie peeked through the sidelight into the living room. "We don't know it was him there on Sunday. It could have been Amy." She tilted her head. "Listen. Did you hear that?"

"Hear what?"

"Shh." She held up her finger. "Did someone say, 'Come out back?'"

"I don't know. We can try it and see." He looked one way and the next. "Which way do we go around?"

"This way." Laurie led him across to a covered breezeway separating the house from the triple car garage. Tiles on the breezeway floor melded into the hardscape that covered most of the back yard, and they walked across it to the covered patio where they'd had lunch a week ago.

"Jack?" Laurie looked around the shady area.

"Over here."

They both looked toward the sound. Jack lay on a chaise lounge under a light fleece blanket. His eyes were sunken, and his skin had a grayish tinge to it. "Hello," he said, holding out a trembling hand. "I didn't know if you could hear me or not."

"Jack!" Laurie sat in a chair beside him and took his hand in hers. "Are you all right?"

Jack moistened his lips with his tongue. "I could do with a drink of water."

Laurie looked up at Spider. "Here. Hold his hand. I'll go get it."

Before Spider could volunteer for the errand, Laurie grabbed him, pulled him over, and sat him down in her place. Then she placed Jack's limp hand in Spider's.

"I'll be back in a minute." She spoke over her shoulder as she trotted to the door to the living room.

Spider looked at the hand he held and then looked at Jack, lying with his eyes closed.

"You're a good man, Spider," Jack murmured. His eyes opened, and his lips curved into a half smile. "I was just yankin' your chain every time I called you Spencer." His eyes closed again, and the smile faded. "I'm glad to have some time alone with you. I've seen that you're a good man to have around in difficult times, and what I've done is because of that, not because of Laurie."

Spider frowned. "I don't understand. What have you done?"

Jack licked his lips again. "Were you going to get me some water?"

At that moment, Laurie came through the kitchen door carrying the soft drink cup that had been in the pickup with the rest of Spider's Pepsi in it. "I rinsed it out," she said to Spider as she carried it by. To Jack she said, "I thought it would be easier for you to drink out of a straw."

"You're an angel," he said, letting go Spider's hand to take the cup.

Spider took the opportunity to slip out of the chair. He motioned to Laurie to take the seat while he moved to one farther away.

Laurie took the cup when Jack had taken a sip. She set it on a nearby table and smoothed back his hair. "What happened, Jack? Did you get sick?"

"It's a bad spell." He spoke in a reedy voice, just above a whisper. "I get them every now and then. Part of the old problem."

"Who's taking care of you?" Laurie looked around. "Where's Amy?"

"She's not here."

Spider sat forward. "She didn't perchance take the pickup and horse trailer and drive over to St. George on Sunday, did she?"

Jack slowly rolled his head from side to side. "I did."

Spider scooted his chair closer. "You drove the pickup and trailer on Sunday? You musta been feeling better then than you are today."

Jack nodded. "It just about finished me off, but I made the trip to Vegas and back in one day. It's hotter than the hubs of hell over there."

Spider and Laurie looked at each other. "Wait," she said. "You weren't going to St. George? You were going to Las Vegas?"

"Yeah." Jack reached for the water, and Laurie gave it to him. He lifted his head and brought the straw to his lips with a shaking hand. "I stopped for gas in St. George, but then I kept on going." He lay back down but kept the cup, resting it on his stomach.

"Why did you go to Las Vegas?" Laurie asked.

Jack's eyes rested on Spider. "Because of something Spider said to me Saturday morning after the pancake breakfast."

Laurie looked at Spider, and he raised his shoulders in an I-don't-know gesture.

"He said I needed to protect Amy from Austin Lee."

Spider's heart sank. Oh, geez. What do you do when someone who's dying confesses to murder?

Laurie had the presence of mind to ask the next question. "How did you do that, Jack?"

"I took her over to a mental health facility in the

mountains outside of Vegas. Very posh. Very earthy. We took Taffy, and she'll go out riding every day. They're going to look at adjusting her meds, and they're going to talk to her about healthy relationships." Jack paused and took several shallow breaths. "I figure she can stay there a month or two, and by that time, Austin will have moved on to someone else."

Laurie took Jack's hand. "Austin is dead. Someone killed him on Sunday."

Jack blinked. The half-smile returned to his lips. "Is that what the questions were about?"

Spider wasn't sure whether Jack was putting on an act or not. He certainly looked like death warmed over. If he had made a ten hour round trip three days ago pulling a horse trailer, he had gone downhill in a hurry. Or maybe he hadn't been in the truck at all. Maybe that was Amy. Maybe Jack knew Amy had killed Austin, and he was trying to deflect blame. "What's the name of the place where Amy is now?"

"Mountain Hollow Residential Care." Jack waved a weak hand toward the kitchen. "There's a card with the information on the counter."

"Will they be able to vouch for the time you arrived?" Laurie asked.

"They'll tell Spider," Jack rasped. "His name is listed as someone they can give information to."

Spider's eyebrows shot up. "Me? Why?"

Jack closed his eyes and didn't answer. Spider waited a moment and then went to the kitchen. The business card was on the counter. Alongside it was a card for Lucky's Horseshoeing in Hurricane. There were also cards for Southern Utah Hospice, Fordham Mortuary, and Major Smith, attorney at law.

Spider took out his phone and bent over to read the Mountain Hollow information. He dialed the number, and a crisp-voiced receptionist answered. After giving his name, he asked what time Jack Houghten and Amy Scott arrived on Sunday. The receptionist put him on hold for a moment and then said that they arrived at noon on Sunday.

Spider did some calculation from the time they were at the intersection. He didn't know whether to be relieved or not to find that Jack's story held up. He slid the card to the back of the counter by the others, and on an impulse, slipped the farrier's card in his shirt pocket.

Then he returned to the patio.

Laurie looked up as he stepped through the kitchen door. She said something softly to Jack and went to meet him. "I think we need to stay here with him," she whispered.

"What? Stay here with Jack? Why?"

"Keep your voice down. He's very weak, and he hasn't got anyone to take care of him."

"There's a card—"

"Shh. Whisper."

Spider whispered. "There's a card for hospice care on the counter. Call them."

"Spider!" Laurie opened the kitchen door and pulled him in, closing it behind her.

Spider spoke in a normal tone. "I'm serious, Laurie. We've got a man in jail that needs our best efforts to find a way to get him out. What do we tell him? Oh, I've got to tend to my sick fourth cousin who, by the way, was well enough to drive ten hours three days ago?"

"The man in jail needs Spider Latham's best efforts. I'm not telling you to quit that. You're the one Brick Tremain hired for the job, so go do it." She put her hands on her hips. "But I'm staying here, and I'm taking care of Jack."

Spider looked down at her and smiled. "Dang but you're cute when you go all righteous indignation on me."

He reached to pull her closer. She stepped back, though a smile was threatening. "Get that look out of your eye," she warned, "because you're going to be sleeping alone at the hotel while I'm sleeping over here."

Spider threw up his hands in surrender. "I'll go get the bags."

"You might as well just check out and bring everything over. We'll stay here for the next few days until—" She looked away.

Spider gathered her in his arms, and this time she didn't resist. "I'm sure it's not that bad. He was just singing with you four days ago. Remember?"

She sighed. "It seems like a lifetime ago. So much has happened."

"Yeah, and so much has yet to happen. We've got to pull a rabbit out of a hat."

They both jumped when Spider's phone beeped. She stepped away, and he pulled it out and checked a text from Marshal Thayne.

"He says he's got the gate log," Spider told her. "And guess what? Tiffany Wendt spent Saturday night in beautiful Defrain Estates."

Chapter 29

◆

THE NEXT MORNING found Spider watching the sunrise in his rearview mirror, intent on making it to Hurricane, Utah, before Tiffany Wendt had a chance to leave the el cheapo hotel where she was staying. The night before, Spider had talked to Tiffany's friend in Fredonia. She said Tiffany had left the area, so Spider and Laurie had spent an hour sitting on Jack's patio, calling a list culled from the Internet. Spider soon grew weary of asking the same question over and over, but Laurie persisted and found Tiffany at an older place in the downtown area. The motel name sounded familiar to Spider, and when he arrived, he recognized it as a place the basketball team had stayed when he was in High School. It looked like it had had minimal upkeep since that time.

The red convertible was parked in front of room 105. Spider pulled in beside it and checked his watch. Eight o'clock. Tiffany was probably still in bed. Should he knock on the door or wait until she came out? What if she slept until noon? Better operate on his own timetable.

He got out and walked to the door, noticing as he came closer that the bright blue paint was peeling from both the door and the doorjamb. He knocked and waited, but no one answered. He knocked harder and then rubbed his knuckles against his pant leg to take away the sting. After a moment he heard what sounded like something falling to the floor and someone called, "What? Who is it?"

Spider didn't answer but knocked again. He wasn't going to have this conversation through a motel room door.

"All right. All right. I'm coming. Keep your shirt on."

Spider waited a few moments more. He had just raised his fist to knock again when he heard the door knob turn. The door opened a crack.

A tousled Tiffany Wendt peeked through with one mascara-smudged eye. "Do I know you?"

"I don't think we've been introduced. I saw you at the museum in Fredonia when I was there talking to Matt Taylor."

"Oh." Her disinterest was palpable.

Spider edged the toe of his boot toward the crack in the door. "I'd like to talk to you a minute. Maybe I could buy you breakfast?"

That seemed to be the magic word. The crack became larger, revealing a bare shoulder and Tiffany's hand holding the bedspread wrapped around her. Spider kept his eyes on her face. "How fast can you get ready?"

"Does breakfast depend on my speed?"

"Yes. How about ten minutes?"

She grimaced. "I don't guarantee the results."

"I'll chance it. See you in ten."

The door closed, and Spider sat on a nearby bench, enjoying the cool of the morning. He took out his phone, and as he did so, the farrier's business card fell out. After picking it up, he stared at it, flicking it with his index finger as he considered. Finally, with no real reason to do so except a niggling in the back of his mind, he called the number.

A woman answered and in response to Spider's inquiry said her husband was the farrier, but he was gone until ten. Spider made an appointment, wrote the time on the back of the card, and sat back to wait for Tiffany.

It took her fifteen minutes to dress, but the results were tolerable. She wore a pair of good-looking slacks and a turquoise blouse, with large hoop earrings of the same color dangling from her ears.

"There's a restaurant a block down the street," Spider said when she emerged from the room. "Shall we walk?"

She fell into step beside him. "What happened to your eye?"

Spider touched the area around his cheekbone. He had forgotten to wear his sunglasses. "I fell afoul of Austin Lee."

She sucked in a breath and stopped in her tracks, staring at him with eyes as big as her hoop earrings. "Why did you say that?"

She had grown so pale that Spider reached out and took her arm. "Because it's true. He had somebody plant a bomb in the car I was driving. You need to be careful about the people you hang around with."

She shook his hand off and continued walking. "I don't suppose you said anything when Little Earth Mother at the museum was dating him."

"Actually, I wasn't around when that happened."

"You're lucky." She continued walking without saying anything until they reached the restaurant, but as he opened the door, she said, "You know he's dead, don't you?"

"Yeah. That's what I want to talk to you about."

Her eyes cut to the door, and Spider stepped between her and an easy exit.

"I'm just interested in information. They've got Matt Taylor in jail for Austin's murder, but I don't think he did it."

"Matt? Kill Austin? You've got to be kidding."

Obeying the sign that asked them to sit wherever they wanted, Spider chose a corner booth and slid in over the slick plastic upholstery. He picked up one of the menus that sat behind the sugar holder and gave it to Tiffany.

"I think you might be one of the last people to see Austin alive. Can I ask you some questions?"

"I remember you now," Tiffany said. "You were at the museum when I came by to pick up Matt one day. Was that your wife that was with you? She could be a stunner, if she just wore a little more makeup."

Spider paused as the waitress took their orders. Ham and eggs for him, the same for her but with two orders of toast. And coffee. Lots and lots of coffee.

"Okay," Spider said when the waitress was gone. "Once again. Can I ask you some questions about Austin?"

"You can ask, but I won't guarantee I'll answer."

"Well, oftentimes it turns out that it's better to

answer in an informal situation like now rather than be subpoenaed to have to testify in court. When that happens, you either answer, or you're cited for contempt."

Tiffany unwrapped some silverware from a paper napkin. "Is that a threat?"

Spider shook his head. "Statement of fact. I can almost guarantee that if Matt goes on trial, you'll be called to testify."

"Because you'll make sure of it?"

"Because your name is in the gatehouse log as probably the last person to see Austin."

"Alive. You said before I was the last person to see him alive."

"Was he alive when you last saw him?"

Tiffany gave a sly smile. "Oh, boy. Was he ever!"

"Tell me about when you left him."

"What's to tell? We spent a beautiful night together. Makes me wonder why I spent so much time and energy trying to land the upright and chaste Matt Taylor."

"Trying to land him?"

"Marry him."

"Why did you? You and Austin seem better matched."

She smiled and batted her eyelashes. "You think so?"

"Yeah. So what was with Matt?"

Tiffany leaned on an elbow. "I don't know. I remembered him all these years, ever since high school. He seemed so in control, so manly. Always driving his pickup into the schoolyard like he owned the hills, but he'd come spend time with us lesser mortals. He was the strong, silent type, and I'd have given anything to be his girl."

"Did he have a girl?"

Tiffany shook her head. "And now I know why. He hasn't a clue about how to treat a woman. His idea of a great date is to drag her up a canyon to look at some rocks."

"But you remembered him, and that's why you came back from California after your divorce?"

"Yeah. First I looked him up on the Internet and found out he was single. Assistant Director of a museum. That sounded like a pretty secure job. Boy was I wrong."

"So why did you tell him you were going to donate all that money?"

"I said that early on, when I was still seeing him through high-school glasses. It was an impulse. I wanted to help him, and the words just came out. Then I didn't know how to get out of it."

"I imagine you were glad when Matt found out."

"I almost did cartwheels. Especially since I knew that Austin and Linda weren't an item any longer."

The waitress brought their order, and Spider intended to continue talking, but Tiffany was eating so hungrily that he let her get through her breakfast before he picked up the subject again.

He watched as she wrapped her second order of toast in her napkin and stowed it in her purse. "Insurance," she said.

"Can we go back to Austin?" he asked.

Tiffany closed her eyes. "It's like one of those romance novels. He was so beautiful. So rich. I spent one night with him, and then he died." She sighed and opened her eyes. "I'll go to my grave with him imprinted on my heart."

"Well, he went to his grave with some imprints, too," Spider said dryly. When she looked questioningly at him, he said, "Never mind. I want you to tell me about your parting. What happened when you left his house? Who saw you leave?"

"Mmm." Tiffany smiled, showing her even, white teeth. "The good-bye was delicious." She almost purred. "He kissed me on the doorstep, and he walked me to my car. He kissed me again and kind of pressed me against the car, if you know what I mean? And he whispered such things that I almost didn't leave."

"And why did you leave?"

Tiffany looked at her fingernails. "He said he had some work to do. He'd be busy all day."

"It was Sunday."

"Was it? He said it was something about the land development. He had an office in his house."

"So, when you drove away, did you see anyone? Someone walking on the sidewalk or in their yard? Another car driving by? Anything?"

She shook her head and spread her hand on her chest. "I was watching Austin in the rearview mirror. I'll remember that image until I die."

Spider caught the eye of the waitress and signaled for the check. "Can I ask you a few questions about your ex-husband?"

"Wendell? What do you want to ask?"

"Is he the jealous type?"

Tiffany's mouth dropped open, and Spider could almost see the wheels turning as she figured out where this line of questioning would lead. "You think Wendell might have murdered Austin because he was jealous?"

"It's a thought."

She giggled. "That's the funniest thing I've heard in a long time."

"What makes it so funny?"

"Wendell takes the Ten Commandments very seriously. Thou shalt not kill. Thou shalt not commit adultery. That's why he divorced me."

"So there was another man involved?"

"How do you think I came up with that red car? Unfortunately, he died on me."

"The family is saying you stole it."

"Hard to do when it was in my own name."

Spider felt things were getting away from him. "Okay, back to Wendell. I understand he's a truck driver."

She cocked her head to the side. "I guess you could say that. He does drive a truck. What he does is service porta potties all around Modesto."

"So you can't see him coming over and killing Austin?"

"I can't see him driving that far on a Sunday. He's very strict about such things."

The waitress brought the check, and Spider slid out of the booth to go to the cash register.

"Do you want your leftover toast?"

Spider looked around and saw the triangular pieces disappear into Tiffany's purse. "No. You go ahead."

He paid the check, and they left, walking side by side back to the hotel. "Things are pretty lean, are they?" he asked.

"I'll be all right," she said. "I've got enough money to get to Las Vegas. I figure I might do okay there."

Spider shook his head. "You'd have a better chance

in St. George. Lots of wealthy people come here to retire. Some of them end up widowers and are looking for company. Less competition than in Vegas."

"But no excitement."

"Sometimes no excitement is a good thing. By the way, how did you find out about Austin being dead?"

"I drove up to see him Monday, about noon. The place was crawling with cops, and they had yellow tape all over the place. I just kept on going. On the way down I asked at the gate what was wrong. The guy there said somebody had died."

"Huh." They'd reached the motel. Spider walked her to her room, took out his phone and tapped an icon. "Can I have you do something for me? Will you call me on your cell phone, so I can have your number in my address book?"

"I'll just tell it to you," she said.

He smiled a self-deprecating smile. "I'm so slow at keying in stuff, we'd be here all morning. If you'll just call me, it will go faster." He turned the screen, so she could see his number.

She pulled out her cell and punched the buttons. "Not only that, but it eliminates the risk of me giving you a bogus number."

Spider's cell rang. He answered it, disconnected, and then added the new contact. "There is that."

There was also the fact that he had just remembered something that hadn't registered while he watched her eat breakfast. He wanted her to key in the numbers, so he could test his recollection.

Sure enough, when she tapped in Spider's number, Tiffany used her left hand.

Chapter 30

♦

SPIDER LEFT TIFFANY at the door to Room 105. He got in the pickup and drove to the city park, pulling over at a shady spot beside the curb, so he could think.

So far, Tiffany was the last person to see Austin alive. Add to that fact her last lover died while they were in a relationship. And, she was left handed. But the wounds on Austin's head indicated a crime of passion. Talking to Tiffany, it sounded like she was in the throes of love's first bloom. No discontent there, unless she was a very good actress. But hadn't LaJean said she was a good actress? Never put a foot wrong, she'd said. Hmm.

Spider took out his phone and dialed Marshal Thayne. He picked up on the second ring.

"Morning, Marshal. I've been over here visiting with Tiffany Wendt. I've got a couple more things I'd like you to chase down." Spider waited for him to get something to write on and then went on. "Tiffany was apparently taking care of an older fellow, and he died. Yes, it was in the Modesto area. What I need to know, was there anything suspicious about the fellow's death? If you talk to Neva, she has a sheet of paper that has the fellow's name on it. It's stuff Karam Mansour got for her."

The marshal said he had something to pass on, and Spider pulled out his notebook and pen. "Go ahead," he said, jotting down the information as it was given. "So, Wendell was in church all day? Okay, then. Don't worry about finding out if he was left handed. But if you can get that other information soon, that would be great."

He rang off and thought some more. Tiffany wasn't the physical type. Would she expend the energy to beat someone to death? He could see her poisoning someone but battering them with a blunt instrument? And then there was the issue of money. Tiffany couldn't afford to feed herself, but the police said that Austin had a wallet full of money when he died. They'd ruled out robbery as a motive. Hmm.

The sound of his phone ringing broke his train of thought. He saw it was Laurie and answered it. "Hi, Darlin'. How's it going?"

"Oh, Spider." Her voice broke. "It's not going well."

"What's the matter? Tell me."

There was the sound of her blowing her nose. "We've just come back from the doctor. Why don't they make house calls anymore? It's cruel and unusual punishment making us drag these poor people out and making them sit in a clinic."

"What did the doctor say?"

"That he was too sick to be up." She laughed a damp little laugh. "I knew that, but how was I going to get him seen? Actually, when I got him there, they took him in and let him lie down in one of the examining rooms to wait."

"Are you sure you want to get back in that harness, Darlin'?"

"What harness? Oh, you mean taking care of some-one?" She cleared her throat. "This one isn't going to go on for years like your mom."

"Oh? How long?"

Laurie's answer came out in a breathy whisper. "Days."

Spider whistled. "Did you mention to the doctor that he drove a horse trailer to Vegas on Sunday?"

"Yes I did. He said that was not unusual, that some-one who's dying does something heroic just before the end. If it's for someone they care for, it's like the spirit takes over and does what the body doesn't have strength to do."

"Are you home now?"

"Yes. They sent a home health nurse back with me, and we've got Jack back to bed. He insists on being on the patio, and that's fine. They've got hospice lined up to help out."

"How's he doing?"

Laurie cleared her throat again, and her voice rose in pitch, like she was on the verge of tears. "He's slipped into something like a coma. It looks like he's sleeping, but I can't wake him up to feed him or give him some-thing to drink."

"Well, Darlin', I'm sorry you've got to carry this load."

"I'm just glad I can be here to help him. Though people have been lining up at the door with food and other offers to help. They each have a story about how Jack stepped in when they had no way to turn and helped them out." She blew her nose again. "How are things going there?"

"It's like one of those ropes with three ends. I'm busy trying to find out which two are really supposed to be there."

"Well, good luck. I'm back to my nursing."

"Good luck to you, Darlin'. I'll be back this evening."

Spider disconnected and looked at his watch. He was ten minutes away from his appointment with the farrier. He pulled out the business card and keyed the address in. Daisuke would've been proud.

The farrier lived just off the highway between Hurricane and LaVerkin in a green little glen surrounded by black basalt cliffs. Spider drove in and pulled around back to where a pickup with *Lucky's Horseshoeing* on the door sat in front of a barn.

He got out and stood for a moment, wondering where the farrier was. Hearing a door open behind him, he turned. A tall, lean man wearing a leather apron came out the back door with a coffee cup in his hand.

"Mornin'," Spider said. "I've got an appointment. Name's Spider Latham."

"Spider, you say? I thought my wife had written it down wrong. I'm Lucky." He came down the porch stairs and offered his hand. "Coffee?"

Spider clasped the calloused hand. "No, thanks."

Lucky glanced at Spider's pickup. "You didn't bring your horse?"

"I just need to talk. You got a place where we can sit? I won't take much of your time."

"I got some chairs under that willow. That do?" Lucky led the way to where two wicker rockers sat on a shady flagstone patio. He sank into one and indicated the other with his coffee cup. "What can I do you for?"

"I'd like to talk to you about a horse with a mal-formed hoof."

Lucky nodded. "I seen a few of those."

"It's a mare, and it's her front off-side hoof. It makes it so she throws it out, just a bit."

Lucky nodded again. "Yeah, yeah. I'd need to see it, but you can help it a lot with the proper shoe."

"I'm talking about Jack Houghton's buckskin mare. I believe you order in special shoes for her?"

"I know the horse. Best mannered little mare I seen in a long time. Whoever trained her done a good job."

"My wife trained her," Spider said. "We owned her before Jack and had our local man over in Lincoln County shoe her. He didn't know about the special shoes."

"That's Rick Owens? He's a good man but set in his ways." Lucky took a sip of his coffee. "You know, I seen another mare just like Jack's buckskin. Off-side front. Same shape hoof. Came in last week. What day was it? Friday? Yeah, Friday."

Spider's heart began to beat and his mouth went dry. "Was it a Palomino?

"Yeah. Owned by a redheaded gal. Said she heard from someone about the special shoes I got for Jack's buckskin."

"Is her name Dorrie Coleman?"

"Yeah, that's the one."

"I'm the one that told her about Jack's horse, or my wife was, anyway. I wanted to know if she got hold of you."

"Why'nt you ask her?"

"I was going to, but last time I saw her, she was in

the process of moving, and she didn't remember her new address."

Lucky cocked his head, eying Spider. "Well, that's kind of peculiar."

"Not really. She told me how to get there, sorta, but she didn't remember the number. I don't suppose you've got it?"

Lucky grimaced. "I've got it, but I don't know that I should give it to you."

"Under regular circumstances, I'd say so, too, but look." Spider pulled out his wallet and opened it to his badge. "I'm deputy sheriff over in Lincoln County. I'm not here on county business. I'm just showing you this to let you know I'm not flaky. A mutual friend just died, and I want to go let Dorrie know."

Lucky raised his cup to his lips and looked at Spider over the rim before taking a sip. "You said your wife trained that buckskin mare?"

"Yeah, she did. Taffy was the second foal born with that deformity. Dorrie's palomino was the first. When we arrived at the ranch looking to buy a horse, the owner had just put the mother down. He was getting ready to put down the baby, but Laurie talked him out of it. We took her home and raised her on the bottle."

"Why'd you sell her?"

"Times got hard in Lincoln County." Spider paused. Would he ever be able to talk about those lean, scraping-by times without his voice going all funny? He cleared his throat. "Jack is Laurie's cousin. He heard we had to sell Taffy. He bought her."

Lucky nodded. "Been through times like that myself.

Give me a minute." He stood and walked to the house, disappearing inside the back door.

Spider looked around at the neatly kept place. A small rust-red barn, spiffy with white trim, stood beside a corral. Beyond, he saw rows of pole beans and a stand of corn with yellow tassels looking like sparklers. Hearing Lucky's approaching footsteps, he turned. "You've got a nice looking place, here."

"My wife sees to it," Lucky said, handing Spider a piece of paper torn off the back of a used envelope. "Here's Dorrie's address. I guess she's setting up to board horses."

"Yeah. I haven't seen her place yet, but she said it'd suit her. Thanks for this." He shook hands and Spider walked back to his pickup.

As he opened the door, Lucky called to him, "I'm sorry about the friend. It's good of you to go tell her."

"She may already know," Spider said, climbing into the cab. He started the truck and headed back to the highway, muttering to himself, "That's what I'm about to find out."

Chapter 31

◆

DORRIE SAID HER place would do her fine, and it looked like it would. A small single wide mobile home sat on the edge of the property, a sop to the necessity of a place to sleep and eat. A line of eight stalls buttressed the left side of a gravel parking area with a barn and hay storage on the center edge and a huge covered arena dominating the right.

When Spider pulled in, Goldie, the palomino, stuck her head out the window of the first stall, and Trey emerged from under the mobile home porch. There was no sign of Dorrie.

Spider parked under a cottonwood tree that shaded the area beside the trailer and got out. He crouched down to greet the three-legged dog as she hopped over to him. Scratching her under the ears he asked, "Where's your mistress? Where's Dorrie?"

When Spider stood, Trey hobbled over to a stand-pipe that had a bone-dry water dish sitting under it. She looked back at him and whined.

"Do you need some water?" Spider walked to the faucet and turned it on, filling the dish. An automatic dog feeder sat under the tree, and Spider noted that there was food in the bottom.

As Trey lapped, Spider put in more water, and over the sound of the splashing, he heard Goldie whicker. He glanced toward the stables and saw her stretching her head toward him. The hair on the back of his neck prickled. "This doesn't look good," he muttered.

He didn't know whether to go to the horse stall first or try the trailer, but he was betting the horse was thirsty, so he headed for the stable.

Her water trough was dry. This was looking worse and worse.

The outbuilding was plumbed with a faucet in each stall over the trough, so it was a matter of turning on the tap. As water poured down, and Goldie crowded him to get to it, he looked around. Piles of manure littered the sawdust-covered floor, but that could be cleaned later. Spider put several inches of water in the basin and left Goldie sucking it up while he went in search of some hay. He found a bale in the next stall and pulled off a couple of slabs to throw in the mare's manger.

On his way to the trailer, Spider tried to push away the feeling of dread that hovered over him like a black monsoon thunderhead. As he reached the porch steps, Trey followed him to the top, whining and scratching at the door. "Steady, girl," he murmured. "Everything's going to be all right."

Not believing his own words, Spider rapped on the door. "Dorrie," he called. "It's me, Spider Latham."

Silence.

Spider's chest tightened, and his palms started to sweat. Should he call the police? Not yet. Better find out the lay of the land first. He pounded on the door again. "Dorrie! Open up!"

He stood on the porch, wondering what to do next, when he heard a sound from inside. Just a tiny sound, like someone shifted their weight. Spider grabbed the doorknob and turned it. "I'm coming in," he shouted, and he opened the door.

The interior was dim because the shades were drawn. The evaporative cooler seemed to be working well, and the air felt moist and comfortable. Spider stepped in and looked around, and what he saw on the couch made him draw in a breath.

Dorrie sat there, staring at him out of eyes that were dark, sunken pools. Her hair lay in a rusty mat atop what looked like a skull with freckled wallpaper stretched over it. When Trey hopped over to her and nuzzled her hand, she didn't respond.

"Dorrie?" Spider was relieved to see her eyes shift ever so slightly when he said her name. He stepped to the kitchen area and started opening cupboards. "You look like you haven't had a drink in days." He found a glass and put a bit of water in the bottom.

"Here you go." He carried it to the couch and crouched down in front of her. "Just a bit at first. Don't want to overdo it." He held the glass to her lips and watched in relief as she swallowed the water. "Good girl. I'll give you some more in a minute."

As he took the glass from her, he noticed a brown discoloration along the palm and heel of her left hand. Gently opening her fist, so he could get a better look, he traced around the stain with his finger. He looked up and met her eyes.

Her lips moved, but no sound came out.

"You can talk in a bit. Let's get you something with calories in it." He stood and went to the refrigerator, holding the door open while he perused the contents. Milk? Not enough sugar. Yogurt? Ditto. Apple juice? Bingo. He grabbed the juice and a bottle of sports drink and carried them both to the couch. Mixing a cocktail of the two, he handed her the tumbler. "Drink just a bit," he said.

Her hands trembled as she brought the glass to her lips, but she downed a couple inches.

Spider took the drink from her. "Let's wait a minute, see if that stays down. Now, what were you trying to say?"

She licked her lips, and the word came out in a croak. "Austin." She turned her left palm up on her lap and pointed at the rusty stain. "His blood." A single tear seeped out and ran down her cheek.

Spider gave her the juice cocktail and watched while she took another hefty drink. "You been sitting here since Sunday morning?"

She nodded as she held the glass in her lap with both hands.

"You been hoping to die?"

She finished off the juice and wiped her mouth with her hand. She looked up at him and nodded again.

He crouched by her and took her hands. "You want to talk about it?"

"I went to see him Sunday morning," she said in a voice that was little more than a stage whisper. "I found out where he lived, and I rode Goldie there to surprise him."

Spider squeezed her hands. "Okay, Dorrie, before you go on I want to tell you that if a policeman asks me about what you're telling me right now, I'll have to tell him what you said."

"Don't worry. I'm going to tell him myself."

"All right. Let me get something to sit on, and then you can tell me the rest." He dragged one of the kitchen chairs over and sat in front of Dorrie. "Go on. Take your time."

She drew in a breath and exhaled a ragged sigh. "I got there about nine o'clock. I was just coming around the garage when the front door opened and this...this woman came out."

Spider didn't try to fill the silence as she paused. He sat, elbows on knees and hands clasped, as he waited for her to go on.

"The woman was hanging all over him, acting like a floozy. She had on tight britches and high heels. Drove a fancy red car. She kissed him and petted him, and he kissed her back. Then she finally left."

Spider picked up one of her hands again. "What were you thinking as you were watching them?"

"I was thinking that wasn't Austin. He wasn't like that. She had lured him into evil ways." Dorrie licked her lips. "Could I have some more water?"

"Sure." Spider took her glass to the sink and filled it half full this time. He carried it back and handed it to her, noticing she was able to hold it in one hand. He sat down and asked, "So, what did you do after she left?"

"I waited a bit after he went in the house, trying to get over what I just seen. Then I remembered that time he said he loved me. That made me strong, so I went and rang the doorbell."

"What happened then?"

Dorrie laughed. It was a wry, sad-sounding laugh, almost a sob. "I was trying to surprise him, and I guess I done that. But he didn't act like it was a nice surprise. He said what was I doing there, and his voice was hard, you know? Like how my papa talked to a lazy ranch hand."

"Yeah, I know. He talked to me that way one day, too."

"Did he? I didn't know he could be like that."

"What did you do then?"

"I told him I missed him. I said I wanted it to be like when he'd come out to the ranch, and we'd go riding or just sit on the porch of an evening. I told him I wanted to be his girl again."

Spider's face screwed up in pain. "Oh, Dorrie." He couldn't bear to think of her laying herself open to the hurt that Austin would and could dish out without a moment's thought.

"He called me a cow." Dorrie's voice was stronger now. "Said I was ugly as a plate full of worms. Said I was dumb. I can't remember all the things he called me. What I do remember is the look on his face." She slowly wagged her head from side to side. "I wanted to wipe that look off his face for good."

"And did you?"

"I did. It happened without me even thinking about it." She chewed on her lip for a moment. "There was this rock thing hanging on the wall. I grabbed it quicker than he could think, and I caught him right over the eye. Kind of where that scab is on your face."

Spider touched his temple. "And after you knocked him down?"

Dorrie covered her face with her freckled, sun-bronzed hands. "I think I went a bit crazy." She let her hands slide down her cheeks and cocked her head, as if pulling something from memory. "It felt so good just to bash and bash and bash. I kept thinking, 'I may be a cow. I may be ugly. I may be dumb. But. You. Are. Dead.'"

Spider rubbed his jaw. "Okay, Dorrie. Let's talk. You're saying you want to tell this to the police yourself?"

She nodded. "But before that, I got to do something about Goldie and Trey."

Spider poured another half glass of apple juice and handed it to her. "You got family that can take them?"

She shook her head. "Before Papa died it was just me and him. Now it's just me."

"Well, you can sell Goldie and send Trey to the pound, or Laurie and I will take care of them until you can take them back."

Her eyes fixed on Spider's. "Would you do that?"

"Would you trust them to us?"

"Well, yes. Of course. Remember when Trey went to Laurie? She's never done that." Dorrie took a deep breath and exhaled. "I feel lighter, like I just got rid of a heavy load."

"You've done a good deed, too, Dorrie. Another man is in jail, accused of killing Austin. He can go free now." He took his phone out of his pocket and pulled up Toby's number. "I'm going outside for a minute and call a deputy from over in Kanab. He'll come and get you. He's a pretty good fellow, and he'll treat you well."

Spider stepped out on the porch and closed the door. He dialed Toby's number, and the deputy answered on the third ring. "Hi, Toby. Spider here. Where are you? St. George? Great. Listen. Tell Sergeant Whipple to start on release papers for Matt Taylor. Why? Because you're going to bring in Austin Lee's real killer. I'll tell you about it when you get here." Spider pulled the piece of envelope out of his pocket and read the address for Toby. "See you in about twenty minutes? Fine."

Spider rang off and went back in the trailer. Dorrie was standing, drinking out of the apple juice bottle.

"I'm feeling stronger," she said. "Lighter and stronger. Now, if you'll help me, I'd like to go see Goldie."

Chapter 32

◆

As SPIDER DROVE up Jack's driveway, the shadows of the poplar trees looked like dark chocolate that had melted and run in the late afternoon sun. The dusky image of his pickup and Dorrie's horse trailer was elongated and cartoonish, too.

The pickup's shadow dropped behind as Spider made the turn behind the trees and drove to the paved circular drive. Braking suddenly, he slowly pulled around the gray hearse that was backed up to Jack's door. "That doesn't look good, Trey girl," he said to the dog on the seat beside him.

Driving around the house, he pulled up in front of the barn, setting the brake before he got out. He held the door open and called to the dog. "Let's go see what's happened in there. A lot of sadness going around today, I think."

Trey scrambled down. Spider closed the pickup door and headed across the gravel to the back of the house where the paved patio began. When he got to the sliding glass door, he told the dog to stay.

No one was in the living room when Spider stepped inside, but he heard voices from the kitchen. Walking to the doorway, he leaned a shoulder against the framework to observe. Laurie sat at the head of the table, frowning at a piece of paper in her hand. A silver haired man in a dark suit sat on one side of the table, and a youngish fellow in cargo shorts and sandals sat on the other. A stack of papers sat in the middle of the table.

Laurie looked up, and her face broke into a smile when she saw Spider. "Hello," she said. "I'm so glad you're here."

The younger man stood. "Are you Mr. Latham? I'm glad to meet you." He grasped Spider's arm above the elbow as he shook his hand as if to emphasize his pleasure. "I'm Major Smith."

Spider took off his Stetson. "Glad to meet you, Major."

"Mr. Smith is Jack's attorney," Laurie explained.

"Oh. Are you in the reserves?"

"I'm not in the service. Major is my name, not my rank."

"Ah. Sorry." Spider looked at the silver haired gentleman, also standing.

"I'm Bernard Fordham. Fordham's Funeral Home."

"I saw the hearse," Spider said. "Does that mean that Jack—?"

All three at the table nodded.

"He went so quickly," Laurie said. "And he took care of everything beforehand. He had given instructions to Major about things he wanted done as soon as he was gone. Same with Mr. Fordham."

Mr. Fordham reached his hand for the paper that Laurie held. "If you'll give that to Mr. Latham, he can sign it, and I can be on my way."

"Sign what?"

"It's permission to take the body."

"Beg pardon?" Spider looked at Laurie and then at Major Smith.

Laurie raised her shoulders and compressed her lips in a helpless-bystander gesture. "Apparently Jack appointed you as executor of his estate. In the absence of any family, you're the one to give permission for the mortuary to take the body."

Spider frowned. "I just got here. I've known the fellow for a little more than a week. Not to speak ill of the dead, but what was he thinking?"

Major took the paper from Mr. Fordham and walked to where Spider stood. He handed it to him along with a pen from his own pocket. "He thought you were a man who could be counted on," he said. "Please sign."

Spider scanned the paper, saw that it was pretty straightforward, and came into the kitchen as far as the island counter. Setting his hat down, he inked his signature at the bottom. He handed it and the pen back to Major, who passed the form on to Mr. Fordham.

The mortician slipped it into a black leather folder and noiselessly pushed his chair in. "I'll be leaving now. As you know, Dr. Houghton asked that he be cremated with no ceremony and no gathering. But, he does want certain people to scatter his ashes. Major has the list of participants and the map."

Laurie stood. "I'll see you out, Mr. Fordham." She followed him as far as the door to the living room, but she paused there and spoke to Spider, still standing at the counter. "If you'll sit down, Major has something to talk to you about."

"I've got a horse I've got to unload," he said.

She put her hand on the doorframe, her brows raised in question.

Spider pointed toward the patio with his thumb. "And a three-legged dog to find a bed for."

Laurie's face grew pale. "It was Dorrie?"

"I'll show myself out," Mr. Fordham called from the living room.

Laurie didn't even glance at him as he made a soft-footed exit. Her eyes grew shiny, and her chin started to quiver. "Oh, Spider! You're sure?" She drifted into the arms he opened to her.

He folded her in, feeling each small convulsive sob that forced its way over her usual defenses. Laurie didn't cry easily. His heart ached for her, and he held her more tightly. Putting his cheek against her hair, he murmured, "Shh. I know. I know." He knew she was crying for Dorrie and for Jack. He knew she was crying because she had been powerless to help either of them. He felt like crying himself.

Instead, he asked, "Do you want to go unload Goldie, get her settled?"

She nodded, her head moving against his chest.

"I'll stay here and talk to Major. While you're in the barn, maybe you could find something for Trey to sleep on?"

She pulled away then, wiping her eyes on her sleeve. Spider spied a napkin on the counter and handed it to her. She blew her nose. "Forgive me," she said to Major.

"No problem." The attorney put his hand on his chair and waited for her to leave the room before he sat at the table.

Spider walked over and sat in Laurie's place. "Okay. What is it you need to talk about?"

Major pulled the stack of papers to himself. "How well did you know Jack Houghton?"

Spider picked up a pen lying on the table and rolled it between his thumb and fingers. "Hardly at all. I met him at our wedding. Probably saw him once a few years after that. We came to Kanab a week ago and in that time shared three meals with him. That's about the size of it."

"You knew he was a successful orthodontist?"

"Hell, he's got it written on the gate to his ranch and on his license plate. You couldn't miss it."

"Well, when he was first diagnosed, it scared him to think that he might not be around to take care of some of the people who depend on him."

Spider set the pen back on the table. "I think we all face that."

"You have to realize that Jack had no real obligation to these people, not like you'd have to Laurie. But he set about making sure they'd be watched over when he died."

"Who are *these people*?"

"To start out, there's Leila Dawn. She manages the clinic."

"You mean the office in the clinic?"

Major shook his head. "Jack didn't want to be bothered. He liked to fix teeth and ranch. Leila Dawn was a young widow with kids to support. Jack hired her and trained her to run the clinic. She hires and manages the staff—including the two other dentists, knows the regulations, keeps an eye on the bookkeeper. She does it all. She retires in ten years, so you'll have to decide then what you want to do."

Spider's brows came together. "What I want to do? Why would I want to do anything?"

Major looked perplexed. "Didn't Jack tell you?"

"Tell me what?"

"That he's leaving the ranch and his dental clinic to you?"

Spider felt his jaw drop, but for a moment he was too blindsided to close it. A dozen thoughts spun through his mind in seconds, the majority of them beginning with *I can't*. Then he remembered Jack's words the last time saw him. *I've seen that you're a good man to have around in difficult times, and what I've done is because of that, not because of Laurie.*

Stunned, Spider sat unmoving. His first reaction was to abdicate, if that was what you did to an inheritance. But then he realized that Amy was one of *these people*. Who would step up and make sure she had the fullest life possible? Who better to be involved in Amy's life than Laurie?

And what about Laurie? Here was her chance to be a successful rancher. Did he deny her that just because he was too proud to accept Jack's bequest?

But could he uproot himself and leave the place his great grandfather had homesteaded, the place he and Laurie had sacrificed so much to hang onto?

However, there was Bobby, saying he wanted to move to Lincoln County, raise his family on the homestead. "It's *qadar*," he said.

Major looked up from the paper he was perusing. "Beg pardon?"

"It's *qadar*—Arabic fate."

"Oh. I thought there was something wrong with your throat."

"There's something wrong, all right, but it's not with my throat." Spider sat forward. "Okay, let's have the whole of it. What does Jack want to leave to me?" He held up his hands. "Mind, I haven't said I'm okay with it."

Major pulled a piece of paper from the stack on the table and slid it in front of Spider. Picking up the pen, he used it as a pointer, indicating the first column. "Okay, first is the practice. You'll notice that it doesn't generate a whole lot of profit each year. Over and above operating expenses, salaries, insurance, rent, those kinds of things, you've got money going into retirement plans and a trust fund for Amy. Then there's a monthly stipend for both museums, the one in Kanab and the one in Fredonia, plus a donation to Care and Share."

"What's that?"

"It's the local food bank."

"And this figure down here at the bottom?"

"That's the monthly profit."

Spider didn't mention that it was twice what he made as deputy sheriff.

Major pointed to the next column. "Here you've got the ranch. Jack runs—has been running—a calving operation. He's had good luck, and he's done well each year." He moved the pen down to the next set of figures. "Here's what he got for this year's crop; here's the profit." Major moved the pointer to the last column. "This is the cash legacy. Jack's personal fortune. He's not a millionaire, but it's substantial."

Spider whistled under his breath.

"Of course the ranch comes with everything. The house. The cattle and horses. The machinery to take care of the alfalfa. Jack's brand new diesel pickup. Oh, the yellow Mustang is to be in Laurie's name."

"That's fine, but why?"

"Jack said since he gave her horse to Amy, he wanted her to have the Mustang." Major pushed the paper aside and placed a many-paged, legal-looking document in front of Spider. "I hope you understand this bequest comes with the stipulation that Amy is to live with you, and you are to be responsible for her welfare. You will be her trustee."

"I got that. Not a problem."

"If you agree, you'll need to sign each highlighted place on every page that has a red tab attached."

Spider pushed the stack of papers back toward Major. "That's something I have to talk to Laurie about." He smiled inwardly, knowing he didn't have to talk to her. She'd give up Lincoln County for Kane County in a heartbeat.

Major nodded. "Fair enough."

"If we agree to do this, everything needs to be put in both our names."

"Can do." Major picked up his briefcase and stood. "I'll leave these, so you can read through them and know what you're going to be signing."

Spider touched the papers. "By the way, who told you my given name is Quimby?"

"Jack did. Why?"

Spider shook his head. "He was a subtle son-of-a-gun, wasn't he?"

"When he was doing good he was as subtle as they come."

Spider stood and walked with Major to the doorway into the living room. The sun had set, and the room was in darkness. "I don't even know where the light switch is," Spider said.

Major swept his hand over the wall by the door molding, and the room brightened. "It's on this side."

"I guess I've got a lot of things to learn." Spider led the way to the front door and opened it. Offering his hand, he said. "Glad to meet you, Major. If we decide to do this, we'll need advice. I hope you'll stay on."

Major clasped Spider's hand. "I'd be honored." He turned and walked toward his car, a sporty SUV parked in front of the stuccoed wall.

Spider stepped back and was closing the door when he saw a flash of lights that indicated someone turning into the circular drive. He opened the door and watched Major pass Martin's rugged SUV as it pulled up in front of the house.

"It's like Grand Central Station," Spider muttered, but he raised his hand in greeting and tried to look welcoming.

Martin got out of the driver's door, a broad smile on his face. There was a spring in his step, and Spider couldn't help but remember how he looked a week ago as the EMTs loaded him into the ambulance.

Neva got out on the other side. She waved and then turned to open the rear door, reaching out her hands for LaJean's canvas bag, so she could hold it as the older woman climbed down. Isaac got out on Martin's side, and they all converged on Spider at the front door.

"We heard you were here at Jack's," Isaac said.

They all turned and looked as a red pickup drove into the driveway and parked.

Matt emerged from the pickup, and a blithe-looking Linda got out on the other side. Matt waited for her, and they held hands as they approached. "We've come to say thanks," the young man said.

Linda leaned towards Matt, and she nodded. "Thanks," she repeated. She couldn't stop smiling.

Spider swept his arm in an *enter* flourish. "Won't you come in? Let's see if we can find some more light switches and brighten up this room. Find a place to sit, everyone. Laurie should be in momentarily." He turned on a wall switch and a lamp and then perched on the raised fireplace hearth.

"We can't stay long," Martin said. He sat on the couch and patted the place beside him for Neva. "We just wanted to come and tell you thank you for freeing Mattie."

LaJean sat in one of the barrel chairs placed at right angles to the couch, and Isaac stood behind her. "What made you sure it wasn't Mattie?" she asked.

Linda occupied the other barrel chair. Matt sat at her feet, and her hand rested on his shoulder. "Who actually did it?"

Spider looked at the floor, wondering how to answer Linda's question. He didn't want anyone celebrating Dorrie's arrest. "The person who did it was the unlucky person who got to Austin Lee first. You'll read about it in the papers, but I hope you'll have compassion. If truth be told, it could have been any of a number of people."

Matt reached up and covered Linda's hand with his own. "Amen to that."

Nobody spoke. The room was silent except for the whoosh of LaJean's oxygen until the quiet was broken by Laurie opening the patio door. Turning away, she whistled. Then she called, "Come on. You can come in."

She stepped inside and waited, and soon Trey hopped over the threshold. After closing the door, Laurie looked up and saw everyone staring. "I didn't realize anyone was here. How nice to see you all." She crossed the room and sat by Spider on the hearth. Trey followed and sat at her feet.

"We've just heard about Jack," Isaac said. "We're sorry about that. He'll be sorely missed."

LaJean reached back and poked him. "What you mean is, his contribution to the museum will be missed."

"I think he made provisions for the museum before he died," Spider said.

"He did?" Martin wiped his eyes and gave a small, quavering laugh. "I'm sorry. I don't mean to be emotional. This has been a day of great and wonderful surprises."

"Would you care for some refreshments?" Laurie glanced from one to the other. "I can make some lemonade, and I think there are some of Amy's cookies in the freezer."

Neva stood. "We can't stay. We shouldn't have come at all, except we had to say thank you for all you and Spider have done for us."

"That's right." LaJean reached up a hand to her husband. "Help me up, Isaac." When standing, she continued her train of thought. "We forgot Jack was your cousin. We didn't mean to intrude, him just passing on and all."

Isaac crossed to Laurie and offered his hand. "Accept our condolences."

"Thank you, Isaac." She stood and went to the entryway.

Spider joined her there, opening the door and trying not to appear anxious to hurry them on their way. "It was good of you to come by. I agree with Martin. It's been a day of surprises. Oh, will you let Marshal Thayne know everything's wrapped up? He played a big part in getting to the bottom of this."

"I'll do that," Martin said as he and the older guests filed out. Laurie strolled out to the Taylor's car with them as Matt and Linda paused in the doorway where Spider lingered.

Linda gave Spider a quick hug and a peck on the cheek. "Thank you so much. You saved Matt's life, but you saved more than that. I hope you realize that."

"Oh?" Brows raised, Spider looked from Linda to Matt.

Matt made an awkward gesture.

Linda leaned forward and said in a conspiratorial whisper, "He said I was like water to a thirsty man." She glanced at Matt and smiled.

Matt stuck his hands in his pocket and looked at the floor.

Spider clapped him on the shoulder. "Good man."

"Come on, Matt." Linda went out the door and pulled him after her. They walked to the car, and just before getting in, she called out, "Thanks again."

Laurie joined Spider in the doorway, and they watched the two cars drive around the paved circle and head back along the line of poplars. "It's nice to finally be alone," he said. "Did you get Goldie settled?"

"Yes. She looks a little poor. What's that all about?"

Spider led her to the couch and she curled up beside him. Trey came over and sat at Spider's feet, laying her head on his knee. Stroking her silky ears, he told Laurie the story of how he found Dorrie.

"We have to be her family," Laurie said.

"Well, if we've got Amy living with us, we'll certainly have plenty of cookies to take when we visit."

Laurie sat up and stared at Spider. "You mean you're willing to accept Jack's legacy? I thought you'd be too proud."

"I was at first. Then I got to figuring that since I was the owner of an E-Type Jag, I'd better live near a mechanic. Besides, I knew it would please you."

Laurie laughed and leaned back against his chest once again. "Isn't it funny how it's all turned out? I mean, we lose your mom, and then at the funeral Bobby says he wants the Lincoln County place, and then, boom, Jack gives us his ranch. It's like—what was it Karam called it? *Qadar*?"

"You're not saying it right." Spider touched his Adam's apple. "You've got to hear it way down here. *Qadar*."

"Wait." She sat up again. "What was that you said?"

"*Qadar*."

"No, before that. You said you knew it would please me."

"Well, sure. Here's a ranch that's got good feed, good water. It's got good-looking Angus and a calving operation already set up. Wouldn't that please you?"

"But you'd be giving up your great grandpappy's homestead. Why would you do that?"

"Because—" He dropped a kiss on her lips and shamelessly stole Matt's line. "—you're like water to a thirsty man."

8. Is there any other character in the book that you consider a hero? Why?

9. Laurie has a special bond with Taffy. Have you ever experienced that kind of relationship with an animal? Have you ever lost a special pet? How did you deal with it?

10. Spider quickly accepts major changes in his life according to Jack's plan for Braces at the end of the book. What motivates him to sacrifice his own plans?

About Kane County

◆

Though *Trouble at the Red Pueblo* is fiction, many of the places mentioned are real.

The Red Pueblo Museum is a hidden gem that sits on the northern edge of the tiny border town of Fredonia, Arizona. If you go there, go in the afternoon so you can hear Dixon Spendlove tell how he found many of the artifacts in the museum.

The Coral Pink Sand Dunes, just north of Kanab, is a state park that is easily accessed. It's a great place to take kids to play.

The Western Legends Roundup, described in the book, takes place each md-August. It's a time when Kanab pays homage not only to pioneer history, but also to the legacy of movie making that Kane County enjoys.

To read about more places to visit in Kane County, go to http://www.visitsouthernutah.com/

About the Author

A native of New Mexico and mother of seven, Liz Adair bloomed late as a writer—her first Spider Latham Mystery was published about the time AARP added her to their mailing list. Though she lived in green, moist, northwest Washington State for forty years, most of her books are set in the southwest.

Liz returned to high plateau country in 2012 when she and her husband, Derrill, moved to Kanab, Utah. Liz had gone to high school in Kanab and neighboring Fredonia, Arizona, so moving there was like coming home. It was natural for her next book to be another Spider Latham mystery, even though ol' Spider hadn't inhabited one of her books for ten years. Writing about him again felt like coming home, too.

Look for more Spider Latham mysteries in the coming years. You can check out Liz's blog at www.sezlizadair.blogspot.com and be sure to sign up for her newsletter.

Made in the USA
San Bernardino, CA
04 December 2014

Book Club Questions

◆────────

1. Laurie encourages Spider to get right to work on this new mystery after his mother's funeral. Have you found working or getting involved in a hobby has helped you deal with a loss?

2. Spider is frustrated with himself for being jealous of Jack. What factors (besides the ones he voices) do you think play into his dislike of Jack?

3. Did your own feelings about Jack change between Chapter Two and the end? Why?

4. Who is your favorite character? Why do you like him or her?

5. Karam, a Palestinian Muslim, teaches American history. Have you taken a class from an unlikely teacher?

6. Karam is detained by the police because of racial profiling. When do you think it's acceptable, if ever, for law enforcement officials to engage in racial profiling?

7. What heroic qualities does Spider demonstrate? Does he demonstrate any unheroic qualities?